I0537363

The Erris Starship

By Denis McClean
Copyright © 2019 Denis McClean
ISBN 978-0-9926814-9-4

All material in this publication is copyright and must not be copied, reproduced, transferred distributed, leased, or licensed without the prior permission of the author and publisher. Unauthorised distribution of any part of the book may constitute an infringement of the author's or publisher's rights and is likely to be the cause of an offence.

Thank you for respecting the work that goes into my books, which is the only way I can create more of them by return. For updates on my published and latest work, please visit me at my Blog, which will point you to my Web-Site and also to my Facebook Page.

http://denismcclean.blogspot.ie/

I sincerely hope that you enjoy this offering.

About …

The Erris Starship was born when inspiration was quite brazenly seduced by impulse while writing 'Erris'. That's the second of my four 'Thin Places' Series novellas. At the time, I wanted to plant a spurious element that I could develop later in that book. I was obliged however, to live within the word-count constraints of a novella but regardless, the planted seed soon sprouted shoots.

Erris occupies the wildest and so far, the most unspoilt north west region of County Mayo, Ireland and it is positively addictive, so I was compelled to revisit. You don't get very many, but even on a sunny day, a rather unique Celtic melancholy hangs over the land like a mist being constantly urged to rise but forever failing. That sombre beauty has lingered far too long after ancient lore based on unlikely facts, or undocumented histories as wild as the landscape. Either way, it's probably the last place on Earth that anyone would ever associate with any version of fantastic star-faring futures and like a mountain, it had to be climbed.

I'm more than happy to let you be the judge of whether I've successfully risen to that daunting challenge because there is much more than one story here.

I should say that 'Erris' isn't a prequel to 'The Erris Starship' because the two books are from different genres but if you like one, you'll probably want to read the other. The reason for that will be desire for more of the Erris narcotic but there is another reason. You'll be sorely tempted to see how a simple seed impulsively planted inside a novella, could grow into a full-blown novel with an even wilder story.

& Dedication.

It's precisely because all possible futures are born from limitless possibilities that I humbly dedicate this work to half of humanity. There are many superbly qualified individuals whom I'd be proud to recall here, but who would be more worthy than the people who make all possible futures possible. That done, they then nurture each unique version of the future until it's time to wave them off, and let each one compete for self fulfilment.

Having patiently guided one unlikely seed to grow into something special, through liberal applications of fearless imagination for fertilizer, I dedicate this book to women. Women daily deliver all of our futures and no measure of appreciation can ever be appropriate to such an awesomely daunting vocation so willingly accepted.

Acknowledgements

My cover graphics are a combination of four pictures, two of which were borrowed from NASA/Goddard/JPL. The NASA website - images and missions, continue to amaze and inspire me. They serve as a constant reminder of the true scale of everything and also as a challenge to us as a species. It is only by uncovering and then understanding the universe that we can truly appreciate our own place in it.

The most striking image is a fabulous shot taken by the crew of Apollo 17. It's of Earth rising above the moon and it was taken quite some time ago, between 7th and 9th of December 1972. Time flies, but the problem with the original picture is the lack of visible stars in it because the Hubble telescope was still a distant dream. So, I appropriately borrowed a rather intense star-field that was captured by Hubble and superimposed it.

That image is of Palomar 12 (Panta Rhei), which is a star cluster originally born in the Sagittarius dwarf galaxy which lies out there beyond the Milky Way Galaxy. These stars were removed by destiny and then set on a very different course using galactic tidal forces. They have their altered destiny in common with this story's protagonist.

The third picture is of a black snooker ball, elongated by GIMP software and the fourth is a much altered image of two people who will always be very close to my heart. One of those is my editor and the taller one is her brother Cathal.

The words at the end of my Prologue are inspired and then rather brazenly stolen from 'The Stolen Child', by W.B. Yeats. I then committed a further atrocity by changing more than one of them to better suit my particular purposes but as a fellow Irishman, I feel I can make a good case for gracious posthumous pardons.

In Chapter 16, I reiterate the lyrics and hopefully, something of the sentiment behind "Wind of Change" by the German rock band, Scorpions. The song was composed and written by the lead singer, Klaus Meine and produced by Keith Olsen in 1990 and long may it continue to inspire us all.

I gratefully acknowledge the tireless and conscientious input of Grainne Pleiades McClean as a proof-reader and editor. Not only does she know a good story when she sees one, but she was unselfish enough to make some significant contributions to make this one even better.

I continue to enjoy the unflagging support of my better half, Gina. She has far more practical interests of her own to keep her well occupied but she still finds time to share in my all consuming passion for stories that take unlikely and/or reluctant heroes and heroines to places we can as yet only imagine or dream about, "... but that's what soulmates do," - she says.

Prologue

On a journey of scenic twists and turns we'd probably save our book for another day. That way, we'll be ready to capture the perfect picture to share with family or friends, even if we later find it afflicted with the curse of a windscreen reflection. Further, if we're not driving then etiquette obliges us to engage in some light banter to foster an ambience of mutual engagement. That's another way of proposing that we keep the driver from getting bored but regardless, that's not the kind of trip we'd expect to take each and every day.

On more mundane trips we invite a book to become the journey and then let it take us away from reality for the duration. In this particular genre, going further is usually better and as long as our book is entertaining, we'll tolerate all narratives from insightful to educational, as long as the learning bits are kept informal and aren't presented like a lesson. That could be too much like work.

So, let's begin this journey with a little insight, which we'll use as a metaphor for gentle acceleration. This is the part where we are just pulling out of the train station, or maybe counting those rumbling runway seconds until take-off, wheels up and then 'Boing Boing'. "You may now recline your seats."

While settling back to enjoy that mile high drink we're quite relaxed, though still alert and focused enough to be able to discern something in a new light, like say evolution for example. Those 'Seat-belts-on' distractions, while clinging to what's left of our main course will come a bit later, preferably when we're already in the zone and hopefully half expecting it.

Evolution plays the most fundamental role in the ongoing perfection of people, but we just don't see it. It's a prime example of not being able to see the forest because of all those trees blocking the view. The problem with evolution however, is that although it's quite literally in our faces, we only notice it in 'simpler' creatures and never in ourselves. It's like we think we're somehow immune to it and that's more than just a little conceited, considering how vast the subject is. Today, therefore we'll need to get sufficiently far away so that we can look back and get an overview big enough to significantly alter our predefined perceptions of evolution.

Let's start by playing the part of your fellow passenger, who's just been sneaking looks at you to see who they've been landed with for the duration of this journey, and don't pretend you've never done that. They won't see the same person that you left behind in your bathroom mirror. In fact, you're most likely not the human you thought you were while savouring that last mouthful of breakfast.

You carry more exotic cells within your body than you do cells with actual human DNA. Crazy as it seems, all of us are apparently more microbe and bacteria than we are sentient, dominant and conceited. Further, any of us who tries to kill off our personal colonies of say, Bifidobacterium or Faecalibacterium will be made to suffer terribly for that crime.
To add insult to injury, the bacteria feeding on the food that we eat, will simply devour our bodies should we interrupt their gravy train by say, inconveniently dying mid-banquet.

A rational conclusion therefore, is that evolution protects the parasites that we host better than it does us.

"Interesting," you might say, "- though unlikely to influence anything on today's personal planner …" and that may be true. But seeing as we're just starting out, let's leave small thinking behind us and consider that we've just lifted the smallest corner of that first thin veneer covering 'Life'. So, let's delve a little deeper. After all, a little dirt under the nails never killed anyone.

Logically speaking, there should be a very clear relationship between life and the way we go about living it, but it's like we're programmed not to think too critically about that. The same evolution that makes little distinction between us and microbial parasites has arrived at neo-liberalism as the best way for us to live life and you know, get things done. So, it wasn't evolution that relentlessly revised that daily planner of yours to the point where master and slave are now almost indistinguishable. That was just neo-liberalism's propensity for further accelerating the pace of its own evolution.

Neo-liberalism has evolved to the point where even the whisper of an alternative is a guarantee of ridicule. Yet the free markets it professes to protect have become so fragile, that something as innocuous as gossip can bring them all crashing down like dominos. Billions if not trillions in digital and virtual currencies can be instantly wiped from share price indices on an idiot's whim.

To clean up the mess routinely made by such unavoidable blundering, we've empowered banks to omnipotently print more currency in the form of 'Quantitative Easing'. That's instant free money for them to squander on bonuses and loans at interest to us. Yet all loans are ultimately repayable only in hard, sweaty and imperfect cash that had to be originally earned from actual physical labour. People who question this absurdity are called 'Conspiracy Theorists' but enough about Central Banks and their minimum reserve monetary policies.

In these overly privatised times, the extent to which our media is either owned or influenced by vested interests can be measured by the effectiveness of their subliminal messaging. Everyone knows, for example, that there's simply no alternative to capitalism on steroids. These perennial sources of insider information give license to elected representatives to place taxpayers on pedestals while continuously eroding citizen's rights to facilitate further division and conquest.

The new taboo is populist debate of global wars waged to protect the profits and jobs of military industrial complexes. How often does the media claim that the result of some 'yes-or-no' poll can be interpreted as suggesting that elections are inconvenient, costly and unnecessary? Such articles will usually conclude by telling us that no productive purpose is served by inviting further instability during 'this-critical-time', as in 'don't rock the boat.'

These are the tools applied by the 1% to frog march all of us blindfolded into concurrent extinction level events and yes, you did read that correctly. We are facing extinction because we are increasingly compelled to consume absolutely everything of any value now, while it is still worth anything to somebody and to hell with the consequences. The global urgency of survival against these increasing odds is a form of induced panic, purposely choreographed to keep all eyes down and ears closed to every sense of foreboding. These are the same senses that have been honed to near perfection during time since the dinosaurs.

"Global warming, oceanic and environmental pollution will be managed in due course," 'They say', "- by increased carbon taxes imposed on people and not on fossil fuel extraction corporations who will in any event, just pass increased costs down to consumers." How come 'consumers' are always 'down' even when the markets are supposed to be 'up'?

We are increasingly forced to wear further alienating labels like unemployed, evicted, homeless, sick and destitute with each of our tributaries flowing the only way they can, which is down. Once there, we join rivulets of refugees to ultimately merge with mainstream masses on minimum wage and/or minimum hour contracts, if they are lucky. While dissent is quasi-criminal, all will slide silently and inexorably into the ever-expanding chasm between the haves and have-nots, for richer or poorer 'til death do us part.

How we arrived at this juncture is not a mystery. The information age wasn't built in a day but once knowledge became currency, small tailor-made deceits were repeated over and over until they morphed into literally indisputable truths. These deceits, like a dusting of snowflakes, will usually melt on contact with the truth, unless solidarity has been chilled in advance for a purpose.

Once that first fall accumulates, layers of lies spread far and wide in a continuous carpet. When ill winds are stirred up, all remaining fact becomes obscured under drifts of delusion until the world we awake to bears little resemblance to the one that we foolishly left unattended, while nursing our hot chocolate by the fireside.

Life may be bad for us but surely it was tougher for the prophets, ultimately destined to lie in the dust at our feet. Just reward perhaps, for neglecting to prophesy total surveillance under facial recognition software. Their unwitting legacy is the earliest detection of any and all post-modern oracles and prophetic reincarnations. In practical terms, the Status Quo has already labelled our unlikely hopes pariahs, or latter-day lepers by the time they raise their heads above our 'Great Unwashed'.

Without those sources of inspired revelation, we can only look forlornly to our mortal and similarly afflicted brothers and sisters. It is perhaps out of desperation that we've grown too eager to acclaim anyone half willing to step forward so we can hoist them up to stand taller on our shoulders. But which of our names, when written in common blood, will decline the collaborator's enticement to stand mute under the right hand of a new master? Who amongst us will ignore the usher's prompts to sit at elite tables? And once seated with napkin on lap, who will refuse to eat and drink as well and as often as their betters, while politely ignoring offers of secret salaries?

The unspeakable truth is our innate jealousy of blue bloods, because we know that the righteous but low caste heart in each of us would sacrifice beats to be considered worthy of any royal summons. From those disdainfully dizzy heights, all other vocations can be seen as temporary aberrations. That minor revelation shows the fundamental flaw in humanity's claim to some insubstantial yet intrinsic form of absolute altruism.

A truly impartial introspection, beginning at the very beginning, will show our default human attributes as broadly negative, with greed, suspicion and insecurity very much to the fore. For the same reasons that the lazy won't confess to lethargy, no-one will break sweat attempting to put meat on the bones of this 'apparent anomaly'. The truth, you see, is that the fundamental problem with us is not with us, per se. The inherent flaw in us lies in life itself, which is spawned in serial deceits.

We routinely begin with stimulants, relaxants and/or intoxicants. Then, in common with the most contagious viral pathogens, pheromones are stealthily released to become airborne as a prelude to our own existence. One sex will then claim the dominant position and carte blanche regarding quasi-conjugal privilege. However, in a contest as subtle as seduction, losing is often winning. In the significant heat of subsequent conquest or submission, people become chameleons in reverse, shedding meticulously crafted but by then redundant alter egos with their clothes, jobs done.

Further, evolution never intended the orgasm to be choreographed. It is pure primal pleasure requiring minimal consideration of any equally egocentric partner and even less of us, soon to become the logical consequence of it. Human gestation ends with us kicking and screaming in protest at being duly delivered blind and helpless into a cold and alien world. Surviving that plunge from previously pristine states of eternal grace would surely demand the most urgent re-orientation, but we're still largely ignorant of just how useless we've been rendered by the supposed 'gift' of life.

When our eyes develop sufficiently to register the revelation of parental devotion, our snot and saliva gurgles are too often mistaken for recognition and even burgeoning love. In reality however, they merely reflect our profound, if undisciplined relief at the miracle of continued survival amongst multitudes of mega-mouthed monsters obsessed with flashing their teeth in our direction.

Sometime after Santa Claus or Father Christmas, talking bears, pixies, elves, tooth fairies and Easter bunnies, we'll be told with saintly sincerity that they actually planned us and then made love. By that time, we'll have learned that appearing stupid is being stupid. So, despite the mind-boggling quagmire of how an unimaginable menagerie of storks, cabbages, birds, bees and rabbits all played bit parts in our creation, with the implicit approval of god himself, we'll feign comprehension but quietly withdraw to reconsider.

Subsequent clarifications will wait until we can discuss the subject in depth and in confidence with like-minded people of superior moral codes. To that end we'll convene clandestine assemblies in tree houses and behind school bicycle sheds or when otherwise secreted with our peers in puerile sanctuaries. All too quickly we'll declare ourselves masters of our own destinies, qualified to build new worlds and to procreate.

To assume that evolution will slavishly stamp any such static circle of life as quality approved is to grossly underestimate this breaker of all artificially imposed bonds. She is the godsent spirit of absolute freedom, an angel of divine and of our own design who will descend to take us higher. All we need to do is cup an ear and listen for her call.

"Come away, O human child
From your waters and your wild
With a faery, hand in hand.
For life's more full of weeping than you can ever
understand."

1 - Starting Over

Despite his best efforts at obliterating most of his own past, some elements simply refused to be erased. Poised precariously over the crevasse separating plebs from their betters however, he was fortunate that all of it was behind him, pending the imminent separation of just one surviving fact from stubborn fiction. That's what brought him into the unlikely setting of Erris, County Mayo in the wild west of Ireland, next stop the 'New World'.

Conor's first impressions of Erris was that it was far too open. He couldn't hide anything in it that wouldn't be instantly found, including himself. Secondly, it just wasn't Dublin, which made it inferior by default. That was despite its wild and unspoilt landscapes, clean air, cleaner water and far fewer outlets in which to purchase overly processed foods. The people were also not immune from summary judgement and they conveniently fell into two distinct demographics.

The summer influx had too much time on their hands and maybe too much money in their wallets. They were intent on squandering both in an effort to create some dubious connection that could subsequently be captured with dedicated cameras, not phones. As for the residents: none appeared happy. That suggested they were stuck where destiny dropped them and were unable to break that same metaphysical umbilical that was so sought after by visitors.

Anyway, his past was just one reason that Conor found himself surveying the same scene that must have greeted his school-going father only a year before his scandalous marriage. As his only progeny, that observation should have been profound but it was disappointingly sterile, imbued with more anti-climax than dejavu. As a result, his disappointment fell with the chill from rocks that had all the appearance of being eternally banished from sunlight.

The narrow, steeply inclined beach was fully enclosed on three sides by cliff walls weeping perennially recent rain. After the initially nerve-wracking paddle from Portacloy beach, he basked in the reassurance of being once more contained within objective boundaries. This was where his parents claimed to have met and his first impressions didn't die quietly.

"What on earth could have brought both of them way out here?" His mutterings didn't get far before being drowned out by a sudden rise in the intensity of conflict between competing cacophonies of gulls.

It had taken him almost an hour to kayak around the point and although he didn't dare to admit it en-route, the gods just had to be smiling on his endeavour. The sea that warmly embraced him hadn't been as quiet for several months, according to local lore. So, relieved to be still alive and within a stone's throw of solid ground, he bobbed indolently up and down until a slightly more significant wave stole up behind to almost catch him by surprise.

He took it as a reminder to never let his guard down and awkwardly steadied himself with an evidently unpractised flail of the oar. The swell this close to the sand was nothing compared to what he'd just been through beyond the cove. It took steely nerves that he wasn't sure he possessed to get through, or rather over them. Focussing only on each wave and nothing else, while praying that death wasn't simultaneously stalking from another angle, was the only way to survive each assault as it advanced to then retreat. Eliminating everything else limited his gaze to measurable rising and falling, while mitigating against the more disorienting churning of the entire visible world when his eyes accidentally fell on the heaving horizon, especially when those bigger swells arrived.

The sneaky upstart behind him was merely impudent and a comparatively impotent imposter. He let it lift him up and then predictably drop him a metre or more closer to his ultimate destination. Beyond the scratched prow of his 'borrowed' two-seater kayak, he counted six seconds until it tumbled onto the noisy gravel, shell and stone aggregate lying beneath the softer layers of sand on top. Conor then reviewed what little he could still remember of Life#1.

Collating newly pertinent facts from earlier, almost forgotten existences turned out to be a particularly painstaking task but he applied himself well and unlike school, didn't shy away from essential homework. His father claimed to have arrived on the same beach to take a breather after an extremely unlikely encounter with two very curious whales. According to Tadhg, that was something that happened not too far off the bigger beach at Portacloy. The same place where his only son had very recently acquired the kayak. Tadhg said that the creatures ushered him around the point rather than let him turn back to rejoin his summer-school friends at the campsite.

Instead of finding some respite however, he said that he stumbled into what he thought at first was a movie scene. He saw two warriors, one with a spear and the other with a golden sword as they confronted two faceless ninjas. An extra, a boy he may have called Daniel, apparently mistook the newly arrived Tadhg for Goliath and tried to take him down with an old-fashioned slingshot. Removed from these action sequences, Conor's beautiful mother-in-waiting was reputedly invoking ancient gods from their beached boat. That was before she was reputedly obliged to slap his father for the insolence of looking at her for longer than he needed to.

Conor couldn't remember what age he was when they gave him that first morsel of a much longer story, but the older he got the more hysterically funny it became. After the day that divided his first life from the others however, it instantly lost the power to create a smile and devolved into a question that would never be answered.

The thing was, his father was young enough to be an older brother and as a result, he was a joker and a kindred spirit more often than he was an oracle and a guiding light. So, it was extremely likely that countless liberties were taken with the retelling of the apparently endless story of how his parents met. Further, everything was a joke to his father and looking back, it seemed like every time he laughed, which was most of the time, she was there to either echo or amplify it.

Some memories are as indelible as they are tactile and the recollection of those translucent green eyes set into contrasting alabaster under a mane of copper-gold hair, still screamed 'goddess incarnate'. Conor knew he wasn't alone in the adulation of his mother. 'Mama's Boys' are not a solely Irish idiosyncrasy and he'd been told more than once that the strong emotional connection he still felt for his mother, was merely a function of her leaving him too soon. There is also the fact that children are perennially simple and still believe in things that we later learn are impossible, like perfection.

When later came, it was a bitter lesson to learn that Gods were supposed to be immortal and also giants and so, he was obliged to demote his mother. Ceide McCarthy you see, was not quite five foot four without her shoes. He knew that because he made a point of getting her to mark her own height above his in the bedroom doorway. Anyway, those feet and inches reduced her to royalty and perhaps a princess but regardless, in the strictly private world that sons share with their mothers, she would always be enchanting if not actually enchanted.

He felt he could lately afford to laugh at such childish naivete, having been rendered a radically altered and much street wiser character by circumstance in the meantime. And yet, the fact that he could never recall his mother lying to him about anything, not even once, had to be just plain weird. It was that small fact that eventually persuaded him to come all this way to see if their beach actually existed, though it certainly didn't live up to his grandiose expectations of it.

It was still too easy to conjure up his default image of Ceide in a warm firelight glow, with the three of them smelling of turf and burnt wood oils. He couldn't stop some of the sillier and more tear-jerking memories rising to the top, like cream. These were not memories he was inclined to share with anyone other than Sonia of course, who also just disappeared though god only knew where she'd got to.

There was something about those shades of fire on hair that made her golden fleece shimmer with every movement while his father regaled him more with the latest chapter of the saga, like it had just been cleared for telling by the censor's office. Looking around, he just knew he was in the right place. He simply had to be because so much depended on getting the most important part of this visit right. Satisfying his personal curiosity could come later but looking at the beach, he smelled the same disappointment that had tainted most of Life#4.

"Anyway." He assured himself out loud and then grimaced when he realised how stupid he'd look chatting to himself like a retard. So, after a reassuring glance around, he clammed up and resumed his ruminations more privately. Once his duty to them was done, he could spend all the time it took to burst that last stubborn bubble of delusion. Then he could begin to write the long promised new beginning to his own story.

He opened a faded and colourfully patchworked haversack without having to look at it, evidence of an enduring ownership. His hands then slid inside to loosen folds of bubble-wrap packaging and his prime purpose was revealed. These were then carefully placed between his thighs while he cleared away the clutter and mentally prepared himself, like a Zen master, eyes narrowing. With those eyes still fixed on their beach, refusing to see which of them was which, he carefully unscrewed the lid of one ceramic urn and then the other. One in the left and other in his right hand, he delicately lowered them over the sides.

When the gurgling began, it was inevitable that some of Tadhg and Ceide McCarthy's mortal remains would reach out to touch their son one last time, but he refused to look down and risk seeing that happen. Then, together as always, he let them slip under the water of their exclusive 'Thin Place', a term they often used but that he somehow never thought to question.

That done, he leaned forward and plunged his arms into the sea as far as each of them would go. This ended the futile clinging of the last ashes to his bare skin, but he kept them fully immersed to wave them off with a heavy heart but no tears. In seven long years he'd cried himself dry and now that he'd also turned sixteen, it was his turn to live.

2 - Life#4 Ends

Stereotyping might be politically incorrect but that doesn't make it fake news. We know from long experience, for example, that young adults tend to instinctively know everything, but seldom look comfortable with their presumably massive hauls of knowledge. To compound that problem, looks are absolutely everything at that fragile age. Living peacefully with the paradox of always having to look great and even unique, though never different enough to be called 'odd'can't be easy. Yet, of all teenage terms and conditions, that one is probably the most critical.

It was with that prerequisite etched into his psyche, that Conor adopted his customary 'virtual-peer-accompanied' mode, to officially launch his incursion a couple of hours previously. Peer pressure weighed constantly and heavily on him, even when it was virtual. So, he was obliged to look as 'normal' as he normally would during that slightly delayed entrance into Portacloy. Practise does make perfect but looking normal is much easier said and done and how much practise was put into it could never be discussed.

To add insult to injury, he had to walk in on foot, like some peasant returning from the fields and this unfortunate turn of events had somewhat undermined his much practised false confidence. As a result, he was already edgy and when that combined with the general absence of anything familiar, he felt far too exposed to hazards so obscure, that highest on the list was the simple curiosity of potential onlookers and a possibly pointed finger.

It was nothing less than 'bizarre' that any morning could pass without hearing a single car, never mind two full days without the reassurance of a physical bus stop. The absence of these perennial life signs was nothing short of phenomenal and it was a constant reminder of how remote and uncivilised the place was. The people of Portacloy and its environs randomly jumped on and off buses anywhere they chose. It was like he'd taken the train west only to find himself delivered to an alternate reality.

To make matters worse he was somewhat embarrassed, even though no-one who mattered would know that he'd taken a wrong turn the previous evening. That mistake obliged him to sleep rougher than planned, and also under open skies on a beach beyond Stonefield and hence the late start to the most crucial phase of his quest. Being late wasn't a huge problem, but it added to the general disquiet of having been lost. He found it pretty much impossible to sleep in such utter silence and the experience had threatened to prematurely freak him out.

It wasn't like he was stupid enough to set out blindly into the 'wilderness'. The thing was, his Maps App had a different definition of what a village should look like because it showed three in the immediate locality whereas in reality, there wasn't even one. Further, the name 'Erris' didn't feature on any road-sign that he'd seen, which probably explained why the place looked so surreally post-apocalyptic and devoid of anything resembling the universally accepted definition of 'population'.

His personal finances weren't in great shape either, and this induced another bout of auto-interrogation that once more demanded to know why he couldn't wait until he landed a job to fund a proper trip. Nothing new was learned from the exchange however. The money problem could only be solved by finding a job that would pay enough to feed him. Job seeking for school leavers had evolved into the contemporary equivalent of enlisting for Homer's Odyssey.

Applicants had to be navigator enough to make Vasco de Gama jealous and have years of experience as a first mate, though ideally with a Captain's certificate and with a history of spilling blood that wasn't their own. The usual solution of bullshitting is impossible where verifiable accolades have become industry standard.

Further, hidden away in illegible small print were the usual T's and C's, extracts of which would be highlighted in enlarged letters, big and bold enough to be seen in the return email. This was assuming that more than one out of every ten applications he sent would merit the courtesy of an acknowledgement of some form. These would politely inform him that he needed at least one other language just to get through the initial screening. In one particular instance he was told that Irish was considered a second language, which made it as probably as useful as Latin, in that it was also spoken by no-one.

Most of the jobs that he could actually do without requiring investments in major training were going to interns prepared to live in abject poverty in exchange for mentored experience in selling cigarettes to over 18's or some such nonsense. That, or two broke foreign students would share a single job. That would allow them to choose which four hour stint suited each of them best. Working for more hours could apparently make it difficult for them to collect benefits or easier to accidentally invalidate student visas.

Lately, he found was competing with retirees and the jobless. The old farts would take any salary to augment their inadequate pensions. Ultimately, it came down to doing the right thing by his parents before finding himself with even less money than an anorexic intern. As it was, what remained of his disposable currency was reserved for real emergencies, like imminent starvation or bribery. He'd already invested in something worth smoking, assuming he could find some genuine people worthy of share it with him. It wasn't 'drugs' as such, if it was indulged in socially.

As it transpired, getting to Mayo with no budget wasn't a contest for someone as streetwise as himself. The ticket inspector in Castlebar train station was no brighter than his Dublin counterpart. Once beyond the turnstiles and back on the road such as it was, introducing his pseudo 'posh' and more respectable South Dublin alter-ego to potential chauffeurs, proved more than enough to get him further into the hinterlands gratis and for nothing. He hated all the pointless waffle but beggars can't be choosers and anyway, talking 'shite' was part and parcel of his 'act' and further continuous practice would ensure that he stayed at the top of his chosen profession.

Having arrived at his destination, however, he found an unanticipated challenge. The secret to street wisdom was people and plenty of them. Crowds offered not just anonymity but also a screen behind which he could operate … and possibly hide things. Nothing overtly criminal as such but in a country where white collar crime paid so supremely well, with the most successful often enjoying immunity as well as unadulterated admiration, dabbling in some discreet opportunism could also be considered enterprise of a sort.

Mayo's open spaces were nothing less than daunting for a specialised opportunist. He felt more than a little exposed on the road into the village or whatever-they-called-it and then, to make matters worse, he was assailed by the local ambience. The fly pestered beasts scattered each side of the road reeked, and they also insisted on shitting all over their main courses. It was almost enough to put him off burgers … almost.

So much for his grand entrance but just then, finding himself on what appeared to be genuine virgin territory was yet another novelty. So, since his mother claimed with some pride to be originally from Erris, he decided to elevate the shaded beach with the undeserved blessing of her name. However, since his subsequent lives were spent almost exclusively in Dublin City and suburbs, he could only sense that something was missing from it. With only time on his hands, he challenged himself with identifying what that might be.

Taking his first few steps was something of a distraction when he was struck by how similar were the sounds of trudging through soft beach sand and of crunching through wet Phoenix Park snow during the previous January. The echo returning from the cliff wall blended into susurrations from tumbling waves, which were packaged by outbursts from the constantly bickering birds. This was more than enough to inform him that he'd arrived alive and well in the wilds of Erris. He'd come a long way and not just in miles or kilometres but also in years and in obstacles overcome and allowed himself a self indulgent smile.

Obstacles simply don't exist for small children, which is probably why it's more natural for them to moan about problems, rather than to learn how to resolve issues. Finding solutions is what big people do to justify their superior status and it's only much later that the walls cave in and real life encroaches. Being orphaned turned out to be a huge problem but the first real obstacles he had to face alone were people and quite often, those who were paid to remove his problems.

Tadhg's parents skipped between being aloof and indifferent to interfering with destiny. So it wasn't really a great surprise when their stint at fostering their grossly premature grandson didn't work out. Conor considered their peculiar way of half caring merely curious until it became commonplace, and not only amongst prospective foster parents. It was also an acceptable modus operandi for the flock of nine-to-five health care professionals assigned to his positive development.

He was promised the sun, moon and stars in non-doctors who healed troubled minds like magicians, casting spells bound with words sans the bitter after taste of medicine. Child psychologists, behavioural and clinical psychologists interspersed with counsellors, school assistants and lesser breeds of mere social workers arrived in droves. At a time when a few kind words from a single stable source would indeed have worked wonders, the system preferred to work in more mysterious and regulated ways befitting the often chaotic input of inept regulators.

Just as a new pair of glasses mandates new eye tests to protect eye testers from extinction, child services run stables of experts with each stable offering the full range of mandatory essential services. What better way to save protected species from extinction, than by declaring their services compulsory and them indispensable? In Conor's case, it was the humble social workers who made the most meaningful inroads when they were needed, usually long after five o'clock and far removed from clinics and consulting rooms as sterile as the rocks surrounding him just then.

The first of many 'adepts' to speak in biblical tongues had a name long since erased by mutual accord. She suggested that ten years was old enough to leave the inner child behind him and Conor was urged to move on. He was offered a new job description in which he would consciously create the boy that he wanted to become. The reason he still remembered it word for word was because of how insane it sounded to him at the time.

That was one of many lofty proposals for an abject snotty nosed reject but it did mark the undisputed end of Life#1 and also gave him a good grounding in the subtle art of spin and double-speak, which would so dominate Life#2. By age twelve he was assigned a senior behavioural psychologist who morphed into a therapist and who was replaced by a real-life counsellor at thirteen. By fifteen he was assigned his own life-coach who predicted that life would imminently be 'great'.

All things considered, it probably wasn't so unlikely that he would ultimately find himself alone on Ceide's beach, searching for signs of a boat that his father believed might belong to entities he referred to as 'Faceless Ninjas'. If there was any place in Ireland where any kind of Ninja could be living under the radar, unseen by everyone aside from his deceased parents, it would probably be Erris, County Mayo.

Years later, he found he no longer knew his parents like their kids should. For all he knew, they were probably having a good laugh at his expense and they wouldn't be alone. There was also one or two of those experts who'd almost sucked him in with their bullshit, and his thoughts turned to abandoning the 'Ninja Boat' element of his quest and heading directly back to Dublin.

With the promised 'Thin Place' burial done and dusted, Erris obviously held no attractions for him but most of all, Mayo was just too bloody empty. Looking good in Portacloy without a crowd of peers to fit into, meant that he stuck out like a sore thumb and that just wasn't wise.

It had taken a really close call with two scammed buskers in Dublin's Grafton Street to teach him that being conspicuous was a worse crime than getting caught, and that looking out of place was the result of poor planning. Staying longer than he needed to stay in Mayo was bound to get him into trouble sooner or later.

Just then, he had to admit that he was guilty as charged on the charge of poor planning and shivered again in his wet clothes. No-one in their right mind goes kayaking in jeans and new, brilliant white sneakers but his window of opportunity didn't quite extend to a wet-suit. Though, it was also true that had he decided to procrastinate more and do less, he would most likely never have made it to their beach for the burial and then searching for a cave that obviously didn't exist.

He'd chosen to let his hair grow so he wouldn't look too cultivated and it was wet enough to slick back, which he did. He smiled wryly recalling how his dark brown mop of hair was a constant source of amusement to both of his ginger haired parents.

"Copper hair always seems to skip a generation in McCarthy boys." His father would laugh and Conor was never quite sure if he wasn't being mocked for looking so different from both his parents. Ceide would purse her mouth until her pink lips creased like a squeezed sponge and point-blank refuse to be drawn into banter that bordered on the sacrilegious if not slanderous, but she couldn't stop those eyes from laughing along with those of his father.

That would be the cue for the same eyes to begin dancing from the father to his son and then back again. Her luminous tresses would then follow every shake of her head when she'd start on his father for giving her son and herself so much good-natured grief. Remembering them play-acting like small kids would become the personal pantomime to get him through quiet Christmas Eves.

With the kayak clear of the water, the pristine state of the small beach should have been the first thing to strike him. The usual human detritus of plastic bottles, broken wood cargo pallets, brittle car tyres and the inevitable residue of unidentifiable multicoloured plastic paraphernalia, aged until faded and worn smooth by sixty decades of human progress, were all absent. What he did notice however, was something else that wasn't there and that the lack of human footprints, even in the dry sand higher up to his left.

He'd probably say that being the first visitor in god-only-knew-how-long, was what might have made the beach more attractive than it first appeared, as he indulged a spontaneous, if fleeting fantasy of maybe staying longer than it would take to dispel an old myth. Truth be told however, he wasn't looking forward to the return journey sandwiched between a sky that went on forever and an undulating sea that mirrored the vastness of it. There was also the issue of those waves and all it would take was one bad one to tip him over and he could disappear without a trace.

He'd have to work up to that but the fact of where he was prompted him to take a little time out to congratulate himself again for a mission pretty much accomplished against all the odds. All that remained to be done was to get back to civilisation and get on with his life, such as it was. But the only route to Dublin would take him through Portacloy first and that would be far more difficult, since there was nothing left to gain from it.

When the shivering started up again, he knew it wasn't going to be easy working himself up to the challenge of rowing back, and he started with some deep breathing exercises to get his fear under control. Minutes passed without the sun coming out to shine any light into the multitude of cold, damp and dark nooks and crannies in the all-encompassing rock face. He needed to get away and maybe the best approach was just to immediately relaunch the kayak and get it over with. But he needed more time and he also knew that indecision was a bitch.

So he looked around for any reason to stay just a few more minutes to get himself in the groove and that was the problem, because a conscious visual inspection of Ceide's beach told him that he'd wasted enough time on it already. There was absolutely nothing to bring anyone to this chilly and perpetually shaded stretch of sand, even though it precisely matched what he could remember of his father's description of it. He was told that it was only accessible from the sea and hence the need to 'borrow' the kayak. Anyway, what kind of idiot stacks canoes and bodyboards like an open invitation to any passer-by to take one, and then just disappear for a siesta or whatever?

Conor could never remember calling his mother anything other than Ceide, so he never had a Mammy or a Mum to demand his unconditional allegiance, as seemed to be the standard relationship most kids have with their mums. Ceide was easily as much fun to be with as Tadhg, who was very rarely 'Dad' and never when he was up to his elbows in the same mucky mess as his son. But those fireside storytelling sessions turned out to be a huge part of who he was and they were certainly more memorable than not wanting to play hide and seek, unless it was to avoid the constant bullying to come.

The central story told by his parents was like a rope of countless interwoven fibres which left it somewhere between dynamic or never-ending. That was because every birthday brought more detail or the offering of a perspective that he wouldn't have appreciated previously. It was probably because the storyline remained intrinsically the same that later sessions were more a process of continuous enhancements, like updating book chapters to use bigger and better words or more grown-up suggestions. That was what made those get-togethers impossible to completely erase, unlike most other aspects of Life#1.

Anyway, the upshot of a saga that took years to narrate, was him standing on the beach where it all began. He was compelled to come if only to invalidate tall tales of his Dad playing reluctant hero alongside doomed ninjas, mysterious flotillas of scary, red-eyed pirates and real magic with more than a hint of religious blasphemy from Ceide. It was only after she left that he began to realise just how different she was from other mothers.

What made the weaving of each episode into unworldly truths for the gullible, was probably down to how Ceide aided and abetted his father with so many of her 'matter-of-fact' asides and insights. These drew him deeper and deeper into the trials and tribulations of life in times so ancient that they were never written. He was probably the naivest kid alive but it was her who made the whole yarn so convincing, like she'd really lived it. That or she was fully sold on his father's version of it.

Tadhg talked most, but it was Ceide who started the storytelling and it developed into something that wouldn't be put off for any reason, almost like a sacred rite. She placed such importance on their sessions that it couldn't be abused, not even as a bribe to get him to do something like keep his room tidy. As a result, the story became a fact of life, like bedrock.

It all began quite casually when she told him one evening that McCarthy was his and his father's family name but that hers was 'Irvine'. He was young enough to assume that they'd always shared the same name, but he couldn't find a practical application for that simple curiosity, so he filed it away for later.

At least a year had passed when it popped into his head that he should meet her mother and father, since she so often included them in her embellishments to the story. He already knew Tadhg's parents but Ceide just smiled and told him they were long gone, which only piqued his interest further. It wasn't like her to put anything off until 'he was older', the bane of curious children everywhere. He remembered being unhappy with her proposal but since he couldn't remember her lying about anything, he simply filed away her promise to one day show him where she grew up and he lately lived only for the fulfilment of it.

In common with the experience of every other kid, when 'you are older' never arrives. It seemed to him that his parents simply evaporated and abandoned him one day and he had a real problem coming to terms with that. Later however, when the McCarthy clan had enough of his tantrums, no-one by the name of 'Irvine' showed up to claim him. Making a total nuisance of himself seemed at the time, to be one of his better laid plans but it backfired badly. The upshot of it all was that he created more time than he wanted, in which to contemplate the mystery of how someone as special as his mother could end up with no parents of her own to introduce him to.

When his only grandmother refused to shine a light on the subject, he had nowhere else to take his questions. It was like living in a bubble but sometime during Life#2, he was obliged to focus on more pressing issues and duly archived his fantastic family compilation of faceless ninjas, ancient gods and their messengers and mountainous seas amid Fomor invasions.

Part of growing up and healing was accepting that his parents apparently went to extraordinary lengths to fill his early dreams with something more substantial than contemporary plastic offerings from Marvel's retro superhero stable. And it was certainly true that as a kid, he was kept busier than Peter Pan with his wild lucid dreaming. Sometime later, when his childhood came under the microscope of Health Service Executive professionals, it occurred to them and subsequently him, that maybe his parents believed tall stories would facilitate his formative development, to use their words.

However, unlike other kids by then evolved into quasi-adults, he had a physical link to that Peter Pan stage of Life#1. That was what finally convinced him to step onto the beach and take a serious, if also brief look around. Having come this far, what did he stand to lose, apart from continued delusion.

He dug deep to excavate it from the tiny pouch above the actual pocket. It was a design feature that had, over the years, become his personal hallmark of what a quality pair of jeans should offer. There were actually two mandatory requirements but number one was the small, almost secret pocket and the other was wide belt loops. The mini-pocket feature was only good for smaller valuables but once something was jammed inside, it wasn't likely to fall out and more importantly, it couldn't be pilfered by bullies.

The only physical memento of those enchanted evenings wasn't much bigger than a two Euro coin. If such a thing existed, it would probably be about the same size as a four Euro coin and easily as thick. Ceide, his Dad and himself stashed it away when he was just eight and he spent the next year mulling over whether to prematurely recover it, despite a solemn undertaking not to do so.

"Go luath." It wasn't just her image that never left him but also the soft lilt of her voice, nearly always in Irish. English was for the in-laws, the neighbours, the local shops and the school teachers, all except the Irish teacher who couldn't get enough of his mother. Anyway, 'go luath' meant that she'd soon be able to explain the mystery of her absent family. It would mean a trip to revisit her birthplace in County Mayo.

They convened a Saturday or most likely a Sunday morning meeting after a particularly lengthy storytelling session the night before and they agreed to take him to their private beach, but only provided he take responsibility for keeping the disk safe in the meantime. Tadhg told him that they'd probably need it if they planned to search for clues to the missing ninja boat.

"Ni raibh am, there just wasn't time," she explained and that was well understood, if only a quarter of the Tadhg and Ceide saga was true. The extended story of their meeting would have resulted in them living it at a bewildering pace.

It was a unique memento, primarily because it just couldn't be scratched. That gave it the appearance of always being newly minted, even years later. Conor held it up to look for wear and tear that he knew he wouldn't find. That was his reassurance of some potential value beyond the merely sentimental.

Two thin rainbow hued triangles slid around on opposite sides as he turned it in his hand. These were evidence of the fine grooves etched into it, like on a miniature data disk but they weren't cut into the surface. They were sandwiched inside the stuff of the disk itself and protected by the clear, diamond hard veneer on each side. Anything that could survive seven years unscathed in the rough and tumble of a boy's first lives just had to be very special indeed. It was also thick enough to see seven tiny stud marks embossed around the edge at equal intervals.

"A key." His father had said, claiming that was the description used by the 'other' faceless Ninja, though the memory of that particular episode had perhaps become hazy over time. That was because he couldn't recall pressing his parents for more information on such mysterious entities. To an impressionable young boy, a masked ninja may have been potentially scary, but totally faceless ninjas were definitely the stuff of nightmares.

Faced with the dilemma of being haunted by something so exotic that he was unlikely ever to come across one, or of inviting reality into his bedroom by learning more about them, he probably opted to live in blissful ignorance. That was despite the very clear recall of being awoken more than once by silent faceless creatures that simply defied later description. Ultimately however, it was probably more logical to ask about something that could be touched at that particular moment in time.

"Key to what?" Conor could still see himself as he once was, wide eyed and innocence incarnate, when invited into the holy of holies to touch what must surely be untouchable. His memory of it wasn't perfect but Conor reckoned it could have been only a month or two before they agreed to stash it away, where only they could ever find it.

"To a boat my dear, though in the oldest dialect of Irish, it can also mean a ship." Said his mother with eyes that couldn't lie and guiding his fingers, she helped him push it inside the wide incision his father cut into the last surviving ash tree in his great grandfather's long garden. As an aid to finding it, Tadhg's incision was cut precisely at Conor's height, at one twenty centimetres.

"Tree scars can heal quite quickly, so you'll need to remember one twenty," said Tadhg. "But if you can't, don't worry because we will."

"One twenty." He must have repeated, though he clearly recalled being unhappy to leave something so valuable outside the protectorate of their house. "But will it be safe out here if we have to move house like you said we might have to?" Standard operating procedure demanded that all treasures be buried underground, and he wasn't short of quoted precedent.

"Finshogue will keep our secret safe but only as long as the three of us do likewise," Ceide assured him adding, "- and don't you worry your dark little head about moving house. Your father's word is always as good as your mother's and as long as we're together, we'll always have a solid roof over our heads."

His great-grandfather's sudden confinement had knocked the stuffing out of his grandson, Tadhg. As a small child, Conor remembered his father looking so distracted that he thought he might have been haunted for a while. He had good reason to remember that look because like his father, he'd soon get his own merciless reminder that immortality, like Santa, was a figment of the imagination. But standing on Ceide's beach just then, his shivering body eased in the warm afterglow of her beatific smile. Though he sometimes wondered about the timing of that little ceremony, so close to what came afterwards.

Collecting useless information comes naturally to most of us, even if the intrinsic value of our personal collections doesn't. Information is also useless when it's not applied and we let it fade into disjointed fragments, like obsolete data on a computer hard drive.

Conor was once well aware that trees were sacred to the ancient Irish and that the characters of the old Ogham alphabet were based on them. He also hadn't forgotten that the Irish word 'Finshogue' referred to the ash tree. So many traumatic years later, those quite compelling points had become inconsequential snippets of useless information. They might one day serve as polite ice breakers at cocktail parties, but only if he could still remember them. Further, as life began to unfold, it wasn't looking like cocktail parties would be something worth planning for.

The Irish that he could still conjure up was proportional to the number of people who continued to defy the odds by keeping it alive on the streets, but they'd become an extremely endangered breed. As an even more naive child, he asked the teacher at school why everyone spoke English and he could never forget how he was laughed at. Speaking Irish at home, as he did, just wasn't in vogue when global business would be conducted in English, Spanish and Chinese plus one other optional but still living language.

The upshot was that he was forced to reluctantly conclude that Ninjas speaking piss poor Irish were probably as logical as extra-terrestrial Jedi Knights speaking English backwards, like Master Yoda, and he laughed or rather scoffed aloud again. Conor peeled off his clothes until he stood in his boxer shorts and then spread each item out to dry on the more substantial rocks higher up the beach.

It crossed his mind that in a place with all the appearance of having his parents as its last visitors, he could also drop the wet shorts. He was about to do just that, until he glanced over his shoulder, more out of habit than anything else. But when he did, his eyes lingered longer on his parents' final resting place and his mind ushered him back through time once more.

He was eleven when he heard some of the school kids say they were sometimes taken to graveyards, but his only grandmother just cried when he asked her where his parents were buried. When he insisted on seeing a grave by throwing yet another fearsome tantrum, she tearfully took him around to the garage.

Once its remotely controlled doors were raised, she hesitantly pointed to two dark ceramic urns kept high on a shelf. They were just above his only grandfather's air compressor. What was it about dark shiny stoneware that suggested 'posh'? But when his innocent admiration made her cry even more, the inconceivable slowly dawned.

"But why?" During countless recalls of asking that question, it always came out as a whisper, a measure perhaps of the callous and fathomless horror that he could still feel sometimes.

"Because I just can't bring myself to bury him, but I also can't bear to look at him in the house every day." But Conor's only grandmother's total exclusion of his beautiful mother haunted him almost as much as the unseen face of the once nameless woman who stole them both away, by simply stopping dead on a motorway at night.

"Depressed." He heard them say over and over like that single word could somehow justify the end of the world.

Over more time than he could be bothered to measure, Conor reluctantly reduced his only grandmother's dilemma to one reason. She apparently blamed Ceide for stealing her son away when he was still too young to settle down. That upset him even more because if no superlative was good enough for his father, then surely his mother was nothing less because they were always a pair.

That was when he decided that he wouldn't leave his parents on a garage shelf, waiting for the day when one or the other would fall to be scattered over a patch of oil stained precast concrete. The mere possibility was enough to push him over the edge. He was furious and that fury evolved until no McCarthy would take him in but by then, he was past caring about where his bed was kept. Apart from his great grandfather, who was the definition of great, the other McCarthys allowed themselves to become strangers far too quickly, and he felt no compulsion to revisit that sad state of affairs.

He beat one of the larger rocks senseless with his heavy water logged socks to temporarily stain it wet and then laid them across it, regardless of no sunshine to accelerate the drying process. The streetwise live with and for opportunity, so he dragged his small haversack around the rock, where it couldn't be seen from the sea. Then, with a wry smile he went looking for signs of the mysterious ninja cave. That was where they should start, his father had said, planning ahead and blissfully unaware that his son would undertake the family quest alone.

From what he could remember, the cave wasn't supposed to be visible from the water, so he marched up the soft sand to stand below the most imposing section of sheer rock wall. Feeling more than just a little stupid but aware that

Ceide and Tadhg were with him in spirit at least, he resisted the urge to look seaward once more and turned his eyes left. Seeing nothing but more rock, he re-planted his feet wider to conduct a more detailed inspection.

Sure enough, there was rock, dripping rock, algae covered rock and simply moist rock. He could also hear water seeping through and down the various rock facades. High enough over his head to induce a bout of vertigo and the start of falling backwards, yellow flowered gorse bushes reached out over the cliff top and stretched almost all the way around the cove.

Conor looked again at his so-called key, a close family secret for fully half of his life and something snapped inside him. He flung it with a mixture of disgust, disappointment and maybe the last of his latent anger. It was heavier than plastic and flew like a miniature frisbee for a second or two. Then it arced tighter and tighter to the left as the breeze caught it and almost missed the protruding rock outcrop but not quite. It pinged off the edge with a totally unexpected sound that sang of ceramics and then continued to travel further than it should have. He watched in dismay as it disappeared into the advancing remains of a broken wave.

"Shit!" He shouted after it and quickly raced diagonally across the sand trying to keep an eye on the spot where it fell. If nothing else, he thought, he should have kept it as a reminder of gullibility and the need to separate sentiment and wishful thinking from real life. He'd learned only too well that life would always be as hard as the sound his disk made on that rock. As that thought dawned and then set, that last bubble of childhood delusion was finally and fully eviscerated.

When he found the shiny silver disk, it was closer to the beach than the spot where it fell and he wasn't sure if he was lucky to still have it, or cursed to be further reminded of hanging on to hopeless dreams. The disk didn't float, but it also wasn't dense enough to immediately sink and so, with the help of undercurrents, it made its way unseen to lie under quite shallow water. He then did what most teenagers do when destiny intervenes for the second time in rapid succession and he threw another minor tantrum.

His semi-precious disk found itself airborne again but this time, the trajectory was reasonably flat and it struck the rock face pretty much straight on, throwing out the same precise ping before shooting upwards in a vertical blur. What little breeze there was, then carried it just around the bluff, where a barely discernible puff of sand showed where it spent its last reserves of kinetic energy.

When he bent down to pick it up, he found what looked like a burrow hole of some evidently small creature. Curious to see what kind of animal would dare to share his mother's beach, he sank to his knees for a closer inspection. Glassy grains of worn sand inside the scooped out hollow were pushed towards him and he felt a wisp of cooler wind touch his cheek. That meant there had to be a reasonably large cavity further inside.

"The Ninja cave?" He said aloud, only to be distracted by the sound of something dragging on sand behind him. The downward curve of the beach blocked his immediate view to the kayak, which obliged him to stand.

"Hey!" "What do you think you're doing?" There were two of them. One was ... bigger and older and making off with the kayak. The answer to Conor's question was obvious. The kayak he'd hauled up on the beach was already in the shallows. It was being towed behind another lolling between him and the breakers. A younger boy was holding position in deeper, water, maybe ten meters beyond.

"He's looking your way Mikey." Shouted the youngest while the eldest, maybe eighteen or nineteen, pushed the lead kayak through a breaker and then pointed it towards his young companion. The way he jumped on board, oar in hand and with a smooth slide sideways, showed he'd done that before. Effortless balance in keeping his body vertical, as the tiny craft sliced through considerable turbulence was equally convincing.

"Ha. That'll teach Ya. Scumbag." The taunt was thrown behind him by the retreating kayaker, while Conor's tethered kayak bounced buoyantly over the breaker in pursuit.

Conor could be quick off the mark when he needed to be, but the soft sand wasn't going to let him prove it. He lost his footing when the desired rate of acceleration proved a little ambitious. By the time he reached wet sand, they'd put enough distance between them to open a leisurely, if not so civilised dialogue.

"You can stay there until you get some respect for other people's property, you thievin' bastard." Shouted the one that the other called 'Mikey' and the younger one laughed like a girl, showing that he was perhaps a little younger than Conor's first estimate of fourteen or so.

It came to mind just then how different things had been for his father on his first visit. Tadhg claimed to have quickly made friends of those who initially attacked him from the beach. Something that was especially true of the one called Daniel, who could have seriously injured his father with an old slingshot. Turning this confrontation around was definitely beyond him, but he had to give it his best shot because there was no other way back to civilisation.

"I'm no bloody thief. I just needed to borrow it." He protested loudly, adding, "Where were you expecting me to take it except back where I found it, once I finished up here?" His open palms failed to add the required measure of sincerity.

"I'd put manners on you right now Scumbag, but I can't take a chance on young Timmy paddling back alone." He looked like he was going to say more but apparently changed his mind and dug an oar into the sea to swivel his kayak away.

"Normally, I wouldn't leave a dog out here alone at night but don't get cocky. I'll be back in the morning with someone more capable of lookin' after himself. Then we can have a proper discussion about ownership before I watch you swim back around to the village."

"What bloody village?" Thought Conor but he also thought better of aggravating the situation.

"Wait! What am I supposed to do out here? You're leaving me no choice but to swim back alone." There was rain in the forecast and his belly was once again objecting to imposed fasts, but there was also a strong element of bluff in his appeal.

"You should have thought about that before you stole my boat, Creep. And I wouldn't recommend swimming back unless you're happy to be taken on a magical mystery tour by those currents out there." Mikey called out as he leaned into his oar strokes and encouraged the younger boy to do likewise.

"It can also get mighty wild in these Erris waters, especially after dark." Shouted Mikey over his shoulder, though the fact that he was prepared to share a tiny snippet of local knowledge suggested that he might not be the hard-man he was pretending to be. If he was, he wouldn't care whether Conor sank or swam, much like Conor himself wouldn't care, if their roles were reversed.

It crossed his mind that maybe he was trying to impress the boy who was possibly a sibling, and decided to use that to his advantage. "Are you scared to come back and discuss it with me now? You're older and bigger than me and in case you can't count, I'm all alone here. Doh!"

Conor was trying to sound 'Macho' but the addition of the three letter exclamation borrowed from Sonia's repertoire made it sound bitchy, taking some of the intended venom out of it. He was too busy to dwell on that however and focussed fully on his predicament. He was reasonably sure that if push came to shove, the younger boy would stay in his boat and Conor wasn't afraid of a little one on one, but his invitation wasn't accepted.

"I know you're alone. I could see you quite clearly from the top of those cliffs when I went tending the sheep, so I knew you weren't heading off to America with my kayak." He laughed hysterically at his own joke.

"Sleep tight." Squealed the smaller one, unable to conceal his delight and the giddy girly pitch to his voice.

Conor watched them exchange small banter interspersed with laughter, no doubt at his expense, until they were out of earshot. Too soon, they angled right at the cove's mouth and disappeared completely behind the inlet's rocky wall.

"Fuck!"

3 - Life#5 Dawns

Conor couldn't get his head around the fact that so much sand had somehow managed to stroll up a steeply inclined beach to then fill a supposedly sizeable cave and make it a rabbit hole. After all, it hadn't been centuries since his parents stood in precisely the same place. That kind of change over such a short time span was truly baffling.

Floating exceptions like lost logs aside, common sense says that anything moved up a beach on an incoming tide will subsequently be withdrawn on the outgoing. It's a natural extension of 'what-goes-up-must-come-down' and if that wasn't a rule set in stone, then Isaac Newton was the earliest example of 'official' fake news.

However, a quietly coalescing challenge to his assumption that all causes and effects were complete, simply because he determined that they should be, was stifled by a shortage of time to sift through all the permutations. He was busy, but the minor revelation registered nonetheless. His perplexed frown only softened when he found no application for the information and filed it away for later, as was his custom.

In a fortuitously more logical universe that held him securely at its epicentre, his father's Ninja cave wasn't yet fact, but a cavity big enough to funnel an otherwise absent wind through a very tight entrance, suggested that it may not have been total fantasy either.

He made a mental note to himself to read up sometime on how something as routine as tides can so dramatically alter shorelines … hopefully with illustrations … and some time frames. Meanwhile, he took a more leisurely tour along the beach to see if there was any hope of climbing out. He did find one option that wouldn't have been outright suicidal had there been no rain for a couple of weeks but this was Ireland. He resigned himself to finding cover and waiting for whatever the next day might bring.

"Bring it on Mikey." He was good enough with his hands and feet not to be intimidated and if he got thumped for borrowing the boat, well at least the most important item on his agenda could be ticked-off and so, smiled wryly.

Conor put his haversack and wet clothes closer to where he now needed to dig. He was fortunate that the local yokel had just grabbed the boat. The obvious advantage of not having too many possessions to protect was offset by the sad fact that everything he carried was pretty much everything he owned, with all of it stashed inside that one bag. He simply couldn't afford to lose anything.

It's another well known fact that animals often mimic human behaviour but Conor was about to demonstrate the opposite. Using canine and tortoise techniques in sequence, he began flailing sand between his hind legs with his front paws. He did that until the mound he was practically sitting upon rendered further flailing counterproductive. Then he shimmied backwards to sweep the product of his flailing further down the beach using his arms as flippers, thus making room for a replacement mound.

With no escape from the beach and rain in the forecast, there was some element of urgency, so he repeated the cycle until he needed a breather, which also presented an opportunity to eat something during recovery. Not an ideal arrangement but then, neither was the situation. A bar of coconut in milk chocolate went down so fast that he barely tasted either element.

The snack was part of a small contribution unknowingly made to his cause by a grocery store cum butchers cum local fuel depot. The combination of sugar and hard labour made him thirsty and he resolved that problem by standing under a dripping rock and letting it flow directly down his gullet. Feeling quite chuffed with his survival skills, he returned renewed to his task.

It was late afternoon when fortune smiled again and he was able to crawl inside the cavity after his damp clothes, duly zipped up inside a cheap plastic rainproof. However, he was covered in sand himself and since he was already wet from the rain, he decided to take a quick dip in the sea to lose the worst of it. But first, he had to unwrap his clothes so he could use the waterproof to stop the sand from sticking again as he crawled back inside.

Once showered and sheltered from the rain, the cavity was amazingly dry and he quickly scooped out a bowl big enough to act as a reclining bean bag. His phone was down to a single bar of charge when he decided to expend some reserve power and make his way further into the darkness. To his dismay, the sand floor fell steeply away to reveal what was most definitely a cave stretching into the distance.

"Bloody hell." He shouted gruffly and cursed himself for prioritising digging over exploration. The echo reverberated throughout the enlarged cave and came back at him in waves. He was quite tired but reluctant to let it dictate terms. Conor had a thing about unseen denizens of both the deep and of the dark varieties. That was part of the reason why he was never likely to swim back to the 'so-called' village alone and especially not after dark.

Things that swam in deep dark water invariably had teeth, while the smaller dry land or dark cave species would likely have matted wet fur and stink to high heaven. That and maybe long dirty tails that could inadvertently slide into a sleeping though partially opened mouth.

He didn't see any animal tracks in the sand but that was no guarantee of absent denizens, so he listened out for signs. There had to be a least one of them somewhere but then he doubled his estimate because denizens always came in pairs. Unsurprisingly, waves gently folding to a rhythm all their own became the dominant sound seeping in from the outside world of fading light and salty sea-weed breezes.

He found himself wondering how loud that sound might be during storms, when they'd be big enough for the kind of coastal earthworks needed to fill up the mouth of a cave but thankfully, the weather was forecast to stay calm if also humid for a few days. Further afield, seagulls continued to squabble over opportunities and treacheries that he could only imagine. In Erris however, they constituted the essential element of any ambience chosen from a truly impressive repertoire.

A breeze that he couldn't yet feel on his face moaned somewhere in the darkness, otherwise he could hear one, two or three sources of slowly dripping water. One fell on rock, another softly on sand nearby and the third dripped into a pool sounding curiously like it was somewhere overhead. That was strange but regardless, he lay back halfway up the slope and continued to listen until the moaning of the wind and the individual dripping patterns were subtly choreographed into a lullaby of sorts. Accumulated fatigue eventually forced him to close his eyes but he continued to listen while his mind went walkabout yet again.

As a ten year old orphan, he'd gone back to pissing in his bed and to giving as good as he got from anyone who had a problem with that. He did the same to experts who talked about him like he wasn't in the same room listening. 'Trauma' they said, and he tried to behave, because otherwise no-one would come to claim him, or so they said.

That threat became prophecy and as it transpired, Life#2 had some things in common with the various sounds of the ninja cave. Every time the moaning rose, he'd be forced to move house to find yet another drip but he never spent longer than it took for the moaning to come back. He was trying to visualise drip number three when Evelyn called him inside for her special stew. How he missed Dear Evelyn.

Life#2. was a series of constant readjustments from one set of foster parents to another. The childcare authority presented each prospective home as Shangri-la but Evelyn and Jimmy Ryan's house apart, they all lapsed into the same stony silences and illogical rule books applied to his coming and going. Life#2 was as endless as purgatory, but he made it bearable with the hope that each day was bringing him closer to Life#3.

Funny how it took a Jesuit Priest named McVerry to take him out of purgatory and deliver him home, because priests normally work the other way around. But Life#3 was to be as short as it was sweet. People can hold some strange beliefs and for a while he became convinced that tragedy was a beast that in its own way, was very much alive. Having successfully fed so close to him, it would logically tend to stay close by, waiting for another easy meal.

Being retired and having more time on their hands than other foster parents produced some sparkling results. It allowed Jimmy to spend more time with him than Tadhg could afford to spend while still alive. And when Jimmy wasn't on overtime, Evelyn worked her magic. She tirelessly and in carefully measured steps, created an older and far from beautiful but certainly a wiser and possibly less impulsive version of Ceide to re-introduce a little love into his savagely interrupted life. Like a patient responding to a potent drug, Conor could eventually share the only thing of value he still possessed. That was what he could still remember of his parents' epic saga, but only at night and only when Jimmy lit a fire, even during the summer.

If Jimmy was younger, things might have been different but they said he couldn't care for Conor and his best friend forever, Dear Evelyn. Poor Eve got lost on her way home from the supermarket and they had a terrible time trying to find her. A few days later, she went missing again during a routine outing to the library. Overnight it seemed, she didn't dare go outside at all and her confidence in safely performing the smallest of domestic tasks simply evaporated. Fear became the beast that would drag her down, just as tragedy threatened to stalk Conor into adulthood.

Like a dutiful, if adopted prodigal son, Conor found a way to make subsequent unofficial visits, but it was never the same without her being there as completely as she was before. Jimmy and her were in every sense a pair, just like Tadhg and Ceide and a pair is an impossibility without both halves.

For once, the Irish Fostering Agency seemed to have got something right and poor Jimmy just couldn't adjust to her loss, though he tried like the soldier he was. On one of those visits he quietly confided to a bemused twelve year old that he just assumed Evelyn would always be Evelyn and so ended Life#3.

On the last visit to his favourite foster-father, Jimmy was looking more and more like a candidate for home care himself. The McVerry Trust stayed steadfast in their efforts to find Conor a new home but there would be no third time lucky for him.

A random vision materialised, in which two ninjas were having a hell of a time trying to squeeze a standard sized timber planked boat into and out of the cave he'd just dug his way into, when surprise surprise, Sonia arrived from nowhere. She just took form centre stage, as she always did and as a result, Evelyn's stew recipe and the exasperated ninjas became instant non issues.

It was unusual for Sonia to smile because scowling seemed to get her whatever she wanted much faster. Conor didn't know if girls worked harder to look older or if that was just in their DNA. Whatever the reason, Sonia might have been younger than him and she was certainly a pain at times, but she was incredibly soft on the eyes.

But what was she doing in Jimmy and Evelyn's house? Back then, they hadn't even met her but regardless, her smile totally disarmed him. Even held captive by his dream, it still stole the time he needed to find an adequate response, especially when neither of them was comfortable holding eye contact like that. He'd do it sneakily and whenever she wasn't looking but smiling was one of the few things she seemed incapable of. Then she topped it all by waiting patiently for him to assemble some words into a coherent greeting. Boy had she changed.

Art, was the answer. He'd ask about her latest Indian Ink drawing and just as he opened his mouth, her face turned instantly dark and her tongue cut him to the bone, like it seemed to do so often.

"What are you gawking at?" She demanded and sure enough, that's precisely what he was doing, but then she smiled again and turned all coy but he'd had enough of her play-acting.

"Piss off, you tease." He said and she got really mad … like she could sometimes. In his peripheral vision, Karl and Anto were smirking in his direction, like they were gauging the extent of potential opportunity from his apparent weakness.

"What?" A single word with the right intonation was usually enough to turn the tables on those two turds. They knew better than to respond to that, so they all pissed off and he was alone again. Sometimes it was easier being alone but he became curious again about where Sonia could have gone to so suddenly. It wasn't like she had a secret family stashed away somewhere and maybe that was part of the crazy chemistry that bubbled up between them sometimes. They were loners together.

"Holy Shit." He said out loud. Too loud by the way his voice returned in bits and snatches of muffled staccato echoes.

He was awake, which meant he'd been asleep and he reached unconsciously for his phone. It still had enough some power, so he thanked Jimmy aloud and again for the gift of it. It was a prehistoric model and not so smart by any current standards but it never let him down and the battery, a very expensive replacement, was even better than the original. It was just after three thirty … in the morning … because it was dark outside … but it was summer … and that meant it would soon be light enough to see.

Summer was great for short nights but after one night spent in a barn, listening for rustles in the hay and another on a beach, fending off man eating vampire flies, he'd apparently been wiped out. He was asleep for longer than most babies but thankfully, it seemed that he hadn't been obliged to entertain the tails of uninvited denizens.

His throat was dry, but uncontaminated and Conor turned the phone off to save whatever little power still remained. He was feeling great if a little stiff and his clothes, cold and damp when he dragged them on, seemed dry enough to feel almost warm. It was just too dark to go exploring for ninjas, so he let his eyes probe the darkness instead.

"Nowhere was completely dark, unless you were blind and even then", they said but he couldn't remember who 'they' were or what 'they' might have seen in the dark. He'd apparently survived a nocturnal denizen foray and point blank refused to contemplate the prospect of another. Anyway, it was surely too close to dawn by then but he needed to urgently change the subject. He had a strange thought just then and wondered whether his eyes were open or closed. How could anyone know for sure, if it was dark, really dark that was?

That dripping of water into water above him was a real conundrum, so he focused on that but without resolving anything other than it was definitely overhead. The soft wind-moan was coming from the same general direction and he made another mental note to start exploring in that direction just as soon as it got bright enough. Then he saw something, or thought he did. A luminescence so pale that it remained imagination for whole minutes, until it quivered like only water can when it's disturbed by something like a dribble building into a drop to then drip.

Another quiver, but the visual clue was out of sync with the three audible drips. The offending spot wasn't far from the cave entrance and a bit further to his right, where the sand was built up closest to the roof but he'd have to wait a little longer. If he could see water in total darkness, he'd see a whole lot more when it began to really brighten up and besides, there was the sound of rain falling mutely on sand outside or, was that something a denizen could do? He shivered.

When the quivering became more defined and then grew a glistening lip with a smoky haze above it, Conor sat bolt upright. There was a hint of dawn beyond the rabbit burrow he'd excavated but just like the visible drip, the beach beyond looked almost as dark as the cave's interior. When a sudden increase in light suddenly enabled 3D discernment, he realised that he was looking at a hole in the cave roof and the haze behind it was the beginning of daylight, or rather daylight reflected from the more distant wall of a separate chamber above.

"Wow."

He crawled over until he was under what was effectively a hole in the roof and then received the reward of a light splash of spray for his troubles. Daylight was coming up fast, or maybe it was because his eyes were so attuned to the lack of it that he could see a depression in the sand where the dripping water was disappearing. Reaching up, he touched wet stone and then eased his hand further through the gap. A small and very shallow pool of water was being topped up by the fourth set of drips from even higher above. These were causing the pool to overflow through the same access hole and ultimately drain through the sand beside him.

Despite the trickle of water and the slippery lip, he thrust his head inside the upper chamber and sure enough, there was enough light to give him a rough outline of a concave wall maybe four or five meters distant … no, make that six.

Being able to see anything at all meant there was another access to the outside world somewhere on the opposite wall that he couldn't yet make out. That access was catching daylight earlier than the north facing beach below and the puzzle of why the beach was still so dark was resolved.

Conor gathered up his gear and threw it through the hole, keeping it well clear of the pool alongside the entrance.

"If the ninjas live up here somewhere, then they can't be much bigger than me." He said to himself, sizing up the tight entrance, like getting himself ready to squeeze up into an old attic but from a ladder that was a tad too short.

There didn't seem to be any hand holds he could use to haul himself up. So, checking above his head once more, he jumped upwards to get some momentum going and then planted his hands each side of the hole to take his weight. He didn't waste any more time and was soon pulling himself up to sit gingerly on the ledge. Instant wet pants encouraged him to stand immediately upright. There was significantly more sound coming in from the outside than was the case in the cave below. The gull chorus was already in full swing but despite that, the chamber seemed aloof from the real world, like he'd found the entrance to an empty cathedral and tried too hard not to make noise.

It was beyond amazing to discover a cave that bore all the appearance of welcoming its first visitor … ever, except maybe for those mysterious ninjas. Despite his best intentions to wait for better light, he got impatient just standing there like a silly statue. Conor turned on the phone, aware that using the flash-light function would most likely flatten the battery completely. So he opted to take a photo with the camera's flash instead. The battery only lasted long enough for him to examine the exposure of a deeply inverted cliff side wall. But the curvature was so significant that most of indented wall behind it was out of focus.

Dragging one foot slowly after the other, so as not to slip on what he assumed would be a wet surface or worse still, a minefield of yet more open holes in the floor, he made his way to the back wall. Head clearance wasn't an issue but only the blind can be truly comfortable in the dark. So, Conor held one had out and the other above until they both came together when the wall gelled into the lowest reach of the ceiling.

With light fast improving, more detail literally stood out. Small crystallised patches became reflective clusters when he looked closer and suggested something like granite embedded in something else. His fingers registered the rough surface as slick, damp and cold in turn, but that changed when he moved further along the wall. A section maybe a metre and a half in diameter was noticeably dry and as a result not so cold to the touch.

Conor took a break to lean against the unexpectedly dry section and perused the chamber from that vantage point, taking advantage of the improving light. The chamber was shaped like a half sphere with a surprisingly flat floor that sloped gently towards the sea. Everything in the cliff seemed to be oriented in the same general direction. There was a suggestion of undulations, like the floor was a much older section of Ceide's beach that had petrified or fossilised. After the brief distraction of trying to determine the difference between petrified and fossilised, he simply excused himself from the exercise and moved on.

A deeper indent took seepage in the same direction, where it presumably worked its way through the seams of the different rock strata to find its way over the outcrop and onto the beach below. Except for the area just under the cliff wall side of the cave, there was a noticeable lack of the same rock pieces that were loosely scattered everywhere else.

That made it easy to see the few small pools on the predominantly dry floor, which looked like an extension of the same rock seam that looked like it must run right through the cliff. He then realised that without the significant build-up of sand below the hole in the lower roof, the upper chamber would have stayed pretty much inaccessible and also unnoticed. Above him, the higher access point to the world of daylight beyond wasn't much bigger than the one he'd just climbed through. From his angle, he judged that it probably looked out northeast, close enough to parallel the cliff face.

He put the curious section of drywall down to a quirk of the different rock formations before realising that the lack of sunlight might also play a part in keeping moss and green algae down, what with no photosynthesis. Surprising himself with that extremely scientific analysis, he decided to challenge it with something totally ludicrous.

"Then again, if there was a secret ninja hangout behind that section of wall, that might also explain the lack of moisture seeping through", he laughed and repeated each word when their echoes returned unevenly. He played with his words, drawing some of them out to produce an overlap, depending on which way he was facing. Conor's Cave had as good a ring to it as Ceide's Beach but if he didn't call something after Tadhg there'd be trouble in heaven, but first things first.

"It's not just a conspiracy theory. Mars bars really are shrinking." He said louder, when he ripped off the wrapping and casually dropped it on the undulations in the floor. The remaining Reeses and Snickers were eased back into the dedicated food pocket of his haversack while he chewed slowly. Mars bars, unlike Bounty bars, simply demanded to be savoured. It was just something that people did - no questions.

"Well if they're making them in two sizes as you suggest, then how come the price is the same as it was, not that I'm out of pocket this time around?" He insisted, still amused by the unusual echo and followed with. "I think I could climb up there." When he saw that the outside wall was far from vertical and looked like it might have a number of hand grip possibilities between the various seams. The only problem appeared to be bright white streaks that he could only hope were dried lichens or something similar.

"It's a really bad sign when you start talking to yourself." He chided himself with a well practised copy of Dear Evelyn's broad Dublin brogue and like her, he continued muttering as he readied himself for the climb. There was also a selection of small crevices that looked good enough for a toehold or two. He just needed to stay to the left to avoid parts of the white gunk that appeared to be quite slick once seen close up.

When he arrived at the top with a grunt, he almost fell back down again. This natural window was caked inside and out with some dried but also not so dry white and green gullshit. With no option but to continue upwards he pushed through, accepting the penalty of white and green streaks on his previously immaculate-white T-Shirt. He was going to find it extremely difficult to look anything close to 'normal' until he found a way to replace his shirt.

"But that kind of T-Shirt", he reminded himself, "-had to be virginal white at all times, coz otherwise, it wouldn' match the brilliant white sneakers." Looking down, he was horrified to find that his foot-ware would also need attention before passing any 'normal' inspection.

"That shit will never wash off," again borrowing Evelyn's overly disappointed tones, even though she'd never lower herself to say 'shit'.

"Sorry for the language Eve." He declared, but totally devoid of guilt.

Once outside, he discovered why the hole through the rock wasn't also caked in mud flowing down from above. The window was more than waist high above the eroded rock below it that was also the roof of the outcrop itself. Above the window was a feature that served as a natural lintel. This was where the rock layer had broken away from the cliff face to leave a section jutting out. It would keep most of the rain off, unless the wind was blowing from east or northeast, which he guessed must be seldom.

He was able to reach the lintel while standing on the window ledge and he hoisted himself up, glad that he regularly did his pull-ups. Once standing on the lintel, he found that he was well on the way to the cliff top. The rest of the route up wasn't as dangerous as it looked from below, provided that he avoid the obviously wet patches of soil by standing only on raised dry rock surfaces or patches of dry grass.

It didn't seem to take very long for him to reach the top, though finding a way through the gorse bushes to get into the sheep pastures beyond them was as dirty an exercise as climbing out from the cave's attic chamber. It wasn't done quietly either and he accompanied himself with a cocktail of Dear Eve's mutterings generously mixed with his own profanities in turn, especially when he discovered just how thorny gorse bushes could be. Just when he was almost through and looking at a very puzzled sheep dripping green spittle from its chin, he remembered his haversack.

"Fuck." Again.

He retraced his steps to the cave's upper storey, cursing every prick of every gorse thorn, every slip and each slide, sometimes more than twice but progress was steady. Soon, he dropped athletically from the lintel to stand looking through the open window once more. There was simply no alternative to getting inside than squatting in the bird crap again while waiting for his eyes to become adjusted to the dim interior. He was amazed at how much detail he'd not seen earlier because back then, he was so dazzled by daylight. An indication perhaps of how much the human eye can adapt to poor light given time. The inside didn't look anything like the same place that he was able to negotiate with some confidence and in far less light.

He decided to take the plunge and was about to back through the window, when his eye caught what appeared to be a smoother and much brighter patch of slate grey rock. It was just below where the ceiling sloped into the opposite wall below. That particular patch was a little unusual in that it sloped away from him while the wall on either side sloped towards him to then join the ceiling. It was obvious that it wasn't part of the same geological structure and the oblique angle, when viewed from the floor below, would probably explain why he hadn't seen the anomaly earlier.

Once inside again, having added to his already impressive collection of green and white streaked camouflage, he backtracked to the bald section of rock to find that it wasn't the same kind of rock that was spread throughout most of the cave. It had all the appearance of slate, except that it was unusually smooth and also glazed over, like it was covered with a thin layer of natural glass, assuming there was such a thing.

A quick look around while also considering the alignment of the floor he stood on, confirmed that all the other layers were pretty much horizontal. This section was out of sync and reaching up, he ran his hand over it and just knew it wasn't rock at all. It was just too artificial and when his finger fell on a small circular inset that was just too precise, he knew someone had to have worked on it at some stage.

So much for discovering his own private cave but his eyes opened even wider when he realised that the impression couldn't be much bigger than a €4 coin, if there was such a thing. Reaching into his 'precious pocket' while pressing himself tight against the normal rock below it, he nearly tripped over an unseen chunk of rock on the floor directly beneath the oddity.

Fingers trembling and clumsy with anticipation, he almost dropped his disk when he brought it up to gauge the impossibility of a fit. Just above head high, his small disk sank seamlessly into an indent so completely clear of dust, dirt and whatever, that it had to be kept clean … by someone.

Nothing happened of course but then, what was he expecting? "Open Sesame." He mumbled, but with volume turned high enough to return unevenly from the high domed ceiling and smaller cavities cut even deeper into the cliff face. The thing was, the disk was such a good fit that he couldn't get a fingernail in alongside it, to pry it out again.

At first he thought it was a trick of the light and glanced over his shoulder to see if someone had shone a light in from the high exit behind him, but there was no-one. The small silver disk was internally illuminated but it was done very subtly, like the weak blue-green iridescence given off by the water trickling down before dawn. Then the disk brightened considerably and filled with slowly alternating colours, like flipping through the coloured bands of a rainbow.

"Holy shit. What is that?" He exclaimed and his outgoing question mixed with its incoming echo, once again straggling back from countless corners, crevices and niches. The colour sequence then slowed until red became strong enough to light the wall section before dimming and turning orange, which strengthened and then dimmed to become yellow. The colour procession continued through green and then blue to indigo and violet but it didn't stop. The pattern was repeated over and then over again, brighter each time, though that could have been down to the increasing sensitivity of his eyes or to an imagination running wild.

The timing of the cycle was consistently even and Conor's excitement turned to impatience with no further developments. He decided to prod the thing as he would if something was 'stuck' but as his finger hovered over it, he was struck by a thought. If the disk was indeed a type of data disk, which it certainly resembled, then a logical response would surely be better than some random prod. So he watched the sequence a bit longer. Seven colours that were, as far as he knew, following the correct rainbow sequence.

It started with red, which meant green was in the middle and violet marked the end of the sequence, so he waited for red to come around again and when it did, he put his finger on the disk. The disk stayed red for as long as his finger remained on it but once again, he became impatient and withdrew it. As soon as he did, the sequence continued as before. So he waited for violet and then placed his finger on the disk again. This time, violet flashed a number of times in quick succession before it extinguished and the disk went dark. With nothing to do but reflect, he estimated seven flashes, which was coincidentally the number of colours.

Convinced that he was definitely interacting with some kind of computer program or automation, he waited eagerly for something different to happen and he didn't have to wait long. Violet flashed four times and then extinguished. He couldn't make anything of that and waited patiently. After maybe a minute that could just as easily have been several, violet lit up again and again his disk flashed four times before dying out as before.

When it was completely dark, he put his finger on the disk and the slow colour sequence began again at red. As it came around to green, Conor withdrew his finger. The way he saw it, seven flashes at violet was an indicator of seven colours to complete the cycle and four flashes from violet had to indicate the middle colour, which was green.

The disk went dark and Conor's heart almost leapt out of his chest when an ear-piercing shriek flooded the chamber and then bombarded him with a prolonged assault of grossly distorted echoes. Something cracked loudly before shattering and to confirm it, great lumps of rock started to fall from the wall to break into smaller pieces at his feet, while dust began to rise in small clouds.

Vibrations running through the floor became more and more pronounced until a large slab of rock broke off to shatter into leg stinging shards around him. He leapt backwards and spun to face the exit hole in the floor, convinced of an imminent cave in. With every muscle taught in readiness, silence fell to be slowly followed by some raised dust and he froze where he found himself for long minutes.

Poised precariously inside a hole that was his designated escape hatch, his butt ready to tense and release him to slide through, he peered into the depths below. A slightly deeper indent in the sand was identified as the target from where he would begin to scamper for his life, but peace prevailed.

The fall of slabs and rocks turned into an intermittent drizzle of pebbles and he waited, though still poised to flee. After several minutes of growing silence, he retraced his steps to find that the grey metallic smooth patch reached all the way down to the floor. It wasn't metallic silver but a sort matte metallic grey, like maybe graphite or something. A series of creaks were clearly coming from inside the newly uncovered section of wall and then, a long circular slit began to slowly open up.

Hot on the heels of that earthquake came nothing less than a volcano, as smoke billowed out through the ever-widening gap and Conor stepped backwards once again. This time he was prepared to dive through the exit if need be. An isolated stone fell far enough away for him to resist visually checking it out while the smell of smoke reminded him of incense, but it was thick enough to screen whatever was inside the still yawning breach.

He didn't realise that he'd stopped breathing until he was forced to gasp and so compensate for too many breaths left on hold. A thick circular door, reminiscent of something that might be attached to a humongous industrial washing machine and in turn attached to a huge curved hinge, cranked fully open and the pleasant smelling smoke began to thin.

With no warning, white light surged out to sting his eyes and flooded chamber with an intensity in utter contrast to the soft rotating light displays. The searing intensity bleached the walls, floor and roof white to obliterate scars that were once cuts and crevices while knots of white smoke, which erupted like incandescent filaments killed off all remaining shadows.

With undetectable rapid transition, the white light became instantly red and the familiar rainbow cycle resumed, but far brightly. As the colours got deeper, so did his ability to see beyond the door, which after due reflection, would have looked more like an airlock except it had no visible handle to lock it.

By the time violet arrived he was peering into a sphere spilling out its last puffs of by then, lilac hued smoke. The machined perfection of the door's inside, now facing out, drew him to touch it. It was gleaming and unblemished, like it had just come off a production line. It was also flat and featureless, aside from a small Perspex slot. Inside the slot was his disk, held in place with two thin overlapping wires.

A glance above the door told him that his disk had indeed been ingested by the door mechanism, much like a slot machine. Inside the sphere, a long semi-reclined seat was built just above the raised floor to follow the same general contour. Slightly above but facing the seat, a wide glazed panel was divided into seven separate sub panels, each one glowing its own rainbow colour and as he watched, the rectangular shapes shrank to form seven 3D orbs about the same size as golf balls. Each orb appeared to be suspended just above the matte black screen that gave it birth.

The console housing the seven panels was a small but quite discernible distance from the sphere wall but also within touching distance of anyone sitting upright in the seat. This arrangement suggested that everything he could see was part of a rigid sub assembly that could move independently of the enclosing sphere.

"Holy Shit." It took him far longer to say those two words than it normally would, but he nevertheless felt obliged to repeat them and then inserted a common profanity between the words by way of elaboration.

The small red orb on the left then pulsed like a beating heart while the orange one strobed before fading. Then yellow took up the strobe and faded until green did the same and then blue and indigo. The panel containing the violet orb wasn't strobing as consistently as the others, but it didn't take him long to realise that it was beating to the same heartbeat pattern intimated by the red screen, only faster.

In fact, the violet orb was keeping perfect time with his own heart, which was racing.

4 - Shaken and Stirred

"Do you think the asshole was able to climb out?"

"No." Answered Mikey.

"How can you be so sure about that?"

"Because, Seamus," said with no small hint of exasperation, "- there's no bloody body lying under the cliff."

That brought a whoop of raucous laughter from the stockier of the two, his closed fist thumped a chest made bare by turning down the top of his wetsuit. Seamus had a face that was faster than most to grow a smile from a frown but also quicker to revert to its default puzzle. In the small community of Portacloy, anyone with Down Syndrome was known as different only until they left school. After that, they reverted to their God-given name, or a derivative thereof, just like anyone else.

Mikey then mimicked a footballer by swinging a neoprene covered foot to playfully connect with the empty rubber arm dangling from his friend's waist. When he made good contact, the floppy arm came close to slapping its owner in the face, which caused one to outdo the other in adding to the human ruckus that was positively invasive for such an isolated spot.

Their purpose momentarily forgotten, oars were dropped where they stood to free hands for some mutual back-slapping and a high-five that turned out to be a medium-three, when contact failed to meet any commonly accepted standard.

"Jayz Mikey, you should seriously think about being a stand-up comic." Said Seamus, wiping tears that seemed to irritate his slightly mongoloid eyes.

"D'ya think so?" Mikey wasn't really asking. There was nothing he'd like more than to make any kind of living doing what came naturally, but he couldn't just up and leave. His parents were no longer up to the chores that needed to be done to eke out a living from sheep farming. He'd lately set a few plots set aside for specialised organic market gardening and one produced potatoes for the local market. He lived in the real world and Seamus knew it, so he didn't bother answering. The rather fanciful Q and A was just part of their ongoing banter.

"Is that him?" Asked Seamus who was also slightly shorter than Mikey but regardless, was already clenching his fists. Summer was great for the extra money brought in by visitors but it could also be relied upon to bring them one or two undesirables.

"How many people can you see Shay?" Mikey patted him on the shoulder as he pushed on towards the approaching stranger while dropping a prompt. "Didn't I tell you he was alone?"

"Oh. Yeah. So you did. So you did." Seamus repeated himself as he sometimes tended to do and fell into step beside his companion as he made his way towards Conor. Over the upstart's shoulder, it was evident the boy had dug himself a substantial hole under the rock outcrop.

"He doesn't look the full shillin'." Commented Seamus as Conor covered his eyes with both hands, like he was having a problem enduring daylight, despite the overcast.

"You're right Shay. Maybe he just woke up," and then to Conor. "I see you tried to burrow under the rocks to escape, just like the scared rat that we know you are."

"Is it only tomorrow?" Asked Conor, looking more than a little dazed. "Or were you already here yesterday … or the day before … but couldn't find me?"

"What kind of stupid question is that?" Barked Seamus, working himself up to the physical confrontation that Mikey said would be more than likely. But the way Conor kept coming at them was making him nervous, despite the youngster being outnumbered two to one and Shay's calloused shovels for hands.

"Did you fall or something?" Asked Mikey, becoming a little concerned that the boy might indeed have fallen from the cliff face to suffer a concussion or something, but Conor wasn't listening. They stopped to face each other from just a meter away, which was a little too close for declared enemies and Shay took one step back. The youngest of the three looked like he'd been rolling around in the dirt.

"I said I'd come back with someone more capable than little Timmy, so here we are. Now, what's your excuse for stealing my kayak, and you better make it good?" Asked Mikey, taking a half step forward until he was almost nose to nose and then poked Conor in the rib cage for good measure. With the battle line clearly drawn, Shay tensed and then moved up to stand on it.

That seemed to bring Conor back from wherever his mind was wandering. "Who are you calling a rat and which of you stole my new sneakers?" His gaze lingered on Seamus' unexpected facial features. He found them a little disconcerting because fighting someone who was handicapped just wasn't done. Then his attention was attracted back to Mikey when he spoke up again.

"I'll give you top marks for having balls lad, but if you think you can take the two of us, then you're really not right in the head. Know what I mean?" Seamus pushed his nose over the line to show solidarity with his friend and mimicked him by getting ready to also poke the boy in the ribs but Conor could see that one coming.

The first lesson of street fighting is to react first and regardless of societal niceties. The younger boy was instantly off his feet and drop-kicked Seamus in the head. The heaviest of the three went down with a look of utter astonishment but the blow wasn't as clean as intended.

With Seamus screaming for vengeance while struggling to his feet, Mikey had already dropped onto Conor's spread-eagled form to keep him pinned to the sand where he fell.

"Holy crap boy. You really don't want to piss Shay off any more than you already have." He shouted with his face so close that Conor could smell the sausages he had for breakfast. "And the state of your clothes. Where did you collect all that birdshit?" His eyes opened wide in amazement when he realised that the boy must have tried to climb out.

"You bloody idiot. You could have killed yourself." It struck Mikey then, that had the boy seriously hurt himself trying to climb out, he would have been somewhat responsible for it by leaving him no choice. "Idiot." He repeated angrily.

But Shay was already on the offensive and kicked Conor in the side but because he was also shoeless, the rubber boots under his wetsuit only softened the blow.

"Stoppit Shay. Can't you see I've got him pinned down? Now back-off till we see what the eejit is on about. He doesn't seem to know what day it is and from the looks of him, maybe he did take a fall."

"I'll murder him for that sneak attack." Shay was scarlet-faced and his eye movements were slightly out of sync. Mikey couldn't say how much of that was down to embarrassment for being caught cold, blood pressure, or the glancing blow from Conor's flying feet combined with the abrasive effect of sand on skin.

"I'm letting you go now, but don't try anything or I'll just let Shay pummel you senseless. You got that?" He paused before adding. "And neither of us has seen your stupid shoes."

"I'm not afraid of two boggers." Said Conor, who was on his feet as fast as Mikey regained his.

"Well you should be. You're giving away a lot of weight, not to mention an extra pair of fists and feet. Now don't be stupid and if you want to stay in one piece, I'd strongly suggest you stop calling the good people of Erris 'boggers' to their faces. It doesn't tend to go down well, Scumbag."

"Then maybe you shouldn't have started by calling me a scared rat, coz I'm neither, but I'm not ashamed to say I can fight like one if I have to." Was Conor's retort.

Shay was about to swing a right but thought better of it when Mikey raised an arm to deny him the space to complete the swing and also glowered his disapproval. Conor was wary of further unpredictability from the one who looked like he might be handicapped, but the two of them seemed to be a counterbalance to each other. The taller one was obviously in charge but he might also be a bit too soft, whereas the heavier one was more impulsive. He'd keep his eyes on that one.

"All right, let's just tone this down a notch," offered Mikey adding, "- and I'm still waiting to hear why you stole my kayak yesterday."

"Yesterday?" Conor was still dazed.

"Of course it was yesterday. When do you think you took it, you tool?" Shay was still itching to establish a semblance of justice. He'd been lulled into a false sense of security by the boy's confused state, though he was definitely faster than he looked. But no-one by the name of O' Rourke had ever suffered the same fool twice and that wasn't about to change.

"Sorry." Said Conor though it didn't sound like an apology, more like an 'excuse-me-while-I-try-to-collect-my-thoughts-here'.

"It seems like a lot's happened since I saw you and that younger boy, that's all." He let his sentence taper off into silence, but they were still waiting for a more coherent offering.

After a silence that they permitted to last for a full minute, Seamus decided he'd had enough and stepped forward again to coax a response out of the boy just as Conor took a half step backwards and held up his hands to claim détente. "My parents met on this beach and there was nowhere else to bury their ashes, so I thought I'd bring them both back to where they met. I buried them out there." Said pointing into the small cove between the two older lads.

embarrassment for being caught cold, blood pressure, or the glancing blow from Conor's flying feet combined with the abrasive effect of sand on skin.

"I'm letting you go now, but don't try anything or I'll just let Shay pummel you senseless. You got that?" He paused before adding. "And neither of us has seen your stupid shoes."

"I'm not afraid of two boggers." Said Conor, who was on his feet as fast as Mikey regained his.

"Well you should be. You're giving away a lot of weight, not to mention an extra pair of fists and feet. Now don't be stupid and if you want to stay in one piece, I'd strongly suggest you stop calling the good people of Erris 'boggers' to their faces. It doesn't tend to go down well, Scumbag."

"Then maybe you shouldn't have started by calling me a scared rat, coz I'm neither, but I'm not ashamed to say I can fight like one if I have to." Was Conor's retort.

Shay was about to swing a right but thought better of it when Mikey raised an arm to deny him the space to complete the swing and also glowered his disapproval. Conor was wary of further unpredictability from the one who looked like he might be handicapped, but the two of them seemed to be a counterbalance to each other. The taller one was obviously in charge but he might also be a bit too soft, whereas the heavier one was more impulsive. He'd keep his eyes on that one.

"All right, let's just tone this down a notch," offered Mikey adding, "- and I'm still waiting to hear why you stole my kayak yesterday."

"Yesterday?" Conor was still dazed.

"Of course it was yesterday. When do you think you took it, you tool?" Shay was still itching to establish a semblance of justice. He'd been lulled into a false sense of security by the boy's confused state, though he was definitely faster than he looked. But no-one by the name of O' Rourke had ever suffered the same fool twice and that wasn't about to change.

"Sorry." Said Conor though it didn't sound like an apology, more like an
'excuse-me-while-I-try-to-collect-my-thoughts-here'.

"It seems like a lot's happened since I saw you and that younger boy, that's all." He let his sentence taper off into silence, but they were still waiting for a more coherent offering.

After a silence that they permitted to last for a full minute, Seamus decided he'd had enough and stepped forward again to coax a response out of the boy just as Conor took a half step backwards and held up his hands to claim détente. "My parents met on this beach and there was nowhere else to bury their ashes, so I thought I'd bring them both back to where they met. I buried them out there." Said pointing into the small cove between the two older lads.

"I wasn't planning on going anywhere else with your kayak and because you have so many, I didn't think you'd miss one for just an hour or two." He finished.

"Ashes?" Asked Seamus, following the boy's finger. "What happened?" His features instantly softening to morph into his default expression of expecting clarification.

"Car crash." Said Conor, shrugging nonchalantly.

This was all very unexpected and the three of them stood frozen for a few seconds. "Sorry for your troubles an'all that lad, but you really shouldn't have taken it without asking. Had you explained what you wanted it for, I would have lent it to you and no bother." Said Mikey, slowly ingesting the boy's story while the tense volatile bubble they'd built around themselves started leaking profusely into the larger and naturally noisier ambience that was Erris.

"Sure … and thanks, but I couldn't take a chance on generosity from total strangers, could I?" Said Conor defiantly.

Seamus had lost his appetite for a scrap with someone who was smaller, lighter and also in mourning, even if he was a thieving city scumbag. It just wasn't done. He thrust out his open hand. "I'm Seamus O'Rourke but you can call me Shay. What do they call you?"

Conor was taken aback by how quickly and how completely the chubbier one could change and accepted the offering, making a mental note of the grip. "Lotsa things to be honest, but my name is Conor … McCarthy."

"Well, Conor McCarthy, only someone from around here would know that this little beach exists, so can we assume that one or the other of your parents was from Mayo?" Asked Mikey, dropping a hand on Conor's shoulder by way of consolation and formally bringing any lingering hostilities to a close.

"Just Ceide, my mother." Offered Conor.

"What was her family name?" In a place where everyone knows everyone else, it was customary to ask. First and foremost, so that anyone who might have known her could be told of her passing and secondly, because country people are notoriously nosey.

"Irvine." Said Conor, adding. "She was born on an island near here, Inishgae, I think."

"Can't say I know anyone of that name who still lives around here but for sure, no-one has lived on Inishgae for donkey's years, so maybe she was from Achill." Said Mikey conversationally but Conor's frown was instant and dark.

"She never lied." Said with a glare towards the tallest, who knew when to let sleeping dogs lie.

"Our 'Mammies' never do, Conor … my mistake … sorry." It was Mikey's turn to extend his hand and he waited patiently until it was taken before adding. "So we'll just wait until you finish doing whatever you were doing. By the way, Byrne is my family name and as soon as you collect what's left of your gear from your rat hole back there. It looks like I'll be your chauffeur back to civilisation, such as it is."

He laughed to finally break the hostile stand-off that was threatening to return by adding. "I'll say one thing though. You must have had a hell of a party out here to lose your only pair of shoes."

5 - Coming Down

We'd expect a finder's fee or at the very least, gratuitous praise and much enthusiastic hand pumping in return for that cash laden wallet we found at 4 a.m., but what if the street was empty? The fact of no witnesses could turn a stranger's misfortune into a case of opportunity knocks for us and all we'd have to do is quietly answer it, like it was destiny calling.

In a universe subject to binary laws, duality, positive and negative, there has to be a rational explanation for the odds being perpetually stacked against us when they should logically average 50/50 at all times, give or take. Mere mortals like us however, must stoically accept that it seems to be our destiny to lose more often than we will ever gain. This is why bookmakers, bankers and bandits generally will never have to sing for their dinners, whereas we practise regularly in the shower.

With no-one else to contest his claim, Conor summarily assumed possession of Pandora's box. It hadn't done anything so far except intrigue him, but there was something about the location, hidden away as it was that hinted at possible riches. The fact that it was impossibly predicted by the only people that ever really mattered to him, was what finally established it as a rarity that would never come around again.

Ownership of the contraption had something in common with opening that wallet and looking inside, hoping to find not one clue of its rightful owner. His smile grew extravagantly when he saw nothing resembling a brand, letter or digit anywhere in that most unlikely interior.

The 'whatever-it-was' was accepted much like the ultimate toy on Christmas morning, though minus an instruction book but regardless, it was play time. Since the thing was obviously going nowhere in a hurry, he automatically visualised himself sitting inside it. But occupying a reclined seat facing a wide partitioned display panel was not unlike entering a cockpit. This one was certainly spartan but nevertheless, any cockpit is usually part and parcel of some highly mobile piece of machinery. Then again, how mobile can something be when it's encased in a rock wall inside a cave and obviously long forgotten … but by whom?

There was also the small suggestion of someone keeping the disk slot clean, along with the puzzle of a cave floor that wasn't covered in the debris of obvious ages since it was planted there. But it was that word 'mobile' that told him to disregard all other considerations for the moment. There would be nothing but time for that.

The only apparently possible motion would be limited to attitude changes within the containing capsule and he concluded that he was most likely looking at a long-lost game simulator of some sort. In which event, the worst thing he could suffer would be temporary disorientation.

The default resting position could also be simply a comfort consideration, for just putting up one's feet up and sitting back to enjoy some antiquated action videos, probably kept on a tape somewhere.

The billion-dollar question of how such an apparently expensive apparatus just happened to be stuck inside a cave wall screamed for an answer, but was ignored. As was the puzzle of a power source for the lights and the automatic door mechanism. The entire setup was so ludicrous that such questions couldn't be seriously entertained while he was still in full discovery mode. So, he pushed them into the future, when more information might materialise from somewhere to provide some answers.

As it was, self-preservation demanded that he do more than simply procrastinate for no justifiable reason. He needed to look for lurking dangers instead of wasting time for the sake of it. After all, when opportunity knocks the door must be opened, yet that was his most immediate problem. Since he was still alive after the gas and the near cave-in, the next issue was one of inadvertently locking himself inside the thing, except that his disk-key was available inside the door. Impatience goaded him to simply get inside by assuring him that the door would surely be opened more readily from the inside than it had already been from outside.

He decided to leave his stuff where it was, partly because the spherical shape of the capsule's interior didn't offer a lot of baggage space, but also just to leave some evidence behind. He should leave some evidence of his presence in the event of a bravado backfire. Yet the more he thought about being locked inside, the more convincing the likelihood became. No-one was going to pay such a well-hidden cave a casual visit. His parents were probably the last people to visit the beach and even they couldn't find it. That made him wonder what Tadhg or Ceide would do if they were there with him as originally planned.

All evidence suggested that his parents were unusual in being anything but trendy, most obviously concerning marriage itself. They were so insanely young that it was a cause of friction between his father's parents and his mother, which in turn soured their son's relationship with them. Conor was once a kid but he wasn't blind and he knew there were problems but he just didn't care about them as long as he still had Ceide and Tadhg.

His small close-knit family were all young, healthy, handsome or beautiful and more than happy with each other if not with the world at large. To him, they were easy to get along with and also easy to aggravate, which made them transparent and predictable.

His father would likely just jump inside the thing and then pull or push something until destiny decided to do whatever it was going to do anyway. His priority would be keeping Ceide and his son safe no matter. His mother was less impetuous, but she wasn't the docile home-maker that domestic harmony sometimes insisted she portray, especially with Tadhg's mother.

Conor's parents could be stubborn and they didn't shy away from standing their respective grounds, so raised voices weren't uncommon when he was a child. So much so in fact, that he considered arguments a normal part of getting along, provided they didn't get too heated.

Tadhg and Ceide clashed almost as often as they didn't, but their arguments seldom produced an outright winner. If opposites attract then people who are alike will argue, but if they are equipped with similar capacities for mutual compromise, then what harm? He couldn't remember any specific episodes of lingering bitterness, so despite his tender years, he felt he knew his mother and father almost as well as they knew him. They never know it all do they?

Ceide suffered from a general aversion to technology and she could raise her voice to the washing machine or to her smartphone as readily as she did to his father. The difference being that she could simply switch those gadgets off, if necessary, by pulling plugs from wall sockets. That meant that she'd most likely volunteer to be the childminder to their son, thereby humouring his father with play-time brownie points. If the contraption turned out to be fun however, she'd wouldn't be averse to beating his father out of the thing, so that she'd also get her turn doing whatever it did. Either way, had the three of them found it together, he was destined to be left behind and that's what finally decided the issue.

He'd assumed the interior might not be rigidly fixed in place and so it transpired when the entire assembly, including the seat, rolled away a little when he leaned on it while climbing through the 'airlock'. That movement convinced him it was some kind of advanced simulator ... buried into a cliff!! He had to concede that maybe he was living a lucid dream fragment that simply refused rationalisation and turned his attention to the door, daring it to disappear. Given its shape and thickness, an airlock seemed to be the most appropriate description ... until something better came up ... or he woke up, whichever.

The seat slid easily back to its original position when he gingerly rested his left leg on it and let it take his full weight. That was when he realised that the entire assembly was probably mounted onto an interior spherical casing that rested or rather, rolled against the interior wall of the external shell. That would explain the independent movement, but it also left some unanswered questions about the alignment of the access door.

However, since the inside of the door had no obvious protrusions, it could conceivably slide under the sleeve holding the seat or possibly retract to let the interior ride over it. He'd worry about that and all the other stuff later because otherwise, he'd get nothing done.

With no obvious on/off switch, he just waited while the seven orbs stopped pulsing and then dimmed when the door swung closed. There was a definite hiss when that movement was complete, which made it a very realistic airlock but what actual purpose could it serve? Cockpits don't have airlocks and certainly not the cockpit of a game simulator. There was also no sign of indicators and complex aviation type gauges. The thought struck him that he might be inside a virtual 3D video player but if so, the screen should be at least as tall as it was wide … unless it would eventually project onto the ceiling above.

With little to do but fidget, his fingertips found the Perspex slot inside the door and it offered no resistance when he slid it up. It seemed only logical to remove the disk and he wasn't surprised when the retaining cross wires turned out to be quite flexible and were easily nudged aside to let him take it. While the three panels each side of it remained dark, the central panel resumed with the steadily pulsing orb of luminous green. Underneath was a thin band of the same colour. He hadn't noticed that feature before and predictably, it appeared to be a reasonable side-on fit for his mini-disk.

Conor didn't have to lean forward very far and the disk practically floated inside the slot. The screen above it then cycled once again through the seven rainbow colours until green came around. Then all screens came alive with the same image of a centred bright green ball.

Simultaneously, an intense blue-white light stabbed down from the ceiling and walls above his reclining head height, like he was caught in the wide beam of a searchlight. It wasn't as blinding as the light that flooded out into the attic chamber earlier, but the surprise element made him jump. It then morphed into a narrow horizontal band of strobing brilliance. This band moved rapidly down and then up the full length of the seat. The sphere walls and ceiling took on the appearance of uniformly opaque glass like that of a light bulb, impossible to see detail beyond the highly reflective surface.

Etched into the ceiling was an impression of his prone body below. It reminded him of the chalked outline of the victim in a movie murder scene and he chose to banish that thought. It wouldn't be quashed that easily however and it took the rising sound of a virtual alarm, like the onset of tinnitus growing louder and louder to distract him from the thought. It produced an intense but thankfully short-lived headache which prompted him to consider recovering the disk from the green slot. Once inserted however, there didn't appear to be an easily identifiable option to interrupt or cancel what had to be a fully automated process.

When he felt something touch his shoulders, it was instinctive to instantly throw out his arms and legs. This defense mechanism would create the inertia his body needed to sit up quickly, but he couldn't. The top part of a restraining body harness was already folding down over his shoulders, chest and waist.

It had just swivelled over his head from an anchoring point behind him, like it was hinged under the seat. Two lower sections, each a mirror of the other folded over from under the lower part of the seat to hold his legs in place from the thighs down. Then the three pieces locked together at the waist with a loud click. He wasn't going to get out of the contraption anytime soon.

He would have been scrabbling to remove the disk from the console to hopefully reverse a process that was unsettling because of its automation, but the harness left his clawing fingers just short of the green slot. In any event, the disk was neither protruding nor visible inside. The seven screens then went into animated 3D mode by first pushing the orbs off each section of widescreen and then elongating them, like they were being stretched and projected towards his face. Once there, they formed a rainbow hued mesh around his head while each orb merged into the next to create a virtual screen that wrapped completely around his head.

The previously opaque screen then crystallised into an image that could have been razor sharp but poorly lit or both. He was under a dark sky randomly flecked with slowly expanding grey spots. Two small levers that could have been miniature joysticks apparently materialised to be conveniently located between the thumb and forefinger of each hand but they weren't real.

His joysticks were virtual products of light focussed in such a way that his eyes registered them as such from that specific distance. Seven illuminated buttons, each in a familiar rainbow colour, lit up to show him that they could be virtually thumbed by either hand. Each button was lit gently like a small LED but the green button was pulsing slightly to make it intermittently brighter than the others.

Conor registered his heart rate as rising steadily and swallowed to stop his throat drying out but those two green buttons were just asking for the tiniest of virtual touches. He did it without thinking because otherwise, he just knew he'd chicken out and then, everything turned upside-down and inside-out. He was wrenched from his dimly lit world so hard and so fast that he must have blacked out.

"You alright Con?" Those three letters wrenched him back to the present. Conor couldn't remember the last time his name was reduced to a single syllable but he never liked it.

"That's Conor with one 'n'." He said matter of factly, but he had to raise his voice when he realised he was competing with the real world of rising wind, water smacking on plastic and the ever present discord of countless seagulls. He also realised that he hadn't contributed much to the rowing effort and, "sorry …," was added as an afterthought.

"Sure thing, Conor. Just making sure you weren't thinking of falling asleep back there coz it's going to get a little lumpy once we round the point." Mikey extended his oar slightly to the right of their course and sure enough, an angry patch of sea seemed to be waiting in ambush. "That patch marks the start of the strongest currents and a swell to match it will be just beyond."

If the sea had been anything like that while paddling out from Portacloy Cove the first time around, he wouldn't have thought twice about turning back and postponing his long-awaited rendezvous with Ceide's beach. It was intimidating but he chanced a look behind to see Seamus pulling up closer than he really needed to be, but the big man just winked at him reassuringly.

"Wow. Where did that sea come from?" Too quickly, he had to shout and Mikey sensed his nervousness.

"What you see there is pretty much the way it usually is on a good day Con … sorry, Conor but don't worry. Just time your strokes with mine and we'll get through it in a jiffy. We'll have to take the waves broadside on for a little while, but if you think you're going to fall in, just dig in with the oar and push yourself upright again. If you do fall over, that flotation thing around your neck does more that you think it can, and I'll just come around and pick you up again. That's if Seamus doesn't get to you first. You ready?"

He wasn't, but he wasn't going to say so. He'd found a far safer route to Portacloy by going through the hidden cave system to the cliff top, but if he chickened out and insisted on going back to the beach, he'd have to share his discovery. There was no way he was prepared to do that.

"Sure. Absolutely no worries." He lied.

It struck him as strange how something as simple as a wave could grow into something so monstrously alive when it had no real wind to drive it, but since he would soon be busy staying alive, he filed that question away for future research. To calm himself, he tried to conjure up an image of the two kayaks being paddled sedately into the shelter of Portacloy Cove in a matter of minutes but then gritted his teeth when survival trumped his imagination.

Another menacing aspect of the sea was how it seemed to boil up in slow motion in the intermediate distance, only to speed up by a factor of ten at close quarters. When the kayak was lifted aloft for the first time and sat precariously on a crest with a sickeningly steep trough on either side, he couldn't see any advantage to climbing the waves obliquely.

He wondered if he shouldn't make the point that turning into the swells to face them directly would be more like a roller coaster, but they'd be through each one faster. But before he could shout his objections, he noticed from the rocks alongside that they were moving in all three dimensions simultaneously. Further, their average direction was seldom where the kayak was pointed. He wasn't in the driver's seat and he'd have to trust Mikey, who seemed to know what he was doing.

When the second wave hoisted them up on its shoulder, his stomach caught a severe dose of the jitters and even more so, when he caught sight of what was yet to come. There was no going back and he reminded himself of where he'd just been and how he'd survived that by embracing everything that was happening and just going with the flow. In a delayed reaction, the enormity of his experience inside the capsule hit him with a slap of cold sea water and he responded with gusto.

The adrenalin rush of each wave surged through him from the pit of his stomach to his open mouth and launched a shout of fear suddenly released to join the hissing spray. For the second time since arriving in Erris, he felt more alive and empowered than he could ever have believed possible.

Mikey heard the enthusiastic whoops being thrown at the elements behind him and beamed from ear to ear. There might be hope for the scumbag yet. "Harder, Conor." He urged. "Dig deeper." He shouted, like he would when urging the junior hurling team to perform minor miracles, and they practically surfed down each trough.

They both felt the roiling water propel them upwards only to drop them down again but they were also moving sideways towards the rocks. Mikey dug in as deeply as he dared on the right to increase their angle of attack to the swell and also to keep a respectable distance from the beckoning needles. That patch of sea had come alive in a seething combination of white-water waves and they were both quickly drenched. But Conor was also exhilarated and set about matching his more experienced partner stroke for stroke, both for timing and depth.

He should be physically sick with terror, just as he knew he should have been while airborne and then spaceborn in the 'whatever-it-was', but he was now fundamentally altered, like he was reborn as someone he was obliged to respect.

There was no choice but to leave Ceide's beach with his two new 'friends' because to do otherwise would risk exposing his secret. Assuming he got the beach intact, he could get back there anytime on foot. Conor was only too eager to do just that and hopefully continue his monster interrupted search for Sonia's alter ego.

It troubled him however, that he slept all the way back and didn't get to discover how the sphere re-entered the cave from outside. In fact, when he'd fully clambered out of it, there was no indication it had gone anywhere, except that he was minus his shoes.

6 - Dark Star

Motion is a blur when the biological modem regulating information flow between our eyes and receptors slash processors in the brain, is suddenly overwhelmed by sheer volume. Some imagery must be lost while the body ramps up capacity to cater for the abnormal event being experienced. Item one on the semi-automatic checklist is to increase heart rate and make more performance boosting oxygen available. There will be time for specifics later.

Item two is putting survival above all other considerations and our random access memory of things that just happened but are yet to be filed away, is flushed away to be largely forgotten. This facilitates the dissemination of new data concerning the ongoing blurred emergency. Survival requires that we immediately quantify risks so that a timely flight or fight response can actually occur. After the fact and when safety is assured, the blurred video extracts are automatically recalled in an attempt to accurately recreate the apparent emergency, and then learn from it for future reference.

Conor didn't give two hoots about how good or bad his basic survival instincts were because at that moment, he was simply an unscheduled passenger, pending receipt of a boarding pass to a destination that didn't yet exist. Still bewildered, a virtual flight pass was transmitted directly to his legs and his body spasmed to achieve a flight state, but his restraints made that option instantly redundant.

Fight response kicked in when his over-tasked brain registered the physical obstruction, but without an identifiable target to counter attack, more information was urgently needed. The brain might freeze but the body can't and continued incapacitation was interpreted as a system failure, which invoked panic mode. This introduced a large shot of adrenaline as a further performance enhancer, while memory was scanned for similar occurrences, working from the present back through his personal archives.

Meanwhile, to cover the growing likelihood that a similar personal experience was not going to be found, hippocampus set about clearing debris from the seldom used neural pathway to access genetic memory from way back.

The reason why a jet-fighter bubble cockpit sits so high on the fuselage nose, is to offer optimum visual oversight to the pilot. Maintaining exceptional efficiency, especially while multitasking, will normally require an equal measure of situational awareness. As a further aid, the most critical information is presented visually within an electronic HUD or head up display. The pilot can then see vital data without having to look away from what's happening in real time outside the canopy. Other data comes in the form of aural prompts and also from instruments that he or she is trained to periodically scan as time permits.

Conor wasn't aware of what a HUD was or what it could do and he certainly couldn't appreciate that the one he was then looking through was quite simply, a fighter pilot's dream. Simple was how it rendered a virtual holographic view of everything outside, even below the seat he half-sat or half-lay on. Further, the image being so stealthily projected from the seven rainbow projectors to crystallize into an identifiable panorama around his head, was fully decluttered to offer the most pristine oversight.

Understandably however, the instant upgrade from two dimensional 7 colour flat panel display, located inside the wall of a sporadically lit cave, took more than a millisecond to be fully appreciated as a complete 360 by 360 degree 3D dynamic and also panoramic presentation, and his untrained brain needed time to work up to it.

He perceived each of the rapidly expanding grey flecks bubbling into grey blots on black. But just before they looked set to dominate the black screen background, they exploded into a million pixels, each coupled to countless others of contrasting colours and shades. To his stunned visual senses, the pixels first became frozen points and then streaking lines and ultimately, a blaze of indiscernible imagery coalescing into something that made absolutely no sense.

The pixels in his Augmented Reality, AR-Spherical Overview blossomed into brighter and brighter shades of grey until they became off-white and then various shades of blue. Looking down for something to relate this development to was automatic, but everything down there was much darker. Below and behind was a very different scenario of a dark grey-green fog, with snatches of something that an experienced aviator would immediately recognise as the indistinct pattern of a retreating coastline, seen through a low-level broken cloud layer.

The G-Forces clawing at Conor McCarthy were telling him that he was already at five thousand feet and accelerating fast, while breaking through the higher overcast into a beautiful sunny evening. But gravity can also slow blood flow to the brain, which can render a fragile human tunnel visioned until blind and then deaf. Conor's body went limp and his personal experience of time came to a rather abrupt stop.

When his life began to tick away again, everything was absolutely fine. Conor contented himself that he was gently re-surfacing from an extremely pleasant snooze, with no recall of how, when or why he'd been temporarily removed from reality. So, he just coasted towards a reincarnation that he was confident would arrive sometime and if not, he wasn't unduly concerned. He was as light as a feather and actually smiled when his eyes slowly opened to discover a most unusual meeting of land, sea and sky. His horizon was somehow deeply inverted to look like a section of some gigantic and outlandish, blue-black on grey-white smiley.

"That's really weird." He muttered, only slightly disappointed that he wasn't waking up and apparently still in dreamland, soundlessly floating under high altitude formations of cotton puff clouds glowing early sunset hues. His total panoramic view however, didn't take long to achieve its design purpose and unsurpassed situational awareness also began to dawn. It wasn't the sky that was inverted. He was suspended face down from a point so high in the sky that the illuminated clouds far below had to be much the same distance again above ground. Then he remembered how he got there and his mouth opened to scream but the silence was deafening.

This was the voluntary aspect of hitting that panic button and his hands shot open, much like those of a startled infant and then immediately snapped shut so he might grab hold of something somewhere to stop him falling, but there was absolutely nothing. The impossible world he'd been literally launched into then spun uncontrollably when the augmented HUD interface registered him pulling and pushing at both virtual joysticks simultaneously. His airborne capsule was trying to respond to impossibly conflicting input commands.

The situation however, was worse than it seemed because Conor had always been agoraphobic and that made him suffer in wide open spaces. It was something that needed constant management and especially when preparing to leave Dublin City behind him for the comparatively unspoilt wilds of Erris. It was also the reason why there'd been absolutely no procrastination when seizing on the unexpected gift of a borrowed kayak to take him where ne needed to go for free. It was a case of taking the bull by the horns and simply surviving, until safely surrounded by the higher horizons of Ceide's beach, where he would breathe easy again.

Knowing roughly where the beach lay didn't make disappearing into that ever-widening triangle of empty sea any less scary, but it couldn't compare with free-falling from the edge of space. Unlike his inevitable encounter with the Atlantic Ocean, Conor couldn't have envisaged this particular predicament while sneaking between the carriages of the Dublin to Castlebar train to evade a roving ticket inspector.

But when push comes to shove, anyone is capable of surprising themselves and then figuring out just how they managed to do that later. Just then, the only reason that registered with him was that desperation came in levels. Panic had obviously earned its evolutionary place by saving people from their worst nightmares but if their predicament was even worse, they could possibly survive as the equivalent of headless chickens for a while. Maybe after flight, fight and panic, an adrenaline overdose would focus the mind on a problem that simply had to be faced and the senses would be forced to contribute to finding a survivable outcome.

Conor's agoraphobia took the form of a pessimistic vulnerability in open spaces. That was where he could expect to find no-one to help, nowhere to hide and nothing to use in self-defence. Having no witnesses to their deaths wasn't something that rational people would worry about, but Conor was terrified of just disappearing without a trace. It should have made the stunning vista facing him unbearable, but he dismissed it for no other reason than he was too busy. That and an unprecedented mental clarity, despite being thrown about like a ragdoll in a spin dryer, came as revelations.

His mind-blowing circumstances stalled rational thought for just a millisecond as he discovered that his vision was nothing less than 20/20 perfect. He didn't ponder why that was just then, because he was obliged to first acknowledge that his breathing was calming down and his heart wasn't quite ready to explode. That done, he felt fine looking down at the spot where he was likely to soon die. It was his only way of accepting the inevitable and his thoughts then, as he spun through the upper atmosphere like a drill-bit through steam, was of the time advantage being offered by his altitude. That had to be something he could use.

Cold reasoning pushed panic outside and into the wake, while Conor wondered how long he might have until the ground rushed up to meet him head on. Unlike a real pilot, he had no idea how fast he was falling, nor of how far he still had to go, so he couldn't contemplate an estimate. He'd already decided to deal with whatever came after life if and when that eventuality arose but, in the meantime, he was simply too busy to worry about it. Becoming a pilot was an ambition he once liked to entertain in Life#1, but that was when all things were still possible.

With no answers inside the HUD, he looked outside and found that the simple act of attempting to look beyond it, enabled consciously selected views of his physical cockpit. The rainbow coloured buttons on each joystick were oppositely aligned with red furthest from and violet closest to his body. That layout had to mean something, so he held both joysticks rigidly parallel as he prepared to experiment and the spinning quickly wound down. He was still plummeting earthwards however, so he wasted no more time and touched the red option with his left thumb and it illuminated brightly to acknowledge the selection but nothing else happened.

He could see individual clouds emerge from the orange white blanket to rise towards him and he prayed, as you do when facing imminent death, that they were really as high above the ground as they appeared to be. He was still feeling no panic; his fear was rational and controlled … but something about atmospheric heat friction crossed his mind.

The thing was, he didn't know enough about the phenomenon to address the implications. So, hoping rather than deducing that his incredible machine was advanced enough to worry about that problem by itself, he chose to disregard the possibility of burning up in a heat friction induced fireball, and continued to work on exercising a hint of directional authority.

He thumbed the violet button at the opposite end of the spectrum and the HUD instantly sprouted intersecting reference and grid lines within a floating plane containing a flashing arrowhead or chevron, which he took to be either a direction indicator or a selector. Taking a chance, he released the left joystick to virtually manipulate the chevron by scrolling in the direction indicated by the HUD and then took a very deep breath.

The machine responded smoothly by gradually levelling out of the death dive but with G-forces that threatened to send him back to sleep. He found himself skimming through the top of a towering cumulus cloud, which caused a series of vibrations to flow through the sphere and remind him yet again of mortality outside.

"How does something the shape of a sphere stay airborne?" Seemed a reasonable question to ask himself just then but that only led to the more obvious puzzle of how it managed to get airborne in the first place.

With no idea how to get the thing back on solid ground, he surprised himself by opting to play with the input controls thereby learning more about his beautiful toy by just making it do things. Further trial and error told him that each button selection from red to violet was a level of automation with red indicating none and therefore total manual control. Violet turned out to be total automation but with manually selectable options. He quickly learned to select full manual directional control by left joystick inputs.

Quite by accident, he found he could relocate them by virtual touch and then drag as highlighted inputs so they would stay resident in the HUD around him, regardless of whatever mode the autopilot happened to be in.

His right thumb did pretty much the same as his left, though at high speed it appeared to exaggerate inputs from the left joystick. At slower speeds, such as might be used for close manoeuvring or alignment, he found he could spin the sphere around on a virtual coin, or flip it upside down. Right joystick also allowed him to pre-set primary functions such as constant speed, constant height, constant angle of attack or climb but also instantly override by manual or right joystick inputs.

Conor was having an absolute ball fooling around until the HUD was bathed in the almost forgotten red pulsing light and an aural klaxon matched it perfectly for timing. He'd completely disregarded the possibility of other air-planes and when the frequency of the pulse and the sound of the klaxon increased, it crossed his mind that he might have attracted the attention of someone's air-force or a ground station below.

"Shit."

He could see very clearly in every direction but there was no visible threat bearing down on him and then he used the HUD to look directly below. He couldn't see through clouds.

"Shit ..." Followed by, "- a missile maybe …"

He was by no means adept, but the nerd inside him was significantly nurtured from playing with the machine, like it was an arcade game. So, he thumbed violet on each joystick and his 'cockpit' immediately complied with his instruction to engage full automatic by arcing steeply to the right and began a steep climb back up to where he'd recently come from. Double violet had to engage automatic pilot, so it stood to reason that it would also incorporate automatic navigation, speed and whatever else it was designed to do, apart from serving as the ultimate flight simulator, minus the simulation.

"Where are you taking me?" He asked as 'it' settled on an apparently 'reasonable' speed while continuing to climb and finally eased out of the turn.

Conor saw three other chevrons converging on the one he scrolled to pull out of the dive and guessed that his machine had a pre-set destination. This was represented by a fat floating star similar to those that usually point 'North' on most maps and compasses. It was offset from both the vertical and horizontal however and the reason quickly became clear. Each chevron would slot neatly into a quadrant of the destination star once the desired level of up/down and left/right were established and he was apparently on course when they all came together.

He figured that he daren't interfere and risk getting shot down or chased around the sky by a homing missile or worse still, running smack into a holiday crowd of 400 people tucking into their cattle class meals in an Airbus. So, since 'his' whatever-it-was seemed to possess more than a semblance of self-preservation, he decided to let it do whatever it was designed to do … for the moment.

The sun was diamond bright but not more, which should have suggested something about glare filters, but Conor was preoccupied with a view reserved for only the most high-altitude flyers. So high in fact, that the sky was indigo and the horizon seemed to getting more sharply defined over time. When the contrast between clouds and sky became total, he chanced a virtual look back over his virtual shoulder. Home was cleanly divided by the line of day and behind that, it was already night time. He'd joined the astronaut/cosmonaut elite and agoraphobia returned with a momentary vengeance that froze him with fear. When nothing untoward happened, he slowly thawed and then took a long overdue breath.

He'd taken three flights in his life. One was barely remembered but it seemed to take him a whole day to fly to Santiago in Galicia. Constant anticipation wore him down until he slept in the hire car all the way to Muros. Then there were two flights to London. One to see Tottenham Hotspurs play Arsenal and another to meet some relatives who made little impression. He'd never seen a real cockpit and yet he was flying higher than any commercial pilot ever. He was also confident that he could land his sphere safely, which left the most likely hazard of accidentally getting himself shot down by someone for being unable to announce his friendly intentions. That made him wonder if the thing had a weapon of some kind but a reasonably detailed perusal proved inconclusive.

The sky was ink black and his HUD showed up each blazing star close enough to pluck like a ripe wish. He knew the main constellations by name, but only because they were used by astrologers and he hadn't a clue where each one should be. He should have studied the stars but when survival is in flux, practical subjects come first. Just then, he couldn't but admire a huge red star and a blazing blue white star and in between them, a river of lesser stars that was probably the central band of the galaxy itself. He'd seen some pictures.

Little by little, the light projections dimmed at their source and then faded until he guessed he must have dozed off. Hundreds of thousands of feet, if not many kilometres high, an agoraphobic adolescent who'd survived his first solo launch into space, was gently breaking out of orbit and sleeping like an innocent by dreaming of absolutely nothing.

Resurfacing the second time around turned out to be a much faster experience than the earlier recovery from his blackout. Eyes popped open to be met by blackness and he was reminded of his pre-dawn awakening inside the ninja cave, when he wasn't sure if his eyes were open or closed. In the console, seven small orbs got brighter and then pushed off their sections of screen and crystal clear surreality was once again presented to him.

The moon occupied almost half of the darkness and he seemed to be curving around it. A glance behind showed the blue and white miracle of the only planet in the universe known to support life but it was shrunk to the size of a soccer ball. The sphere shook when he registered his aloneness and his hands twitched sufficiently to glance off a virtual joystick. So, he froze while he faced down demons telling him he was destined to die alone, unseen and very silently in space.

Coming around at him, from the dark side of the moon, which wasn't really dark at all, was a megastar that looked weirdly different from every other source of light piercing the blackness. In the first instance, it was glistening when all the others were shining and something told him that if he kept curving around the moon like he was, he would find it dead ahead. That was when it struck him that he was falling down … or weightless … but his stomach hadn't alerted him by suddenly spawning a billion butterflies. He wasn't in control, but he could be if he chose to be and confidence grew slowly, like the darkly shining hole in space that was definitely bearing down on his position.

He checked both joysticks to ensure two violet LED's and full automatic pilot. The thing was, he couldn't fly an aeroplane and much less a space-fighter or whatever. There were rules about weight, thrust, speed and aerodynamics for flying and mass, inertia, gravity and vectoring for whatever this was. He was confident enough to try manoeuvring at slow speed and up close, but how fast and how close he was to anything was a complete mystery. It was by then obvious that his machine had to have a very sophisticated computer system and he wasn't ready to compete with it in the matter of his own life and death.

Another weird thing was that all the G-Forces he'd so far experienced were all either positive or non-existent, like he was always accelerating, falling or just drifting through the air or space, even when he knew that couldn't have been the case. The only explanation was that his sphere was constantly rotating so that when he slowed, it swivelled around to mimic a feeling of acceleration when he braked. That meant that the HUD orientation would seldom tally with what he should be feeling and as a result, he should have been sick with disorientation but he felt just fine.

He put it down to the fact that he'd figured out how to interpret and therefore anticipate course and direction from the HUD chevrons, and that knowledge must be overriding his gut feelings. It wasn't a very convincing deduction but it was more than good enough for then, because it was clear that the strange dark star was something even more wondrous than a distorted black hole in space. It was solid, in the sense that a black and almost spherical mirror could be and it was simply humongous. It was like a lake of elongated mercury reflecting back the darkness in which it floated.

It was so vast that even when he drifted over it, he couldn't see his sphere's reflection on it but he could see every star in the universe shine back from a hull that had to be several kilometres in diameter. From his angle, it was a giant flattened and totally featureless spheroid that could have been a genuine black hole for all he knew. He was eager to get closer and maybe discover more but also afraid to play with the controls so close to something so totally awesome. It was a majestic impossibility that utterly defied him to contemplate how or when it could have been made, not by people but by something closer perhaps to gods.

That word put the thing in some perspective. Someone somewhere had to have physically built it and that only hinted at the wonders that must lie hidden behind the cold black vacuum that it defiantly turned inside out.

But sunrise happens, even high above the moon and he flinched from the stabbing intensity of light needles piercing his irises and was forced to look away. There, on the really dark side of the moon were the lights of a gleaming city and he instinctively knew what the black star was.

In space, there's no need for sleek rapier wings or a needle-sharp nose to satisfy aerodynamics. If you want to travel in a vacuum, the optimum ship shape should be spherical, like his recently acquired flying machine. But if you wanted to bring lots of people a really long way, then you'd need to induce artificial gravity by spinning up your sphere, and the best shape for that is a spheroid. The huge dark star spheroid looked both impermeable and indestructible, like everything would simply bounce off it, including cosmic radiations that would kill any fragile biology that dared venture out amongst the stars.

Conor McCarthy had just flown under a giant starship anchored over the dark side of the moon, where no-one on Earth could ever see it. But even more amazing was the gleaming starfarer city built inside the massive crater below it.

"But we've been to the moon and someone must have seen all this … surely?"

More positive G's but in the HUD, he could clearly see a cluster of illegible digits losing value because every so often, the line of eight became seven and then six and then five. He was dropping out of orbit to meet them.

7 - Crystal City

There's normally not a whole lot to see from an air-plane window, and that's probably as true for the pilots as it is for us in seats 11E and F. Landing is more often a matter of twiddling buttons while reading checklists and scrutinising the movement of intersecting lines on a computer screen. It's only on clear sunny days that we can expect to proceed visually west from the motorway roundabout and do so at a height where the road layout is clear but not low enough to read the speed limits. In any man's language, that would be just asking for trouble.

There might be a few discarded electric vehicles on the moon but no motorway. It's a sterile waste where everything is the widest contrast of black and frigid at night or white and irradiated by day. The first things to literally stand out during descent are shadows followed by the real extent of those craters and lastly, the heights of some of their thrown-up rims. Coasting silently over the line separating day from night, shadows pointed long and then even longer fingers to show him the way. Two bright but unbelievably jagged peaks jutting up into the last of the sunlight became beacons behind which Conor was quickly plunged into darkness.

Dark Star reflected the blackness around it along with a slice of daylit moon below, while glints of smaller and brighter stars tried feebly to escape its mysteriously magnetic embrace. A quarter moon should have shone back brighter but the light was scattered and much reduced by its convex mirrored surface.

In the HUD, four chevrons converged on a central green star that was itself centred on the axis of the larger directional star and the digits were reduced to 3. However, it was becoming clear that the zero numeral was represented by a dot like Arabic, like he'd recently learned from something. That was because two of the lines were preceded by dots and he was by then so low that one of those lines had to be an altitude readout. He had no idea however of whether height was measured in miles, metres, feet or miniscule fractions of a parsec.

Conor was nervously compelled to keep checking that both virtual joysticks were showing violet LED's, which would confirm that everything was in full automatic mode. When he looked up after yet another check, two lines of strobing green lights had blossomed in the darkness alongside. One line on the left and the other on the right pushed their strobing elements ahead of him, where they seemed to visually converge inside the city.

Whether the lights were real or another virtual function of his magical Head Up Display, he couldn't tell. He could only assume that if he'd selected manual mode, the lines might change colour should he drifted away from the green centre-lines, but he wasn't feeling cocky or stupid enough to check that out.

His sphere continued to glide glide smoothly forward and he felt some gentle acceleration, which paradoxically had to be interpreted as braking. All the while, chevrons continued to close on the small green star at the centre of the navigation section of HUD. He thought it odd that he had no sense of the sphere turning around when engaging its high-speed braking.

As it happened, that wasn't such a big deal because as long as the HUD showed the vehicle's directional orientation, rather than his own inside it, it was something he'd already gotten accustomed to. It did strike him however, that although a propulsion system could be used for high speed braking, it wouldn't be very practical at lower speeds when the sphere would need to be continually rotated for manoeuvring. He had to wonder what the cutoff speed might be and whether the sphere could also use small vectoring nozzles.

Anyway, the fact that he was acutely aware of so many technical aspects was something of a revelation and it considerably boosted his confidence even further. Being capable of remaining so calm and collected meant that he was really on top of his game and he needed to be. After all, he was on final approach to an alien star-faring colony on the dark side of the moon.

The more he thought about that, the more ridiculous it was, because there was absolutely no reason for a common or garden variety of man/boy like himself to be associated with such a fantastic flight of fancy. In what had to be the most extreme and yet genuine case of perverted logic, it was the insane surreality of it all that kept him playing along, like he knew he would most probably be unaccountable for any mistakes, like he knew it was all a dream.

With no alternative but to see everything through to the end, he did what he had to do and just kept going. From directly overhead, or as near as made no difference, he'd seen no sign of a dome but one moment he was sailing through the blackness of an unknown lunar crater at night and the next, he was inside the city boundary. In his peripheral vision, a wide curtain of light was simply pushed aside, like he'd just forced his way through self-sealing veils of a tightly woven light matrix.

After what were successive ages of uneasy silence, a much-muted klaxon sounded and the sphere's interior was bathed in warm red light that began to pulse to a familiar beat. The violet LED's under each thumb were gone to be replaced by two reds and the converging sets of guiding green lights evaporated into thin air. It was that rather innocuous observation that offered further evidence of his sanity, because he found it belatedly amusing that air of any thinness could exist on the moon. But he quickly lost his smirk when it struck him that maybe the semi-visible dome was capable of containing an atmosphere.

"Why not?" He asked himself and then felt the need to elaborate.

"With this level of tech, surely anything is possible."

His heart began thumping as he took the virtual joysticks in his hands but almost panicked when he forgot which hand was speed and which was attitude. Yet again, he surprised himself with his own cool response.

He abandoned both sticks and manually zoomed in on the HUD with hand and finger gestures until he found the central green star again. This had to be his destination relative to his surroundings and not too far away, was the chevron depicting the position of his sphere inside the circular city perimeter. So, he simply tapped on it to tell the guiding computer that was where he wanted to stop. At low speed, he felt the braking as braking and his smirk returned. He was right about the low speed braking mechanism but stopped congratulating himself, because it still remained for him to get visually oriented on his actual position relative to the buildings.

At first glance, and aside from the unworldly location that in any case could only be fully appreciated from outside the dome, the city could pass for any small, new generation city. These are the newer type of new towns that are purposely positioned for our ever-expanding urban populations, except this one was just too bright. Under normal circumstances, that would hide the usual scars of poorly maintained streets or socially deprived communities displaying the latest art or graffiti, until daylight at least.

But as he peered longer, its biggest flaw was an unlikely symmetry to the graph-like clumps of buildings that could suggest functionality, except nothing was moving except himself. There was no funneling of headlights by street from one direction, or red tail lights being channelled in another, the normal signs of nocturnal life. There was also no greenery which made it colourless, compact and sterile. It was the enigma of a beautiful futuristic city at first sight, but when all of its empty windows were taken into account, it was more like an industrial city yet to be commissioned. There was little reassuring about such an outlandishly expensive facility being so obviously empty.

Each of its uniform windows were small and rounded, reminding him of ships portholes or perhaps of air-planes but every single one was brightly lit from within. The intensity of lighting inside buildings still waiting to occupied suggested that power wasn't a consideration, and was being squandered to highlight only affluence. The sparkling effect was offset by the walls of each building, which were translucent. This created the illusion of glowing glass or crystal as he got closer.

His approach had taken him around the city perimeter in a tightening spiral that was closing on the outermost, lower level constructions. When he judged his speed to be little more than running pace, the sphere turned more sharply to the left and began to enter the outskirts. After a while, he could have been looking at a display of ornate crystal night-light holders stacked increasingly higher towards the central cluster but there was no flickering flame effect. Each building was a facade through which escaping light was as uniformly cold as it was bright.

Above the city, the clear black vacuum into which a soul could simply vanish to be no more, was gone. The dome dominated and it was subtly illuminated to suggest a very physical structure despite the apparent ease with which it was punctured by the sphere on arrival. The inner surface was glossy enough to throw out a warped reflection of the city contained within and below. Conor could only guess that the dome might be about five kilometres across, making it considerably smaller than the Dark Star that overshadowed it. Wherever the reclusive or sleeping citizens might be however, he could see that they could never get lost, because the outline of each narrow street was clearly visible in the reflected 'sky' above them.

Using the right hand joystick, he slowly swivelled the sphere until it was visually aligned with the automatic destination that showed as a green star and then eased it forward. The tallest buildings in the centre of down-town looked to be no more than about ten stories high and they were built in a central square cluster. Outside that, the surrounding square clusters were reduced by a floor and so on until quite close to the dome wall.

Already at the edge of town, he made ready to ease the sphere over the smaller 3, 4 and 5 storey buildings when the roof of one in a 3-storey cluster visually stood out from the others. While all the buildings around it glowed the same steady and uniform white light, this one shone the same shade of red as the sphere's interior.

So he made a minor correction and steered directly for that. As he came closer, he could see that the red roof area was patterned with sixteen circles in a four by four formation and each was a deeper shade of red. Arriving directly overhead, it became clear that they weren't circles but tubes and for some reason, one of them was missing but just then, a tube began to pulse invitingly.

Selecting the manual close manoeuvring function from the HUD, Conor dropped the sphere down as gently as he could but apparently missed his intended mark. There was some light buffeting before the machine was guided into the centre of the tube's sleeve. Nothing bone jarring and more like a series of small jolts reminiscent of an old elevator misbehaving to sometimes test the occupant's balance. Regardless however, red was instantly replaced by violet and he let his machine do whatever it wanted to do in full automatic mode. It was easy to consider such an immediate transfer of control as a rap on the knuckles by the powers that be, unless it was just part of the automated process.

The virtual head up display then became pixelated and quickly lost definition. It unwound from the back to shrink like a curtain closing towards the centre. He was then faced with a flat two-dimensional display suspended halfway between his face and the widescreen panels that were projecting the multicoloured lights that made it all possible. But the actual console was all he could see through it and the loss of external visual reference was as profound as being struck blind.

More than 360000 km away and almost a year before, he lifted a pair of yellow tinted night vision glasses from a pharmacy, having mistaking them for regular sunglasses. The downside to the art of smoothly pocketing easily marketable merchandise was the tendency to disregard the small print. So as soon as he was safely around the corner, he popped them on and only stopped wearing them when they were damaged beyond repair in a late-night fracas outside a pub about three months later.

He called him his 'Happy Day' glasses because aside from making everything so much clearer, the yellow tint made the world in general a much warmer and therefore a better place to be. So much so, that it was actually depressing to see the world daubed in drab shades of reality whenever he took them off and so, he never bothered, not even at night.

Losing the HUD was even worse in that he really needed to see everything that this new environment offered or threatened. One moment was limitless freedom with literally no horizons, and the next saw him stuck inside a claustrophobic shell. The seven beams of projected light that made the HUD hologram possible, was reduced to displaying a duplicate of the partitioned screen behind it in his console. The reason for that became quickly clear when he found that he couldn't touch the physical screen because of his restraints. The only interface was the flat console projection.

Under the projection of the central screen, the green 3D orb flattened and lost many shades of colour to become 2D and underneath that, the virtual slot into which he'd originally inserted his disk-key glowed the same dull shade of green. He virtually touched it and the three-piece restraining harness clicked over his belly and then lifted smoothly away from him. Each of the three sections opened like flower petals to then swivel back under the seat, while the virtual console moved away to become one with the physical original of seven flat screens.

When he sat up, the mini-disk was waiting for him in the console slot and when he took it out, the slot in the door to his left gently pulsed also in green. All other lights went down until the green slot in the door was the only light remaining. He wasn't about to be offered another option.

Taking a deep breath, he inserted the disk-key into the door and after maybe ten seconds, a loud clunk was followed by the same airlock hiss he'd heard when it first closed and it immediately started to swing wide open. The sphere had evidently dropped out of its red tube sleeve to sit on the floor of a glass cube emanating white light from five internal surfaces. The sixth was a glass wall with a thick glass door insert.

Bare millimetres beyond the furthest reach of the opening airlock door, the glass door was being manipulated by a tall, skinny and very strangely dressed man. He continued to pull it open until it lay flat against the outside glass wall structure. That done, the freaky looking man joined an identical colleague with an equally narrow head and Conor's curiosity took command.

They had small holes for nostrils and above those, inside a darker band of skin, beady little yellow dots for pupils were set into inky black irises but they had no indented sockets. Each had a small tight lipless slit for a mouth and maybe it was because they were so devoid of expression or the means to generate one, that made them look faceless.

Both looked like they might have been decked out in some kind of fancy dress but the room … no … the corridor behind them was so bright that it was difficult to get more detail on what their clothes were made of just then. Conor found himself squinting before doing a double take … because aside from their misshapen heads, those darker bands of skin covering the top half of their heads made them strangely reminiscent of masked Ninjas. An image of Tadhg telling him how he acquired his disk flash-backed for an instant and he made that vital connection.

The corridor beyond them was quickly filling with a discordant crowd of surreally normal people in an apparent one-way rush to get to the same destination. It was like his sphere's arrival and his actual presence, together with his small reception committee was the most natural thing in the … well … moon. They were all animatedly calling out to each other or chatting far too loudly, as one might expect of people going about their absurdly normal business.

Above a sound suggesting countless gaggles of geese, a tannoy was spouting some instructions that he couldn't quite grasp, though that just added yet another absurd element. Aside from the faceless ninjas, the corridor could have been inside the departure concourse of any busy international airport terminal during the summer holiday season.

Looking as stunning as ever and just coming alongside, surrounded on every side by others in the extremely casual crowd, was Ceide … and Tadhg of course, hand in hand. They hadn't changed one iota since he was nine, but they were so absorbed in their own conversation and so totally oblivious to him staring mutely back, that they never saw his jaw land squarely between his feet on the floor.

He had to do something but the noise ramped up a hundred percent when someone at the head of the crowd started cheering, and it carried down the corridor like a wave.

"Dad ...?" He called and then realising that his voice was just a whisper, he raised it to a shout.

"Ceide!!!"

8 - Phantom Procession

He was mad, not angry mad but stark raving mad and it was so all-pervasive that it couldn't possibly have resulted from any single occurrence, no matter how weird. From the moment that 'his' sphere invited him inside for a flight of fancy, reality was skewed in phases that he really should have taken some time out to question. Instead, he just fell from one disaster into the next. He swallowed all of whatever it was, hook, line and sinker and the collective upshot of that gullibility was this very sobering insight into the mind of a lunatic.

Shooting through a cliff face to get airborne was more than just surreal, as was physically drifting above that psychotic upside down sunset. Arriving at the moon to witness a gargantuan starship anchored over a crystal crater city was so weird that it simply had to be drug induced. Conor McCarthy wasn't a stranger to drugs and he knew of one or two that could do that.

The final nails in reason's coffin were the Ninjas that his father claimed to have seen on Ceide's beach before he was even born. The sphere, or the physical manifestation of their long-lost boat was just the anchor that his drug damaged dunce of a brain got snagged on, so as to hold the entirely fanciful sequence together.

It was all subliminal smoke and mirrors and he couldn't believe he was that desperate to cling to a past that was as dead as his parents. Nothing was really there but he just had to keep his eyes shut to freeze everything as it was. That was the only way he could hold the nightmare in stasis. He had to stop it from evolving any further while he figured out how to reboot his life. What he wouldn't give just then, to simply open his eyes and be back in that stupid cave, looking at nothing more exotic than last month's rain filtering timelessly through limestone walls.

The thing was, if he dared to open his eyes and if those things still existed exist, he'd probably lose his mind for good. But he couldn't think because the noise was too much and so he screamed to drown it out, because now he was really getting as angry as he was genuinely mad.

Four deep and very slow breaths later, it dawned on him that the best way to tell what was real was by touching something. If his mind was lying to him through his eyes and ears, then he'd use the always infallible touch of his fingers. So, he shot out of the sphere to confront his demons, but ended up tumbling across the corridor to smack up against the far wall. He couldn't stop himself because he was too light. There was no way he could get traction on the shiny floor and so stop his own momentum.

The jolt was more than enough to fully refocus on the circus parade still passing by. He'd never seen Dear Evelyn look as frail as she did, clinging to Jimmy's arm just then and he assumed that like his parent's ghosts, they wouldn't see him either. But Eve freed her other arm by carefully placing a shopping bag full of groceries on the gleaming floor, like she used to do when there were eggs inside.

Then she reached out to him while Jimmy just smiled knowingly … the way he did sometimes but without looking at him. He didn't have time to dwell too long on what Jimmy could have possibly known about life on the back side of the moon, because that thought was gone faster than it arrived.

"Eve?" Conor muttered and reached out to take the offered hand, though how someone that feeble was going to help him up was something he'd have to work around. Just then, all he craved was the warmth of human contact. But her fingers passed right through his and the shock of seeing it do just that caused him to whip his own hand away from what had to be her ghost.

The inertia induced by that sudden movement flipped him onto his back and looking up at the ceiling, he realised that he didn't understand a single word of what was being said, shouted, screamed or broadcast over that equally insane tannoy. Then he caught sight of Dear Evelyn's back, shuffling unsteadily away, arm in arm once more with poor old Jimmy.

They weren't real because none of it could be … except perhaps for the Ninjas, who weren't even people. It was probably the automatic association with masks and stealth, but he wasn't sure if masks and Ninjas were ever really a thing. The two waiting for him to do something more meaningful looked like their faces were covered with a second layer of skin above their tiny nostrils. All around him however, there was just too much happening to focus on any one aspect for very long.

The steady procession of people with bags, coats, umbrellas and briefcases filed past. They chatted or thumbed phones as people do and yet the strangers walking between those who were more familiar to him, weren't so strange as he watched. He looked away to see where they might be going and caught sight of something even more unexpected.

"How in hell did Sonia manage to get past me?" His heart skipped a beat but she was quickly swallowed up in the crowd, some of whom he was beginning to recognise.

They were all people he'd met, conned or scammed at one time or another but there were also those who played more significant roles in his life. The Jesuit Priest, McVerry and Justine from the child welfare agency glided past but they didn't see him either. Their heads were huddled quite close together, sharing some latest development as they often did, or maybe it was just so they might hear each other over the din.

Everyone was being swept along in a surge of unseeing and uncaring faces. Ceide and Tadhg were already gone and only the Ninjas seemed to be somewhat aware of his existence, but they did little to affirm it.

"Well?" He demanded. But the Ninjas might well have been statues and he looked each one up and then down, daring either one to do something so he could retaliate and vent some of his pent-up rage. The one on the left turned about and reached up over the opened door of his sphere. He couldn't call it a 'He' because it didn't look human enough, but it turned around with his disk between its long slim fingers and offered it to him.

"Keep." It said in a voice that didn't originate from anywhere near its thin unmoving mouth.

Conor wasn't just light but also light headed and his forehead only began to throb as it had during the pre-take-off tinnitus episode. It was a belated reminder of his head meeting the opposite wall. The pain had arrived unusually late but it was severe enough to make him wary of stepping forward to accept the disk, in case his brakes or balance failed him again.

So, in slow motion, he shuffled closer with hands extended, not just to accept the disk but also as insurance against falling over and his face inadvertently meeting the ground. He was so light-headed that he was almost floating. The feeling came as such a shock just then but as he thought about it more, his body must have experienced near weightlessness for so long that it wasn't an issue until he stepped out of the sphere.

The words being bandied about by people were infuriatingly meaningless, like he just wasn't up to the concentration level required to make sense of them, yet they had familiar tones. His mind moved of its own volition beyond any consideration of time and he just squandered it on simple observation as it arrived. He was busily rejecting so much of what he was being subjected to that he found himself somewhere between asylum mad and simply lost in some out of body experience. Luckily, he noticed a pattern emerging from the random chaos in the corridor.

Dear Evelyn and Jimmy shuffled past again and there, turning the corner behind them was Tadhg and Ceide, also coming around once more. In between, the same people he'd known or met before, but there were fewer of them than last time. If the same trend continued to develop, the duplicates of those who played the most significant parts in his life would soon outnumber his duplicate victims, casual acquaintances and the shopkeeper in the Erris grocery, who didn't even get to come around a second time.

So, he moved out into the thinning phantom stream hoping for just one solid contact before they were all gone but he was disappointed. One after another, they walked up to him with eyes alternating between the mid to far distance and those they walked and talked with, and just passed right through him. The even stranger thing however, was that they all carefully avoided the stationary Ninjas, whereas he didn't exist.

Then he had the thought that maybe he was also a ghost to them. Maybe he'd died and this was something like the scenic route to some intermediate stop like purgatory, on the way to hell, cos even at sixteen he knew he wasn't likely to see the pearly gates of heaven.

"OH MY GOD!!!"

"IS THIS WHAT HELL IS LIKE?"

Sonia's spectre approached again but unlike the others, she was very different this time around. She'd normally be covered from beautiful head to toe in black on black, with black cropped hair and heavy black eye make-up. Sonia never dressed down and showed only her face and hands, ghostly white from staying out of daylight. Black was her standard uniform and she wore it to stop people from gawking at her, or so she said. In truth however, her clothes were as much to cover the marks she cut on her body, though not many people knew that. But this version of Sonia was something radically different.

This time around, she was positively glowing and also decked out like an angel, not that the real Sonia could ever be called ugly, but this one had bare skin and bright clothes. When she got close enough, Conor was gobsmacked to see that she even had cleavage and then, when she pushed through the last of her fellow phantoms, her long flowing gown. However, he was simultaneously occupied with a problem of a more practical kind.

He had to figure out how to walk without falling, like he was either drunk or in some drug induced stupor and it occurred to him that he would weigh considerably less on the moon. One seventh, he remembered from maybe reading it somewhere. That would mean that he could really be precisely where he seemed to be and not necessarily en-route to some metaphysical dream-time afterlife. The oddball Sonia then did something really weird and looked directly at him when she was just about close enough to touch.

"Why can't I walk like everyone else?" He asked himself and moved forward to see if this Sonia had any more substance to her than her previous version, but it was like walking on ice and he was quickly decked again. As he looked helplessly on, people he barely knew strolled towards him like he wasn't there and then strode casually through him.

He was light as a feather but inertia was still a major issue and his head met the floor, despite the fact that it seemed to take an age to get all the way down there.

"...OK? No monster?" She said, like maybe she was stoned.

'Wow." Sonia was also barefoot and showed her scarlet painted toe nails when she dropped to one knee. Her mouth was moving but it seemed out of sync with whatever she was trying to say, like her video was being streamed but with severe time lag. Since he was obviously concussed but more to the point, so delighted to see a real friendly face, he decided to let those initial observations go.

"Yeah. I'm OK." Her hand of all hands was something he'd never refuse, even if he didn't expect any physical contact, but she was really real. It just brushed his, though it might have been a tad cooler than he remembered from last time. He couldn't be sure about that because she pulled it back before his fingers could close around it. He was curious more than he was peeved because he'd heard nothing from her for months and her phone was going straight to messaging.

"Sonia? How the hell did you get here?" But he was so pleased to see her that he lunged forward without thinking about the consequences.

It seemed that Sonia wasn't as happy to see him and her mouth opened as wide as her eyes, like he'd turned into a vampire or something. She was about to scream but thought better of it and was up in a flash, but she wasn't going to hang around. She rose so fast that she kept going up in the low gravity. This Sonia was also well practised at handling it, because she floated away backwards and swivelled to literally hit the floor running a full three meters distant. Sonia had a really weird way of running, more like one of those ballerinas who took really small steps to make smooth movements and with no shoes, so it was all very silently done.

"Sonia!" He shouted but not so loud this time. The background noise was already thinning out with the reducing phantom stream. There was already a hint of an echo to his call when she decided to turn her head.

"Monsters ... Coming ... Go Back." She threw the four words at him but they didn't sound like they came from Sonia at all. He remembered the way she used to toy with an extremely dynamic collection of accents but even then ... she sounded ... very foreign. She'd also let her hair grow out and it was tugged this way and that after her as she ran. Then she did something really amazing and like a practised athlete, leaped to meet the oncoming wall. It was patently obvious that she was moving too fast to make the T junction at the end of his stretch of corridor but apparently, she was in total command.

"So that's why ..," he mused, "- only real people like himself and Sonia have a problem with the low gravity ... which would make ghosts of everyone who just appeared to be walking normally ..."

"Oh, I am is ...Tess ... No ... Sonia." It was thrown at him like a reprimand, but in a flurry of flimsy gown, flailing legs and shocked hair she sank lower and lower towards the floor and then launched herself feet first into the T junction wall. She stayed down there while still moving forward at speed and used one hand to keep herself from falling flat while she changed direction. Then she sprang back from the wall she just bounced from, to land semi-upright and disappeared around the corner.

"GO BACK NOW." Was the last he heard of her.

"Maybe she got a modelling job …" He muttered sinking to the floor to try making sense of casually meeting up like that, only for her to take off as she did … yet again. The thing was, he was barely able to stand upright and there was no way in hell that he was going to try sprinting after her.

Nothing changed, not even the silence that mocked him for only adding to it. He stashed the disk away in his small valuable pocket and then, taking his cue from Sonia, Conor removed his shoes and socks and placed them under the sphere door. It must have closed up when the Ninja removed the disk. Mimicking her moves precisely, he was soon able to walk and then trot and then run but not so fast. It would be some time before he could perfect her technique of turning without slowing down first, and then he realised that she must have arrived at least that long ago.

Seen from above and before 'landing', there were maybe 16 red tubes on the roof but he counted only four in that square of corridors, with each of them opening out into its own small section. Since the building appeared to be maybe three storeys high, that meant the other tubes or rather, the spheres inside them, had to open out onto different levels and maybe even a basement. Conor was particularly pleased with that rationale, because it meant that maybe he wasn't completely mad just yet.

It was only the slightest of physical touches that saved him from tipping over the edge and since it happened, the phantom procession became a trickle and then stopped. Appropriately perhaps, Tadhg and Ceide were the last to casually stroll past him, still hand in hand and seemingly immune to the low gravity. It still took considerable willpower not to capitulate to the easy option of letting his tenuous hold on what remained of reality, slip away. The most important thing at that moment, was being able to tell what was surreal and what was totally absurd.

Somewhere in the surrounding 25 square kilometres or thereabouts, multiplied by the average number of floors in each building, was his inexplicably disappeared ex-girlfriend. She apparently still didn't want anything to do with him, but boy had she changed in just a few months. He decided to first eliminate the other levels in the same building because although phantoms can travel in the mind, Sonia didn't walk all the way from Dublin to the dark side of the moon.

Of the twelve other red tubes that had to open onto floors above or below his, he was guessing that at least one of them held another sphere. Bouncing was much easier than running in 'slowmo' as Sonia had done, even though it meant looking ridiculously like a beachball caught up in a breeze. He followed the same route that she had and was just around the first corner when he came across an open access into a square room. Running around the walls was an angled ramp on which he could turn right for up or left to go down. Apparently, 'they' didn't do steps on the moon.

The inconvenience of no safety handrail made a rather unnerving job of something as simple as leaning over the edge to take a look down, even though there was ample light pouring through the walls and ceilings. Sure enough, he was able to quickly confirm that he'd landed on the ground floor but there were at least three or four basement levels below.

The futuristic building was so sterile that it was reminiscent of a newly constructed hospital or a mental asylum pending the fitting of furniture and medical equipment. He could almost hear the echoes of his own breathing and that was why he was completely unprepared for the savage roar let loose by someone or something on one of the floors below. It made him literally jump and then he knew he hadn't misheard Sonia, when she said something about a monster.

Conor froze everything, including his breath and fully expected the primal bellow to be followed by a cornered girl's scream, because logic told him that she had to be in the same building. He jumped even higher however, when that roar was repeated but from a point much closer. It wasn't difficult to convince himself that no scream was proof that she was already somewhere safe, and he beat a hasty retreat.

The glass room with his sphere inside wasn't too far away and he was more than relieved when the heavy glass door was easily nudged out from the wall to swing silently closed after him. As an added bonus, the airlock opened without obliging him to repeat the earlier rainbow inspired aptitude test. That had to mean that his personal disk had additional data imprinted on it to make it even more personal, but he wasn't expecting what came next.

At first, he put it down to time spent breathing the purified air of Crystal City, but he could still detect the lingering odour of incense when the door closed, though he didn't get long to dwell on it. The sphere went instantly red and then straight to violet for fully automatic, despite the fact that he hadn't yet inserted the disk into the console slot. Further, he felt he was already moving before the cage of the body harness audibly locked around him.

"That thing must be really dangerous." He muttered and then agreed with himself because whatever it was, it sounded extremely pissed off. Then, the weirdest thing of all because he inexplicably dozed off after popping out of the 16 cylindered roof to quietly punch through the Crystal City's dome. He couldn't remember anything of his trip back to the Erris cave.

"What kind of moron sleeps through something as spectacular as a return flight from the moon?" He wiped his eyes while his fogged-up brain told him he'd been out cold for the best part of a day or possibly more.

9 - Real Erris

"These have seen better days, but they'll get you back to Dublin if you don't try walking all the way." In a surprising number of ways, Mikey's mother could have been Mayo's answer to Dear Evelyn. There was a definite age difference, though with women of that vintage, it was hard to put an accurate figure on it. They did however, present equally warm and generous smiles with natures that more or less matched. However, she spoke with a broad Mayo brogue that demanded Conor's constant attention because unlike Dear Evelyn, she tended to speak without eyeballing her intended target.

"Now sit down there next to our Michael and help yourself to some stew. There's always some extra in the pot. Isn't that so Michael?" Seamus O' Rourke had already gone home to dinner in his own house, which was the next one uphill after the closest neighbour. That said, Erris neighbours tended to live much further apart than their suburban and city counterparts in sprawling housing estates.

Normally, he wouldn't be seen dead in a pair of old bogger clogs but they were better than trying to explain that he'd left his only pair of real Nikes on the moon. Young Timmy, the boy he'd seen kayaking with Mikey the day before, lived even further back in the hills but was apparently a regular visitor to Mikey's house. He was already sitting in 'his' spot and he didn't look too pleased with Mikey for bringing home a stray.

That could have been because Mikey, or Michael, as his mother insisted he be called, had just been informed, in code, not to eat as much as he normally would. That way, there would indeed be some extra in the pot. Timmy was apparently something of a regular at dinner time and was by extension, also expected to exercise restraint while the new boy gorged himself silly.

It was standard Irish hospitality and Conor knew precisely what Mikey's mother was getting at, and he winked at her son to see if he could rile him. But that was water off a duck's back and Mikey just shrugged good naturedly in reply. Conor took that to mean that unexpected guests were probably a regular occurrence in Boggerville.

The stew was a revelation but it was followed by a rather lengthy and whispered discussion in the kitchen next door, from which he was pointedly excluded. That wasn't hospitable at all but Conor was elated to be offered almost a half of a home-made apple tart for dessert by way of compensation. That would leave Mikey and Timmy with less than a quarter of the tart each, and even less if they planned to keep some for Jack, Mikey's father.

Mikey didn't seem to mind and just winked, leaving Conor to guess that his sponsor's mother must have been told something about why he was discovered on Ceide's beach. Only that would justify getting half an apple tart for showing up cold, drenched and barefoot like a pauper on her doorstep

"You'll stay a while of course young Conor, since there's no reason at all for you to rush back to Dublin after you've only just arrived. Michael will see to it that you have plenty to do so you don't feel indebted to anyone and meanwhile, you can treat this place like your own home." She was nothing if not direct and Conor beamed his gratitude.

"Thanks very much, Missus. I wouldn't normally even think of taking advantage, especially after getting a free feed like this, but I really would like to see a little bit more of the place where my mother grew up." He could be as disconcertingly smarmy as any well practised confidence trickster, but he was also genuine in his wish to stay a while. Not so much to see more of Ceide's County, though that was an unexpected bonus, but more to revisit the cave using the privacy of the dry land route to hopefully revisit Sonia in Crystal City.

He felt genuinely guilty about leaving her behind to fend for herself like that but consoled himself with the thought that it was better to live and fight another day, than to volunteer painful and pointless mutilation by irate space monster. Still, there was absolutely no rush to get back there and the reason for that was that Sonia was unlikely to be actually there.

Conor, Mikey, Seamus and to a lesser extent Timmy, were living proof that the prevailing Irish sentiment of City

Dwellers getting everything on priority, while their rural counterparts did little, apart from hoarding government subsidies, was absolute claptrap. When Mrs Byrne, (Conor just couldn't bring himself to call her Nellie as she requested), told him he'd have plenty to do, she wasn't kidding.

Mikey's father, Jack, was a warm-blooded ghost. He was gone by sun-up only to return late, reheat dinner and eat while his wife alternately played waitress, cook, confidante, gossip and scullery maid. Mikey never stood still and when not tending, nursing and rescuing sheep from cliff ledges, he was weeding, transplanting, fertilizing, thinning, transporting, buying and selling. Seamus and himself often overlapped by working each other's family farms and plots, which reduced dependence on expensive and reputedly unreliable casual labour.

At weekends they played Gaelic Athletic Association football and every parishioner who could walk, even with the aid of a stick, was expected to turn out in support, regardless of weather. He found it strange that they still regular used words that would be considered either redundant or archaic in Dublin, like 'parishioners. When not actually playing a game or training, Mikey was busy with the water sports equipment, the small camping site and a grocery store manned by some of the more mature local children on a school holiday rota.

Seamus helped out at weekends with the sports and leisure equipment and especially during finer weather, when visitors would literally crawl out of the scenery. The weekly dance at the GAA club was in constant need of responsible stewards and bouncers to keep alcohol consumption amongst the kids to an absolute minimum. It was a venue occasionally frequented by the local police and Conor could be relied upon to gel into the background for the duration of such visitations.

Conor couldn't shirk work even if he wanted to. He might have been a 'chancer' by trade, but free board with three meals was exactly what a bankrupt vagabond needed, and he wasn't going to risk losing it and besides, there was a code.

After a few days, he fell into the routine of finding himself absolutely wasted most nights and not because of intoxicants. He'd sleep dreamlessly but never for as long as he wanted to, because there was so much to do. There was something about simple labour that allowed him to think, and his impression of these practical, hardy and extremely tolerant people grew as he himself became pretty much indistinguishable from them, apart of course from his accent.

He was thrown hand me down clothes and someone's rubber boots with clean socks from time to time and even a handful of Euros most weekends. He didn't need undue levels of concentration or expertise to complete most of his tasks, with the result that his priorities became clearer. It was about the same time as he interrupted a small drug purchase at the dance, and Mrs Byrne scolded him with her eyes for not praying before eating, that he knew the time had arrived to get back to Crystal City.

Like him, Sonia was sure to come and go, though how and where she'd found another private sphere was anyone's guess. The chances were slim that she'd conveniently be there waiting for him, whenever he might get around to a visit. If he was honest, and he might have been getting closer to that, he'd also admit to something of a phobia concerning unseen monsters. They were a larger form of denizen that tended to grow more bloody teeth each time he thought about them. But they were also welcome, in that fear of them had inexplicably replaced a previously very debilitating form of agoraphobia. They were even rational, given their surreally irrational circumstances.

Amongst his Dublin peers, he often played the part of the dealer in illicit drugs at one or the other of specially selected nightclubs where his work made his obvious youth irrelevant. He'd recently graduated to bulk purchasing, but despised mixing with the real city scumbags. They were the dealers who could apply considerable pressure through special offers, so their distributors could quadruple profits, or so they claimed. More often than not, these arrangements would descend into outright blackmail. The thing was however, as someone who'd proven himself reliable, they'd set their sights on promoting Conor to deal in the harder stuff.

Officially, he was still thinking about that particular business proposal, but his thoughts had recently become complicated. It was easy enough to tell who was doing what particular drug in a Dublin Nightclub, where he would be the youngest person there. In Boggerville however, which in his vernacular meant anywhere beyond the Pale, it was normal to have a plethora of really young kids at the Saturday Night Dance. Most of those were too young to buy alcohol, so any who chose to take drugs would stick out like a sore thumb.

It was probably a case of overexposure to Mikey, who took it on himself to look out for all those kids and of course Seamus, who had to be the softest person ever to work as a bouncer, when you got to know him. To make a long story short, there was some dealing going down and Conor knew the stuff was just too dangerous for kids of that age group. So, he didn't think too hard about it and just waded in to confiscate the stuff before Mikey got to hear about it. There was a bunch of them who paid a lot of money for the stash so he had to approach Seamus to back him up with the threat of unpredictable muscle.

It was all done fairly quietly, though not before Mikey noticed that something was out of place. As far as Conor was concerned, it was a mixed blessing. Sure, those involved were going to get barred for a long time, which he thought was unnecessary in a place where there was little for young people to do anyway. The bonus though, was that Mikey could hand the stuff over to the police for brownie points but the incident was a milestone that forced him to consider the unthinkable.

There just had to be some kind of drug involved in tripping to and from Crystal City. Arriving back so soon from a trip that would have to take a week was a giveaway, except for his lost shoes. Coming down from a trip with fewer functional brain cells was all part and parcel of recreational drugs, but arriving without his shoes meant he had to have physically gone somewhere.

Coming down from drugs was also something that he'd grown uncomfortably comfortable with, especially in the run up to getting close to Sonia, whom he probably tried too hard to impress. Anyway, coming down always brought a great sense of loss and yet his biggest actual loss had to be Sonia herself. Once inside the sphere however, he lost days going to and coming from Crystal City. It wasn't the same thing, because Erris was a different kind of drug but he still lost a month far too quickly and seeing Sonia again only brought that sense of loss into a sharper focus.

Sonia was definitely weird, but she was always weird and no less so when he was first drawn to her. He winced because they usually refer to the girl as the moth drawn to the flame but with Sonia, he knew he was likely to get burned, and so it transpired. It was unlikely but not impossible that they both had trips in their respective spheres in common and Conor told himself that maybe that was why she took off first, without a word.

They'd done quite a few trips together and maybe she saw Crystal City as the perfect narcotic destination without him tagging along but there was more to it than that. She sounded very different in Crystal City, but also very genuine. Regardless of everything else, he couldn't come close to explaining why or how she could change so much so fast, but he had to see how profound those changes were. Maybe she'd be ready to treat him like a human for a change.

Sonia aside, there was also a star ship hanging useless in the sky, like it might be waiting for something significant to happen and he wanted to be a part of that. The thought did cross his mind that maybe it was as empty as the moon beneath it. It also occurred to him that the starship and crater city could be derelicts but only if they were real. Coming down from any drug was only the return part of the trip. Getting up there was touching an alternate future that was never likely to happen in reality and yet ...

Just as his father was way too young to marry his mother, Conor wasn't old enough to be unduly concerned about buying his own home one day, but everyone agreed that owning a place, any place, was only marginally more expensive than shelling out a fortune in rent for some stinking rich 'Land Lord's' health hazard. But the fact was, buying a second-hand or more likely, a third-hand car was less than the price of mandatory insurance, so there was nothing to lose.

None of the kids would depress themselves by talking too much about owing anything meaningful beyond what their parents or better off family members could gift them for birthdays and so on. Conor was compelled to consider if his sphere wasn't induced by some extreme wishful thinking drug, if such a thing existed. No kid that he'd come across had got a fair crack of the whip from a job or from life in general and they didn't expect one. That was just life.

Coming down from a trip was the loss of euphoria induced utopia and it made the most resilient of people depressed enough to do stupid things. He'd seen some of that damage. littering Dublin's streets most nights, but coming down after his latest two trips left him feeling just fine. He was, in his own way optimistic and that was additional to being able to walk appreciatively through the solitude of mountains searching for missing sheep, without the irrational fear of dying alone and unseen up there. Where did he get that from?

Whatever drug was being used in the sphere, and he suspected that it smelled like incense, some more of it could only improve his options even further. He never thought he'd warm to people as easily as these people warmed to him, because they just had to know that he wasn't as squeaky clean as Mrs Byrne liked to pretend he was. If she really was like 'Dear Evelyn' she had his number as soon as he walked through her door but like Eve, she gave him the benefit of any doubts.

There was also something about Mikey and the fact that there weren't many years between his age and his dead father's, when he was alive. That made him the nearest thing to Tadhg that he could still imagine. But there are two sides to everything and lately, he'd also come to understand why young Timmy wasn't so pleased to see him arrive that day with Mikey's arm over his shoulder.

As it turned out, he was more than just a little jealous and Conor thought that was hilarious at first but he learned to look past it, just as everyone else chose to do. It seemed to be something that people preferred not to talk about and if he had any real issues with Timmy, it may have been that he was just a tad too soft. But then, how many people were just too hard on others and themselves? He had to admit that he might be guilty as charged and that as long as people didn't make life more difficult for anyone else, there was room for everyone.

Mrs. Byrne had to know that her Michael wasn't going to get married to Nuala McGrath, who wasn't as besotted with him as some people thought she might be. Mikey was never likely to live the traditional Erris way, but she was keeping 'Mum' about it. The thing was, as he learned more about those stoic people and as they learned more about him and his parents, he felt obliged to share what he knew with someone. Unlikely as it would have seemed a month before, Sonia and the sphere was beginning to fester like a dirty little secret that urgently needed to be aired.

10 - Terminal Madness

Who, in their wildest dreams, gets to take a second trip to the moon before their 18th birthday while also bypassing stringent astronaut training and selection? The trip was even more mind-blowing than it was the first time around, mainly because he knew how to survive it. That gave him the opportunity to soak it all in. Yet despite a proliferation of sights to see before dying, a closer flypast of the enormous starship was the most anticipated.

It was an absolute behemoth of a machine and the fact that such a wondrous construction could get itself up there to where it floated, meant that countless technological secrets bordering on miracles had to be stashed beneath its black imperious hull. That's what made it latent compelling power in Conor's greedy eyes and within its vast dimensions were limitless possibilities.

In Erris, he didn't get much time to get up to speed on the subject of interstellar travel, because internet access wasn't quite the human right it was in the city. Second time around however, he had some inkling of what it took to sail between the stars and knowing what little he did simply being in the same time and space as something like that was humbling.

It didn't need to grow much bigger as he approached. That was because it was already awesome when it slid into view. He could almost feel its power, like static waiting to crackle across the darkness and strike his sphere with bolts of lightning. The way the enigma just hung there, a perfect if silent spheroid, made it both scary and inviting at the same time and sheer size seemed to bring it close enough to touch, if he dared.

The eighth wonder of all worlds was overwhelming and yet, the colour of it was literally in the eye of the beholder. It appeared black, but whether that was because it mirrored the blackness of space, or if it was actually black, like a slightly flattened black snooker ball, was debatable. From as close as he could get, where all points of individual reflected starlight drifted slowly away from its apparent centre, it could also have been a black hole into which things of less significance than itself could simply vanish without trace.

It was very much off limits however, because he quite deliberately crossed some mysterious distance threshold twice, only to find that red manual mode automatically disengaged and the sphere switched to violet. That particular colour meant that an unseen computer had assumed total control. His limited experience of computers insisted that someone had to first establish and then set all automatic parameters, but the fact of floating through space in a sphere like he was just then, had to be no less a puzzle.

He wanted to attempt a third approach but the red LED's on his virtual joysticks became stubbornly unselectable. So he found himself on the same flight path flown a month previously and was soon skimming over the rim of the crater containing Crystal City.

As on that first trip, it was night time in the crater area but the scenario was familiar enough to let him anticipate the gentle deceleration as acceleration. The only explanation he could come up with, was that he wasn't actually facing forward but backwards. That in turn suggested that a single mechanism was providing thrust and reversing it meant pointing the sphere in the opposite direction. Then again, if all of it was nothing more than hallucination, what would practicality matter? He decided to forget about it and just settled back to enjoy sights that hadn't been seen by anyone since … Sonia.

Conor had never been overly technical as such, but with little else to do, apart from admire spectacular views, he could only wonder if that disorientation was indeed a technical issue or if it was part of the whole psychosis. Impossible as it was, everything appeared to be even more surreal than his first 'Trip'. That was the only way to explain the sharpest definition imaginable to everything outside.

He was however, wiser and more confident than before and while en-route, could afford to squander time that he was obliged to use more constructively on simple survival the first time around. He was even able to consider the lofty question of mortality inside this very convincing if overly defined unreality. The previously strong waft of incense, which he suspected was the drug that induced the delusion, wasn't as strong as he expected but it appeared to be no less potent. He was there one moment and quite literally, gone the next.

At that particular moment, he chose the role of impotent spectator punching effortlessly through the insubstantial yet internally illuminated dome wall, to line up on the roof top that was still red-lit. For the sake of possibly causing a different effect resulting from the same cause, he declined manual control and waited to see what might happen. The sphere's internal ambiance simply changed back to violet and the touchdown roof of almost 16 tubes immediately followed suit. Everything had to be monitored from somewhere.

There was a tube missing from the second row of supposedly four tubes furthest from him, which he hadn't fully appreciated the first time. Under that was where the access ramp to the other floors lay. One of the tubes in the group of four that was closest to him became brighter than the others and the automatic drop-and-stop through it was almost indiscernible. He had to admit that it was an improvement on his previous manual effort

Some processes couldn't be automatic it seemed, and the red slot in the door simply pulsed gently to remind him it was waiting to receive his mini-disk. This time around, he knew precisely what he needed from his trip, but the smoke of so many burnt Erris bridges was still taking time to clear.

At first, Mikey didn't take the news of his intended departure very well. So he had to tell him about the sphere, though not everything, like the cave where it was waiting. Cutting out the detail of discovering the sphere, he skipped straight to flying to the far side of the moon and the amazing sight of the giant black starship, then Crystal City and of course, the briefest of reunions with Sonia. He left out the phantoms because that was just too much. Mikey's face morphed out of human shape and he went absolutely crazy.

"After making us all believe that you might have turned a corner, you just kept some of those fuckin' drugs for yourself … didn't ya? Are ya still high, is that it? No … never mind giving me more bullshit for an answer. JUST GET OUT." Conor didn't need to be told twice.

But he didn't get very far. Seamus was on his way over and from the combination of Conor's packed haversack and sulky demeanour, he knew something was wrong and demanded to know what had happened. Rather than spill the same beans and most likely get the same results, all he offered him was the outcome.

"Mikey's gone fuckin' crazy." Followed by. "I'm outta here."

Seamus often did something that made him uncomfortable but it was just something that he did. He hugged him tight until Conor had to squirm free. "He didn't get err … too friendly with you … did he?" It was easy to conclude that Mikey being gay was probably the worst kept secret in Portacloy.

Feeling a little guilty about breaking out of a bear-hug that was as innocent as a child's and simply a way of expressing with a gesture something he might struggle with in words, Conor placed a hand on the shoulder of Seamus by way of apology, but he needn't have. You had to work seriously hard to insult Seamus. The truth was that he was more than aware of being different to most people in Erris and he found that it was easier to remain largely oblivious to all but the most intentional insults. Seamus had shoulders as waterproof as a duck's back meaning that most insults, like water, just ran off them.

"No. It was nothing like that and anyway, he knows I'm straight. I mentioned Sonia before, and he seemed happy enough to know more about me. I can't explain why he went nuts this time. He called me a junkie!"

"That makes no sense." Said Seamus, who took him by the elbow and started guiding him back towards Mikey's house. "Just wait outside and leave this to me. Don't go anywhere … OK?"

"Mikey?" He pushed through a door that was never locked. Crazy Boggers.

Conor didn't really want to share the same experience with someone else. The more he thought about it, the more logical it seemed that he'd get locked away for insanity or for doing drugs, whatever. If Mikey thought he was really tripping, it wouldn't take long to convince Seamus. Timmy would believe anything that Mikey told him and the three of them would soon turn Nellie against him. So, staying in Erris would be pointless.

When he heard their raised voices, Conor knew he should use the diversion to get away. Seamus would be expecting him to take the road south but with both of them temporarily out of sight, he ducked around the back of the house and disappeared east into the fields. That would take him up to the higher grazing above the cliff. If he hurried, he'd have enough light to safely climb down to the cave. If it turned out to be too dodgy, there was a crude stone shelter for the sheep to use during storms. It could hum a bit in warmer weather but it was better than suicide.

After touchdown, it only remained for him to slip his disk into the door slot and it duly hissed before something clunked and released it to smoothly swing open. Touching down had to be more precise than he first imagined. As before, there wasn't much space between the fully opened airlock door and the thick glass wall of the bright room in which the sphere rested. That forced him to consider how much manual control he'd ever really exercised over the sphere during that first touchdown.

The seat rolled a little as he moved towards the airlock exit and there, on the floor under it and a just a little to the side, were the shoes and socks he'd removed last time to get more traction on the slippery floor. A door made from the same thick glass material as the wall was already pulled out and lay flat against the outside wall. This time around, he noticed the set of three solid and stubby hinges made of the same, almost transparent material.

In the door frame was the first of two narrow headed Ninjas. Their robotic beady yellow eyes fixed on him as he moved to climb further out, but very slowly. The low gravity episode of the first visit wasn't something he was likely to forget.

Above him, was a circular patch of roof that he guessed had sealed shut after releasing the sphere from the tube above it into the glass room. Whether there was a vacuum beyond it was yet another mystery, but for the moment he would have to assume so.

Multiple attempts to determine whether his 'trip' was real or the result of some psychosis had not produced definitive answers but they pointed towards some kind of mind bending. For that reason, he discounted the possibility of being humanity's impromptu ambassador to an alien star-faring race, and took his tactless time as he prepared to moon walk again. That meant removing his other shoes and socks, which he placed beside the other pair while admitting to himself that they had to be the definition of 'incongruous' as they sat side by side on the dust free floor of a lunar interplanetary or even interstellar passenger terminal.

That gave him the opportunity of a quick glance under the lip of the sphere's airlock door. He wanted to see how it could rest so steadily, despite a supposedly single point of contact with a floor that could have been one huge ceramic tile. He didn't find an obvious answer to that question and added it to his growing list of mysteries to be resolved later.

"Nice to see you too." He was certainly more subdued than during his first arrival, being careful to ensure that every move was slow and deliberate, even if that also meant being predictable.

Squeezing past one, he brushed as heavily as he dared against the other. It was his reassurance that they wouldn't be taking part in some phantom procession, but neither seemed in any way perturbed by a move that could have been interpreted as aggressive. Unfazed, the one nearest the sphere reached up above the door to remove his disk and then handed it over him with cold skinny fingers but no words, this time. That was twice that he'd forgotten to take his car keys out of the ignition and it made him wonder if there really was anyone else around, who might be tempted to drive away in it.

When no noisy phantoms disturbed the total silence of Crystal City, he had yet more of what he didn't need. That was time to once again question his own sanity, which he refused to do and consciously focussed on reaffirming the reasoning behind this second trip instead.

He should have totally overlooked Sonia's brief appearance, which was obviously what she wanted from him. So many radical changes had to be an indication that she'd already moved on since they were both an item, assuming of course, that the Crystal City version of Sonia was as real as the real one. His main reason … well … the only reason that wasn't a lost cause, or human curiosity tinged with inhuman recklessness, was the starship.

If some long-abandoned contraption in a forgotten cave could take him this far from the drudgery that he and most of his peers could expect from life, then it stood to reason that a starship could take him all the way, assuming he could get himself on board. Everything so far had come not just free and without apparent risk, but also with some significant personal enhancements, such as his lost agoraphobia, increased confidence in his own abilities and a new sense of purpose bordering on aspiration. Ultimately, there was nothing to lose.

Having thought about it at some length, he concluded that he should be immortal in Crystal City, and that carried the bonus of having little to fear from lurking space monsters. Though he found himself emphasising that word 'should'.

First things first however. There were 15 tubes aside from the one his sphere had just used and he was obliged to examine 15 rooms under each tube for signs of Sonia's sphere, just in case. It was an extremely long long-shot, because there was no guarantee that she'd ever come back, except that maybe they had that in common. If he'd found a good reason to return, then she might too. During the short time that they were a 'thing', she often surprised him by how much they had in common … some days. Then again, he found himself contemplating the most probable numerical value for 'some' and muttered. "Not many."

If he had to wait around for her to show up, then he'd let himself be drawn to the sparkling attraction of the city beyond the sterile terminal arrival place. Maybe he'd find some clues that might prove useful in getting to the starship but if not, it would be very interesting to see what was going on over there. His Vasco de Gama alter ego was growing bolder.

He was 90% sure that 91% of what he was experiencing was only happening in his head, so the same would logically apply to any monsters, not that anything in Crystal City was truly logical. He wasted no more time and left the Ninjas behind him. Bouncing was as effortless as he remembered it and much safer when done barefoot and so he started off in the opposite direction to that taken the first time around. Beyond the glass fronted cubicle containing his sphere, were another three that opened into the same length of corridor.

The rooms were empty and each inset door was locked tight, like a plug. He was then able to take three consecutive left hand turns to circumnavigate the stretch of four adjoining cubicles. That was enough to convince him that the delivery tubes were divided into sections of four. The square access ramp to the other levels occupied roughly the same dimensions as a glass cubicle and it explained the loss of symmetry to the 16-tube layout on the roof. The sides and rear of the 'arrival room' section was also something like glass but it was opaque, so he couldn't see anything of what was inside.

Three turns meant he should be back at the end of 'his' corridor and sure enough, the ramp to the other floors was immediately to his left in the next block, precisely as he remembered it. With 16 tubes divided into 4, as suggested by the group of four behind him, a further three levels, above or below, would contain another 4 on each level. That left 3 square blocks out of every four on every level hidden behind opaque walls and only god would know what was in there. The Ninjas were nowhere to be seen, but he had a feeling they weren't too far away because he hadn't seen them go anywhere. He couldn't shake the feeling that they might be watching everything he did.

This was the same spot where he heard the monsters last time, but reassured by the logic of his own immortality, he tried to saunter down the inclined ramp, even though it had no safety rail or steps. In a further display of confidence, to whoever might be spying, he was tempted to jump over the side and sort of float down to the bottom level. The problem with that was that the more he looked at it, the more it looked like it could be a leap of faith too far.

There were three levels below and three above his. The building looked like it had a total of four levels above the moon's surface when seen from approach, so that would give it three basement levels but since each tube needed to have a glass arrival or docking room built under it, all those sections of floor above the arrival cubicles would be filled with nothing but sections of tube.

All in all, there was a hell of a lot of wasted floor space. He couldn't imagine what the architect was trying to achieve but it further supported his fomenting theory, that everything was illusion and wouldn't necessarily adhere to logic. Except of course for the shoes … and the Ninjas. He touched the wall … just to be sure it was there and despite cracking his head on one just like it the last time around.

With no landmarks, placards or signposts anywhere, he'd have to work hard at keeping his orientation intact. On the level below, the four arrival rooms were behind him, relative to the floor above. He found the room directly below his own arrival room, to be just another block of opaque glass. Each of the designated arrival rooms was found to be empty and locked. On the lowest level, he found two closed spheres, but the glass cubicle doors were also closed and locked. Inside each of the doors, at about the same height as the disk slot above his sphere's door, was the curiosity of a patch of almost invisibly thin wiring looking vaguely like a circular barcode.

Conor made his way up to find another closed sphere on the level above his, but in a different direction and orientation to the rooms below. On the upper levels, so much of the building had to be made up of empty tubes behind opaque walls that the construction plan was just insane. Three tubes from the fifteen had spheres inside but any of those could be Sonia's and if it was, then she wouldn't be too far away.

The thing was, he couldn't keep tabs on all three at the same time and he had to remind himself that he shouldn't bother trying, since the purpose of his return was the starship and not Sonia. Still, there was no harm in looking out for her while at the same time, looking for starship clues. It wasn't like he had a deadline or anything though it was beginning to look like Sonia was a pointless exercise.

After all, she might return to her cubicle and then fly her sphere away while he was on a different level, or in a different part of the terminal, or even in the city beyond the terminal. What if he was successful in getting on board the starship while she was lost somewhere? Maybe that was the perverted purpose behind the crazy design. It was a maze but the silence was becoming oppressive, so he decided to cut to the chase and on impulse, he called out.

"Sonia." Then louder, "SONIA', and then louder again, "SONIA."

Two monsters roared back. They were quickly joined by another but he had no idea where the sounds were coming from. When two of them roared once more in rapid succession, his deduced immortality died and he started quietly backtracking to his glass cubicle and the safety of a locked sphere. That would be the one with shoes outside, but what if the door was locked. Then the purpose behind the circular barcode dawned on him. He was very pleased with himself for solving that little mystery but was horrified to find himself doubting what floor he was on.

"Fuck."

Then "Shit", when he realised his first profanity wasn't the whisper that he intended it to be.

He turned back to bounce his way around a small block that looked something like an empty car dealership showroom. It was, as expected, divided into four glass rooms but none of them contained a sphere.

"Sonia?"

Curled up in a corner was the longer haired Sonia, but her head had grown bigger and her eyes were like two daubed patches of black with glitter or something. A monster roared from so close that it had to be in the next corridor.

He couldn't see the door seam which had to mean it was locked, with her inside. Conor banged on the thick glass. "Let me in."

Then he whipped out his disk and held it up against the barcoded patch of glass. The small wires momentarily glowed like an electric bulb filament, but red … for manual control. He was locked out.

"Sonia?"

"Please …"

far too soon, the thing belly flopped around the corner, like it had come directly from a nightmare dimension. It seemed to be dependent on touch as it felt its way around the corridors with a pair of extended sensors, like some huge snail minus the shell, but this snail had a mouth and attitude. It growled again and again, like maybe it could sense he was almost close enough to touch. The stubby head then split in two to show two lines of serrated teeth, but it had no eyes as such, unless they were the small globules at the end of each waving sensor.

He would have to take a chance on it being blind because otherwise, the eyes would be built into the head like any normal monster. That would have been amusing but smiling might well be the last thing he had time for. If it was blind, Conor realised he could use the low gravity to jump over it … but only if he had to.

"Sonia?"

She was shrinking even further into the corner, covering her head with her arms. He could barely see her inside the flowery layers of gauze that she seemed to think could hide her from him.

"What's wrong with you? Hiding under your frock won't help you. Open the fucking door and maybe both of us can keep it closed against the bastard." But the toothed blubber thing wasn't deaf and the darting feelers quickly extended themselves down the corridor toward him. They were quickly followed by the abomination that could apparently slide almost as fast as he could run.

"Shit." He could see very little beyond the creature. That was because its concertina mid-sections were so bloated, they almost filled the corridor wall to wall and floor to ceiling. Then he had a terrible thought about those sensors.

"What if it can smell me?" Having become quite proficient in judging the length of his strides by varying speed, Conor was suddenly very serious about launching himself down the corridor.

He hadn't long to convince himself it could work and decided that retreat might offer a better chance of survival. He'd circle around behind the thing and get back to the ramp room that way. Once there, he could verify which floor he was on by simply looking over the edge. His target was the middle level … how hard could that be?

When he turned around, a blast of warm fetid something almost made him puke. There was an even more grotesque beast behind him and a cold quivering feeler globule brushed his face at the same time as he was assailed by a belch of exhaled stench.

"There's no bloody way these things can be real …" But they didn't appear to agree.

11 - OyanNisTess

The strangest things can cross your mind when you're facing imminent death, provided of course that you don't panic. If you don't take off like a headless chicken, you should experience the contradiction of a timeless and yet momentary aloofness from it all. This will be something like taking a back seat while destiny abstractly pulls out an audit checklist, to record how you're facing up to your impending demise.

It's impossible to say for sure why this happens but we do know that everything evolves. So, it may simply be the automatic collation of data for evolutionary purposes. It will perhaps be used to further refine the last moments of the next unfortunate to make the same fatal mistakes as you just did in getting to this juncture.

Three specific items would be etched into Conor's superego and remain there for as long as he took breath, and maybe even beyond. The first was that he didn't panic. He didn't quite know why that was, because most people would in a situation that wasn't likely to be recorded for posterity or at least, not by them. That being the case, item two became an instant re-run before his unblinking and thinking eye.

Whether it was a scene from a movie or a crazy don't-try-this-at-home video would have to be decided later, if there was a later. In that particular scene, a driver with a temporarily lost name was racing through a tunnel and needed to avoid a roadblock or a wreck up ahead. The critical fact however, was the way it was filmed, like in IMAX slow motion. Just then, Conor had something in common with that driver because time for them both was slowed to such an extent, that it may as well have stopped to allow them to make their final calculations.

So, if it could be done in a car as a movie stunt under normal gravity, then Conor should be able to generate sufficient forward momentum and directional inertia to do something similar using his own muscle power instead of metallic horsepower. That was because his weight was effectively reduced by six sevenths. Using only his legs, he reckoned he could generate enough speed to stay airborne for long enough to clear the most distant obstacle that was blocking the corridor.

It could only be done if he adopted the same spiral motion as the stunt car did while climbing up the tunnel wall. The centrifugal force would create virtual gravity and that would make it possible for him to follow the contours of the walls and ceiling. As long as he could avoid the teeth at the front of the beast, it wouldn't matter if he landed a little short. The important thing was to just keep moving until he got to the ramp room connecting the floors and then hide away in his sphere.

The third item was his unexpected ability to multitask while devising the spontaneous plan that would hopefully see him live to fight another day. Something that Sonia said, or rather shouted, as she ran away from him to summarily end that first fleeting reunion. It was a name, 'Tess' and it was followed by the mention of 'monsters'. In retrospect, it was most likely that the word association had served as a trigger for his recall of a forgotten memory.

Their Dublin City peers tried to be discreet about their obvious differences but failed because kids don't do discreet. Most of them agreed that Sonia was just too different to be compatible with him and since their relationship didn't stand the test of any meaningful time, their judgement was correct. No two kids are the same however, and their juvenile idiosyncrasies were exacerbated by Sonia adopting a different accent for each day of the week. If that wasn't challenging enough for a guy who stupidly fell for her infrequent charms, she also liked to randomly change her name.

Sonia was razor sharp and she didn't expect everyone to use those adopted names, because that would leave her with no friends at all. So, he was charged with not simply remembering how she preferred to be known but also understanding everything she said using her phoney improvised accents.

He couldn't remember how many names she summarily discarded during a tumultuous couple of weeks but those names marked the beginning of the end of whatever it was they might have had. If he couldn't remember her latest choice, then he obviously didn't care enough about her, or so she claimed. Justification perhaps, for their trial separation made unilaterally permanent sometime later, when she just disappeared.

The much-modified Sonia, cowering in a corner behind her locked glass door, was doing her best to hide behind the veils of fragile fabric that she wore. The real Sonia was nothing like her Lunar reincarnation but maybe, just maybe, that was what she was trying to tell him earlier. Maybe her currently adopted alias was 'Tess'. This version of Sonia looked nothing like a 'Tess' but then, he didn't actually know any others and since time wasn't on just side, he just shouted as loud as he could. "TESS."

It was too late to gauge her response because his attention was instantly and fully re-focussed on the ugliest creature, which apparently had acquired a taste for his particular bouquet. Like a gigantic bloated gastropod, the abomination facing him was coiling its bulk tighter like a concertina ready to exhale. The next move would see it expand so the teeth could seize something more substantial than merely the whiff of him.

With no distance between them in which to build up some much-needed speed, Conor backed away and then down while he turned about. He coiled his own legs under him and then took a deep breath to boost them as he shot away. It was done quite fluidly with eyes glued to the point on the floor where he would leap up and then forward onto the wall. Then he eyed the point further down, where he would touch the ceiling in a long loose spiral. Even without practise, he reckoned he could land a safe distance beyond the ghastly head, assuming he could avoid it on the way up

Just as he made ready to release every fibre of every sinew and muscle he might possess, a lightning quick tightening snagged his right wrist and wrenched him powerfully off his feet. Momentum and inertia were instantly and irrevocably divorced and the two monsters swapped places while the corridor cartwheeled and he exited stage right to be slammed up against an opaque glass wall that was miraculously, inside Sonia's arrival cubicle. Whatever had grabbed him was cool but left two reddening and warm weal marks, one on his wrist and the other, further up on the forearm.

While he tried to figure out how he'd just come through such solid glass, Sonia whirled away from the door which thudded heavily into its inset frame. The enraged creature slammed up against it, which only closed it harder and faster than she could have. Then, just as when he'd seen her do her specialized turn off the wall while cornering at speed, Sonia was a flurry of arms, legs, floral patterned gown and that unusual haircut as she shrunk back into her foetal position in the corner.

Outside in the corridor, the two monsters went at each other instead. They did so with bellows that sent shock-waves through the floor. Since being heard above that din was impossible and with Sonia already traumatised, Conor just looked on, absently checking himself over for damage and fortunate to find none that would really matter, all things considered.

Maybe it was something to do with their bulk, because the monsters didn't seem to have much staying power for heavyweights. For all the noise and throwing around of their considerable mass, they didn't actually engage each other with teeth. They preferred to haul, push and nudge each other backwards and forwards and quickly forgot about their human meals watching them. After maybe fifteen minutes, they backed away from each other, like two lead footed wrestlers fighting for a purse unworthy of their best efforts, to reassess the situation and maybe encourage the final bell.

The two Ninja's appeared from a direction that suggested they'd somehow just bypassed one monster from the rear. After a moment's reflection on all that empty 'office' space secreted behind the opaque wall opposite, he put it down to a well concealed door somewhere. Regardless, the Ninjas had no fear of the bellicose beasts and they simply split them up to take one each down opposite lengths of the corridor until silence eventually muted their echoes.

Conor was beginning to get accustomed to being speechless in surreality and did nothing to dispel it, until he needed the reassurance of his voice to convince him that he'd actually survived.

"Did you see that? They took them away like they were nothing more than cows being brought back from the pasture to the milking parlour."

When he realised what he'd just said, he knew he'd stayed far too long in Erris but thankfully, Sonia didn't seem to hear his overly agricultural analogy because she didn't look up. If anything, she seemed to shrink even more into herself when he spoke. She was terrified, but she'd also just saved his ass.

"Thanks Sonia … Tess I mean. For a minute or two there … I thought you were going to sacrifice me to whatever gods made this place. Ha-ha." His phony laugh upset her even more. So he slowly made his way over to find she was physically trembling. Where was the kick-ass girl with a penchant for whipping out her old-style razor when threatened … or not?

"Wow … easy now … everything is OK … Tess. They're gone." Like he did with the frozen lamb stuck petrified on that Erris cliff ledge, he reached down and then closed the distance between them, talking softly but constantly until there was option but physical contact.

"We're fine now … thanks to you. That was very brave of you … seeing as you were more scared of the bastards than I was …" He lied and placed his hand very gently on her shoulder, which was really soft. Truth be told however; he could recall little that was soft about Sonia.

"What do you say about us getting you home Sonia … err Tess? We'll give it another half an hour to be sure, and then we'll make our way back to my sphere."

"You have a pod?" She sounded even more foreign with her head sunk into her chest.

"Sure. Don't you?"

"No pod … they sent it away … without me inside."

"They just took it?"

It never crossed his mind that 'they' would do something like that. He'd been to Crystal City only twice but each time, the Ninja reception committee made a point of handing him his disk. From that he just assumed total ownership if not control. Could those who sent her sphere away be the same, apparently mindless Ninja's? It didn't seem like they had enough grey matter between their ears to decide critical issues like that.

"That would leave you stranded here." The implications bubbled up like methane from a swamp and he followed up with. "Wow. How long have you been here … alone … Tess?"

Something as uncomplicated as a new-born lamb will quickly respond to human empathy when it is offered with calm reassurance. A bond is formed that might last or not but at that moment when nothing evolves into something, any bond becomes everything.

It wasn't his imagination because her head really was bigger … and so were those big black eyes. Her hair had a funny feel to it when he touched it hanging over her shoulder, like the strands were too thick but also too soft. Then he knew why she seemed to move with a flurry of legs and arms. Under her long loose dress, she had two sets of each and the outermost, which was the uppermost pair or arms were actually tentacles.

"Holy … "

He was already falling back and away from whatever it was, but it didn't immediately react to his instinctive retreat with an attack. It just cowered there with an expression that could have been human, resigned, vulnerable and sad, inviting him to identify even more attributes. When his buttocks eventually met the floor, he found that he'd stifled a scream that had already taken too long to build. He wanted to add the word 'lost' but found that it just didn't convey enough of what was there.

The scream became stillborn but its twin turned out to be a revelation that survived. Tess wasn't human but she was definitely 'She'.

While that sank in, 'she' managed to project the same passive pose for his protracted perusal. He didn't know fully why, but he was embarrassed when he spoke. "Tess?" He asked, slowly and maybe too softly.

Her liquid eyes opened wider, and then wider again and her image shuddered for half a second, like the camera of his own eyes had been nudged by his own clumsiness.

"Oyan Nis Tess." It … she … said, through a mouth small enough to be a child's … with no teeth.

"No monster … OyanNisTess." It was a peace offering with a strangely oriental suggestion to the sound of it.

The fourth unforgettable thing about that meeting, was how he knew what to say next. How she could impersonate Sonia's general appearance and movements to the extent that he couldn't see what was really underneath, would have to stay a mystery for a while longer. The thing was, she'd run away from him last time when he tried to embrace her, simply out of the sheer relief of meeting someone so familiar.

She obviously wasn't a monster like those other things, but she seemed to think that might be how he saw her, which in turn suggested that she must have seen him as a monster too. And yet, despite all that, she opened the door when he called her by name. She had to be really desperate.

"No monster … Conor McCarthy."

12 - A Meeting of Alien Minds

Time had stood still twice in an hour. In a way, the first was like a game cheat, because that instance of frozen time created more of it for him to devise a plan that ultimately, he didn't need. The second event was still ongoing but if he didn't break that silent impasse soon, she might once again see him as something of a monster.

"So. What are you?" He blurted and her head went to one side while she fully ingested and then masticated his very direct question.

"I am one with the Oyan people and of the clan we call Niss and you already called me by my chosen name. So now, What are you?" The act of putting an equally strong emphasis on the word 'are' only highlighted the fact that he'd done the same and he realised how superior he must have sounded.

"I'm sorry. It's just that I've never spoken to something … someone who wasn't … isn't human."

He was puzzled by two facts that only become obvious when he saw her as inhuman or rather … not human. The most significant was how it spoke English and the other was why she had so suddenly clammed up, like she was inexplicably lost for words. Then it struck him that she was probably waiting for his answer.

So he rattled off his credentials. "I'm human, I guess, and my clan is Carthy, you might say and everyone calls me Conor."

Her head turned the other way and for a crazy moment, he was reminded of the way a dog does the same thing when trying to figure something out and decided to lose that train of thought. Dogs were almost human but the association just didn't seem appropriate. He was looking at a real live alien.

"Before .... when I first saw you, you had painted toenails but now, you don't even have feet. How in hell did you do that?"

Time passed while she digested some unintentional implications and then responded by slowly pulling the ends of her tentacles under the fabric of the dress. He'd obviously insulted her and the unspoken reply was both human and understandable but also very weird, because she used both a tentacled arm and a shrunken trunk to coyly move the material down.

"Oyan don't have toes to paint. That was just something you wanted to see and therefore, you saw it, just like the one you call Sonia. You will not find that Sonia here."

"Why not?" In a way, he was relieved that Sonia wasn't on the moon, because that meant he didn't have to go running around looking for her at the risk of meeting more monsters, but she seemed very positive about that.

"Do you Conor, know where we are ... where we really are?"

There was a definite time lag between what she appeared to be saying and what he was hearing and again, her image could shimmer slightly from time to time. Maybe that was something they could figure out together but this, 'Tess' had apparently been abandoned in Crystal City for quite some time, which meant she had to know a lot more about it than he did.

Strangers are not to be trusted on sight and especially strangers who weren't even people, so it crossed his mind that she might have a separate agenda. There was no guarantee that she'd share what she already knew with him, which made him hesitant to offer his own thoughts.

The deceptively human shaped creature seemed to be breathing easier and was visibly expanding back to her previous approximately human female proportions. It occurred to Conor that maybe she was fishing for information ... but then ... she did open that door.

"We may be inside some space settlement on the dark side of the moon, but this place is so outlandish that it could be something like a lucid dream or a trip, right?"

"Drugs?" She asked after a moment, eyes even wider than before.

"Sure. Do you really think all of this could stay hidden from a planet of billions of people only a few hundred thousand klicks away?" Then added. "Also, we do have satellites."

She took so long over that one that he had to follow it up. "Or maybe they let you guys build all this … in exchange for … what?"

What he didn't say was, "- assuming that it is real."

"Can you see from one end of a 'Klick' to the other." He must have missed her small mouth forming the words.

"Yes, of course. It's short for a metric kilometre … a thousand big steps if you like … for one of us …"

"So, you think there's a habitable planet just over our horizon?"

Totally black eyes and no discernible eyebrows made body language impossible, but it sounded like she was taking the piss, and that could get him angry.

"Like I said, Tess. We may be drugged or dreaming or something, but we are on the other side of the moon, where no-one on that big blue planet can see us directly. It's that, or we never left the big blue planet … and we are still there somewhere … maybe not too far from County Mayo. Who knows … we might even be in a clinic or an institution?" Now he was fishing.

Tess started to shrink again but stopped when he posed his question and it wasn't lost on him that she found his raised voice threatening. Whatever she was, she was more lost than he was because he still had a sphere … he hoped. "I'm really sorry. I'll talk softer."

He touched her shoulder area again but then jumped when a tentacle brushed the back of his hand.

"I'm really sorry." The sound just blossomed in his head.

"We'll have to be careful that we don't scare each other and I'll promise you that whatever you think I am, or see that I am, I won't harm you. As I see it, we're together in this place and we'll break out together in pretty much the same way as we got inside." Said Conor as sincerely as he could. Then he took the end of the tentacle and found it only a little colder than himself. It was extremely soft and pliable and the merest touch caused it to change shape as it yielded to his fingers.

"You are very warm."

"Thanks, Tess. You're kinda cool yourself." He laughed at his own joke and she instantly shrank.

"Shit. Sorry." He backed away to give her space but two tentacles reached out to take an arm and a hand each but they did so with unexpected gentleness. It was even more remarkable when he remembered the power of her earlier grip on his wrist.

"Maybe I'm still a little scared of everything ... maybe ... but tell me how many times you've been to this place ... in total." She asked.

"Just twice ... and you?" The quick switch of topic suggested that she wasn't asking simply to satisfy idle curiosity.

"Too often I suspect and I've come to believe that's why they stopped me from going back to my home." Whatever about their obvious physical differences, she was also different in other ways. She'd gone from running away on sight, to cowering terrified of his voice to sharing his private space far too quickly.

If Tess wasn't touching him, usually on the arms or hands, she was simply swapping tentacles to do so, and once she was standing upright, she was right in his face most of the time. It was like an invasion of privacy and more than a little off putting, probably because she wasn't a real female but she didn't stink or anything. He'd just have to get used to it or risk insulting her. Maybe that would be a diplomatic incident. He grinned and she looked at him curiously with those big black eyes.

"So how many?" He lost the grin and not just because she was holding his hand with her other left arm. It felt every bit as weird as it looked, but he needed to stay conversational because that answer could be important.

"Four times." She said and he let the subject drop because that wasn't very many and he had a feeling that it could have a huge bearing on what they might do next. He couldn't help but wonder if her sphere, or pod as she called it, was the same as his and if so, would it respond to his disk?

There was no indication that she was aware of his growing uneasiness. In fact, she seemed quite comfortable in the company of an alien who was mulling over what he might do in her situation.

"You probably have no concept of how ugly you were earlier, but I'm beginning to see you are much better now. I think that could be an indication that you have a deceptive nature and that's the attribute that makes you look … monstrous sometimes."

Did that mean she had a sense of humour? He couldn't let that pass. "Don't take this too badly Tess, but before talking to you here today, someone would have to have double dared me to get into the same room as you." And despite his darker thoughts and his commitment not to do so, he laughed too loud again.

"Shit." When she shuddered again.

"We'll need to stop saying sorry and just try to be a little more considerate." Again, the words didn't originate in her tiny toothless mouth.

"Yeah." He agreed. "Let's try to be friends and that means real friends … by looking out for each other."

"Agreed." This time, he saw more movement than he expected and her eyes became tiny, to match her mouth.

"Then, I suggest that we exchange more data and since I have more of that than you, you will be inclined to be guided by my advice." Her eyes started growing again.

Conor had a lot to gain from being friendly, but he wasn't going to be told what to do by a creature that wasn't human, regardless of how benign it appeared to be.

"Agreed … but I don't take instructions well, Tess." He gently squeezed the tentacle that refused to let him go. When it wasn't actually touching him, it was hovering bare millimetres over his head or hands, always ready to touch.

"I said guided because I would never assume to instruct you without your agreement, unless you were in danger, like you were out there." The eyes went tiny again and he stroked the tentacle which in turn stroked the back of his hand.

"Yeah … I really should thank you again for that."

"Isn't that how friends are made?" She was the most graceful creature imaginable and all she had to do was flow to one side and then stand beside him. She was pretty much the same height as Sonia but she was like elastic and could apparently double or halve her height on a whim.

Up close, the dress was more of a shapeless shift that made Conor wonder what he might be truly capable of in Crystal City. After all, if he could unconsciously conjure up an image of Sonia's cleavage as he'd done previously, how much of his surroundings were adulterated imagination? Also, it wasn't like he'd ever seen that much of Sonia in real life to be subsequently capable of re-imagining it.

Tess had a large round head on a neck that looked too delicate to support it. She had a tentacle off each rounded shoulder that was as elastic as her body was, and a stiffer and maybe more powerful pair or arms rooted into each tentacle armpit. Each arm sprouted four fingers in a configuration of two thumbs to the rear and two digits forward, but they were all muscle and sinew. Close up, Tess had no obvious bone structure, except maybe around the face.

The legs and leg tentacles above them were rooted in the lower chest and back because her trunk was very short. That effectively put one pair to the front and the other to her back. But because she moved diagonally like a crab, she effectively had a pair of arms and legs facing forward from the side and another two pairs facing backwards. That made her incredibly mobile, impossible to push over and super dextrous with hands and feet combined. She was also very powerful and Conor was belatedly thankful that she didn't initially respond to him as the threat that he obviously appeared to be.

Despite her totally alien appearance, she wasn't scary or hard on the eyes and she glided from point to point in the low gravity with a confidence that made him jealous. There were no monsters in the corridors and none in the ramp section but regardless, they continued to talk in whispers.

"Your disk is the same as mine." He commented when she raised it towards the almost invisible barcode patch built into the glass door. He pushed the door out and she had no shortage of limbs to catch it and then close it quietly behind them as they left the empty cubicle.

"How do you open it again, because there's no handle to pull it?" The seam was perfect and impossible to prise open, even with her overload of biological equipment.

"Disk opens." Said Tess with tiny eyes.

Her eyes seemed to grow when she was scared and then shrink when confident, and even cocky but he remembered to keep his voice down and also to exercise more patience. She could sound human but he had no idea how she was actually thinking.

"But it's glass and I can't see any motor. Something has to push or pull something else to open it, but there's absolutely nothing inside the glass apart from the wires in that barcode thing." He ran his hand over the door seam again, barely able to feel it.

"There is little here that functions mechanically but right now I feel exposed out here in the corridors. Monsters come and go to no logical pattern. So, let me explain more when we're secure in your pod."

"Sure." But he was no longer sure and this time she knew it because the talking stopped and Conor put more distance between him and the touchy-feely alien female. That separation was easy enough to maintain as the two made their way to the ramp area, one gliding along as easily as an octopus through water. The other meanwhile, trying to stay some distance ahead with a comparatively incongruous slow-motion bounce, still reminiscent of an erratically blown beach ball in a variable breeze.

For Conor, dependence itself was proving to be as addictive as any drug. Meeting a real live alien was terrifying at first, what with all those tentacled limbs. Who would have believed that real aliens would really have tentacles? But after shock came tentative efforts to not appear or sound terrifying to each other and eventually, the dawning that in this place they only had each other as possible friends and collaborators. He'd let his guard down and now he was stuck with the consequences.

What if she used her over-abundant limbs against him? If she could pull him off his feet and into her cubicle with little apparent effort, then she could easily use her disk in his sphere and she'd be in total control. She could go home to whatever weird world produced her and he'd be stuck in

Crystal City. There was no doubt in his mind that after being alone for all that time, she'd very likely done all her thinking well in advance.

13 - Parley

From the outset, body language was looking like it could pose problems between two sentient beings with only their sentience in common. But learning is what evolution does best and Tess was quite obviously unhappy, because her eyes were huge while she waited for Conor to open his cubicle door. Four tentacles and two arms were splayed on the glass. She could have been simply scared because she admittedly didn't like roaming the terminal's spooky corridors, but she could just as easily have been anticipating a struggle.

Despite his apprehensions and their commitment to a mutually productive friendship, the sphere was just too important to Conor. Tess had lost hers, through no fault of her own, but that was her account. There was no way to avoid it, he needed to take full control and then keep it until they decided their next steps, or until he unilaterally made a decision for them both, by just leaving. There was nothing to stop him from leaving, except Tess.

"I need to ask you something."

"Can't you wait until we're inside." Her heavy head was swivelling on a neck slender enough to be feeling the effort. She was starting to tremble, which for her was probably the nearest thing to a girl … a real girl starting to cry, but he stuck to his task.

Then she turned on those huge liquid eyes and moved closer. Taking his hand so gently that he couldn't tell precisely when the first contact was made. "I'm afraid." She made it sound like a confession.

"Me too." He replied and she countered immediately. "Now open the door."

"Can you open the door?" He asked and the question seemed to stun her into silence for some moments.

"I tried some doors before, but my disk only works in the cubicle that my pod arrived in. Maybe it will lose all key functions when my pod is assigned to … someone new." She froze like she might have heard something but he heard nothing and besides, he was the one with ears.

"Yeah, but did you ever try it on a cubicle with a sphere inside. Not all of them are empty." The pressure of her hold on his hand instantly increased.

"You tried your disk on my door but it didn't open for you. Don't you remember?" But she didn't wait for his answer. "Now please open, Conor." It was a command.

He remembered only too well but there was no sphere inside her cubicle and there was so much at stake. "Do you think your disk will work in my sphere?"

She was still looking away down the corridor.

"No." She was emphatic about that but it wasn't the reassurance that Conor needed.

"Did you ever try your disk in another sphere or pod?"

"No. I told you that it only opens one door but surely you know that I must have tried to use it on so many doors, not just to these rooms." Then she understood his reluctance and turned slowly to face him.

"Do you think it's logical that I could take your pod from you, when I can't even open the door?" Her eyes were as big as they were when the monsters were bellowing outside her door.

"I think maybe someone or something took your pod and maybe your solution is to get my trust and then take mine because, to be completely honest, that could be something that I might do." She dropped his hand like it had just been replaced by a hot iron and slowly produced her disk from some mysterious pocket on the inside of her shift.

"If you want to hold this … and if you decide not to return it … I would always be wandering these corridors and you know I would suffer too much from that. Could you do that to me, or to anyone?" She moved away from the door and away from him.

"This is survival Tess. I can trust only me."

She put more distance between them. "It was also survival when there were monsters at my door but I opened it for you when you called my name. So, open this door, Conor McCarthy."

"But you had no sphere to risk losing, Tess. What would you do if our situations were reversed?"

"I've already done that." She moved further back. "Goodbye … Monster."

14 - Software

The two most perplexing puzzles posed by the sphere were the levels of automation and delusion built into it. Superficially, it was capable of round trips to the dark side of the moon, but only if the pilot-slash-passenger was technically gullible and also not colour blind. A basic appreciation of what historical lunar landings actually entailed would make 'Conor's' sphere the most valuable piece of research and development technology in existence, or the ultimate in drug induced virtual or alternate realities. Either way, it was potentially very valuable, though cashing in on the surreality it created, was not going to be easy.

Its potential was further boosted by the fact that the mysterious drug it freely dispensed carried no damaging side effects. Quite the opposite in fact, because Conor never felt more mentally capable, if still somewhat confused about the precise purpose of the equipment. He also wasn't totally overawed by his surreal predicament, though that wasn't necessarily good news. He understood narcotics and the selling point of so many was the false sense of confidence bordering on reckless blasé that they could induce. His internal jury was still deliberating specific physical benefits beyond simply feeling better than he could ever remember being before.

But for every apparent positive there is a negative and the downside of his commercial aspirations required Conor to dehumanise Tess and that could only begin when he rendered it sexless. The mystery of his mistaken association of the creature with Sonia was hard to explain, much less forget. If he could do that, important decisions could be made based on hard cold facts, even if these were also in short supply.

"Anyway," he mused, with a clarity of thought made possible only by the elimination of all distractions, "- if the alien octopus thing was correct, I could embark on the return leg of my second round trip and still have the option of making a third sometime in the future but that would have to be that. According to it, a fourth trip would most likely be a one-way affair, and that would take it off the menu."

There was so much to think about and he had to get it right. Instinctive suspicion told him that the Irish Government wasn't likely to invest in what he would have to claim as salvage and would most likely seize it. So he'd need to sound out potential foreign investors by trawling the dark web. But since no-one spends hard cash on hearsay, any potential investor would want to see the sphere tested. Luckily, there was one trip left in the tank before the Ninja's bosses, whoever or wherever they were, impounded or confiscated the thing, just like they did the alien's. People who bought and sold valuables on the dark web were also not likely to simply walk away after being duped, so it was going to be a risky business, once he got home.

The upshot was that somebody at some stage was going to take that last round trip and it would either be for serious money or for the attempted rescue of a stranded shape shifting alien with dubious motives. It should have been impossible to be so blasé about his plans, having met such an exotic creature but the surreal circumstances of the whole thing made it easier to stay under awed. The only real fact of life was the existence of the sphere itself and it was marketable.

So he sat inside it, turning his disk over and over in his hands because once he placed it inside the console, he had no way of getting it back again until he'd wake up back in Erris, where all those bridges were most likely still smouldering away.

The craziest thing of all was that the creature who called itself Tess wasn't in any real danger. Only an idiot would give up the opportunity of a lifetime to save the life of something that either didn't exist, or that was effectively immortal. He'd seen no restaurants in the Crystal City Passenger Terminal and he was never hungry anyway, so it was patently obvious that he couldn't die there either. Yet, the monsters couldn't just be disregarded and there was still the mystery surrounding the shoes that he'd left behind on the first trip. What that meant was that Crystal City had to exist somewhere.

"Tess!" He tapped on the glass door but after an initial flutter, the insignificant bundle of pastel coloured rags in the corner settled even closer to the floor.

"I'm sorry, Tess. Please let me in." Guilt pangs had him feeling like he was revisiting the scene of a capital crime, where he'd upset a girl so much that he really made her cry. But since Tess wasn't a girl, kicking a kitten was probably the closest analogy he could come up with. Either way, he'd behaved like a total asshole.

"OyanNisTess." Using her full name made no difference and if anything, the rag pile skulked even lower.

"Oh come on … please ..." Nothing.

While trying to come up with a better approach and out of little more than idle curiosity, he fished out his disk and placed it over the door's barcode patch and wasn't too surprised when nothing happened. Looking down however, to ensure he put it back in his small 'precious' pocket, he saw hers. Light from the illuminated floor was shining through it, making it almost as invisible as the web-thin wiring of the barcode mechanism.

"Jeez Tess. Is this your disk?" He pressed it against the patch and the door swung silently out to meet him. "Holy crap. I don't think it was locked."

"Go away, Little Monster Boy. I'm waiting for something with more presence than you or better still, for the narrow-headed bipeds to come along and take me into the city for a change of scenery, like they sometimes do with the monsters. I've had enough of being alone in this place and I've decided to change my situation. Now leave me to it." If she was a real person, that last part could have sounded like a threat.

Because he could only see the top of her head, he was surprised at how much sound she could push through such a tiny mouth. Just how loud that was only became evident when it rushed out the door and reverberated through the corridors until it found a distant monster, who gave it an even more irate reply.

He'd spent what felt like several hours mulling over his options, but no matter how easy it was to convince himself that making up with the alien was the dumbest, what should have been a minor consideration had grown into its own monster to haunt him. The alien had opened her door to save him and when push came to shove, he couldn't find it in himself to reciprocate.

A sixteen-year-old part time confidence trickster, scammer and small-time drug retailer would appreciate more than most that there's no place in business for emotions. But the most routine commercial transaction depends on some level of tit for tat for success. A flowery and very faded greeting card once told him that friendship makes no demands, but no-one needs to ask for something that will be given automatically. There's also something binding about a hand shake, even if one of the hands had only four fingers. If he couldn't at the very least do for Tess what Tess had already done for him, then the proposed friendship of a non-human that he was only too eager to disregard, was too good for him.

It was the jam smeared in the butter irritant that stopped him from fully exploring his more rational options, like an itch between the shoulder blades that just couldn't be scratched. But having eventually done the right thing, he didn't expect to be insulted by the thing calling him a little boy. At his age, when memories of being little were still fairly fresh, it was likely to hit a nerve, and it did.

"So does that make you an elder, like my mother or something?" It sounded childish and mental repeat found him guilty as charged. Conor grimaced at the impotence of being unable to retrieve it so he could swallow it and then pretend it was never said.

"Not a mother." She said sulkily, slowly pulling the rest of her bulbous head out from under the folds of her voluminous shift.

The eyes were tiny and Conor knew that interpreting alien body language and mannerisms was still a work in progress, because those little eyes had to be far from happy. He pulled the door behind him and then used her disk from the inside to lock it against the monster that Tess had just invited for a visit, and then went over to sit by her side. It was pointless going anywhere with one of those things prowling around.

He tried not to notice the paradox of humanity in eyes that grew into liquid black pools from mere dots and shook his head when he remembered how easily he'd mistaken it for Sonia. That was just insane. But her body also filled out and he gathered she must have been spread out on the floor, pretty much like a large balloon only half filled with water. It was either that or she could deflate and then inflate herself again.

"It's true that I'm probably older than you but that was never likely to affect a mutually perceived equality, until you decided to behave like a … child by disregarding what was in any reality, a momentous … achievement, a most unlikely consensus that might never happen again in any universe."

Conor was back and as far as he was concerned, he didn't have to crawl into her favour, but in view of her exotic status, he decided not to make a mountain out of the molehill that was her obvious disappointment. What was done was done and it was time to move on.

"I admit that I might have made a mistake, but I already apologised and I'm here now. As soon as it's safe to do so, we can go back to the sphere … if you still want to do that, so we can decide what to do about … well … everything."

She was quiet for a few moments. "Since it would appear that I disturbed another monster, we may as well talk here. After that, I will decide for me whether it is better to leave my key outside the door again or to go with you to your pod."

Conor was horrified. "You deliberately left it out there ... Oh my God! Are you nuts?"

But she was anything but irrational. "We Oyan are a very sociable people and I have had enough of solitary confinement in this madness. Strange as it may seem now, it was only the hope that you might return as something more than a little monster that kept me sane."

Conor read somewhere that the octopus was the nearest thing to an alien life form on Earth. Something to do with their truly unique evolution but back then, he found reading such articles boring. How was he to know that he'd meet a person sized variant, who could talk ... about being pissed off at him and who was scared of being alone?

"I shouldn't have refused to share the sphere with you but to be honest, I was afraid that you might be more devious that you looked. You are an alien after all and how could I just trust you like that." Something about that statement didn't sound quite right but he went on regardless.

"As I saw it, you were more likely to use our agreement as a way of ... well ... gaining my confidence and then stealing it … and we human people don't like being alone any more than you Oyan."

He barely felt the end her arm brush the back of his hand but when he did, he slowly turned his hand to take the twin sets of pliable digits between his fingers. When she stayed quiet, he tried to lighten the sombre atmosphere.

"So, how old are you anyway, to feel you're entitled to judge me like that?" He tried to smile and her eyes became smaller again. After such a promising beginning, she really was impossible to read.

"There is nothing wrong with unbiased judgement once all facts are known. What is unacceptable, is to judge too soon." But she didn't let him dwell on that and immediately went on.

"I could say I'm five … ten ... twenty … or thirty," - her tiny mouth was once more out of sync with her spoken words and for the umpteenth time, she shimmered before continuing, "- and what you would hear is five … ten … twenty … or thirty, but that's not what I said at all." This time a tentacle reached out to take his other hand just as he'd taken her 'hand'. "Does that confuse you?"

"Yeah … it sure does." And his fake smile morphed into genuine puzzlement.

"I say that because software is automatically translating my communications for you, and then presenting what you say to me in a form that I can understand. It is either removing a language barrier, or applying a common language that we are both unaware of."

His eyes opened wide. "You think it's software and not drugs?"

"Maybe it's a case of both, possibly augmented with something else again, but words between us have very little meaning. First, tell me how old you are, but tell me how you measure age before you give me your answer, otherwise software will over simplify and I won't learn as much about you as I need to." When he realised what she was getting at, he couldn't resist a small gasp of appreciation at her powers of rationalisation.

"Wow … of course. OK then … well, Earth goes around the sun once a year and it's done that sixteen times since I was born … alone." He added the last word for good measure. He remembered the same octopus article saying that an octopus can produce thousands of young but only once, before it dies and it seemed appropriate to elaborate, since he'd already called it … her … a mother.

Those alien eyes seemed to swallow him and his words whole, but she masticated them quite slowly. The eyes then grew huge, something like they did when she was scared of the monsters but this was more gradual. She was also silent for long minutes before they started to shrink again.

"So," she began, "- that blue planet that you claim is on the other side of this moon is also home and you call it Earth, but since you measure age in cycles, do your moon's rotations affect the numbers in your age?"

"Yes, it is and no, the moon is unimportant. It goes around the Earth about twelve times a year but aside from causing the tides and maybe lighting up the sky for a couple of nights each month ... except when there's rain, it doesn't do much because it's dead … just like this place … outside the crater." He shrugged and she once again took time to ingest his offerings.

"Let me begin by telling you what my job entails. I am an anthropologist, which on my home requires me to be something of a xeno-anthropologist as well, so let me share some thoughts, but do tell me if I get something wrong."

"Sure." He agreed, but far too quickly because xenoanthropology was something he'd have to think some more about before risking a comment that could show his ignorance. As far as he could remember, it was either the study of ancient humans or the study of ancient non-humans. But then again, xeno could mean human to an alien. So he decided to listen more and think less.

"Sixteen to you is twenty to me because your primary arithmetic model seems to be based on ten. That's not completely logical because although you have ten digits on your hands, I can't understand why human people would disregard the same number of digits on your feet."

Conor looked down at his bare feet and laughed. Tess jumped but then squeezed his fingers reassuringly when he started to apologise for startling her yet again.

"We have eight limbs, so your standard multiple of ten is eight to us and we count in octals. Anyway," Tess could be quite the conversationalist when relaxed, "- the last figure I need is your age expressed in a decimal of a galactic year."

"Wow. I really have no idea how to calculate that." He mumbled.

"Then tell me the age of the galaxy expressed in Earth years?"

"Wow." Again. Conor was beginning to feel decidedly stupid.

"Never mind. Maybe you know the age of the universe?"

He just shook his head slowly. "Astronomy was never my strong point." He offered weakly.

"The first cause? Creation?" She hinted.

If this was school, Conor would already be in the corner and then he remembered something. "The Big Bang?" He blurted.

"Wow." It was her turn to gasp. "It seems that software has no translation for that except word for word, just as you expressed it, because it means nothing to me except noise. Was 'The Big Bang' your creation event?"

"I guess so …"

They both looked at each other like they were seeing each other for the first time.

"How long ago?" Asked Tess.

"Maybe twelve, thirteen or fourteen billion years. I can't remember which … sorry."

"That's OK. I'll take the middle answer, so are you ready?"

"Shoot." Which only delayed the proceedings as she tried to make sense of the translation and failed. After thinking about it again she decided to disregard what was probably just slang because his body language suggested that he was waiting for her answer.

"There is some calculated guessing on my part but it seems that you still live on your original home-world which, given your bipedal projected form means that your civilisation is still in its infancy."

"Young?" Conor interrupted. "But we have writing that goes back maybe ten thousand years …"

"So, it seems that I'm correct so far." She was about to continue when his question registered as a question, but since he didn't follow it up, she disregarded that also.

"A moon of this apparent size orbiting twelve times in a solar year would have been a major factor in accelerating evolution for all life on Earth. Since you don't see my own projected biological form as a monster, it would be reasonable to assume that your Earth is still endowed with a wide variety of life forms. Personally, I find the concept of a blue planet with periodic rains very appealing and something that we exiled Oyan would cherish like the last flower in the universe."

To Conor, ten thousand years in the past was quite literally the stone age and truly ancient history, and he wondered if he might have heard Tess wrong when she claimed to know something about anthropology, but he let it slide. The fact was, he found her insight more amazing than any variable definition of 'young'. She could extract so much from just talking about his age, but what came over most was the fact that she really was a real alien. It wasn't such an abstract concept anymore.

"So, ask me." She invited, with big eyes again. It crossed his mind that she was also something of a hypocrite for calling him a child when she could so easily act like one herself. She was so obviously enjoying her little game.

"How old are you OyanNisTess?" A double tentacle with hand squeeze showed her appreciation for the courtesy of her full name, which in another time and place might be considered condescending. Tess however, was pleased for another reason and that was the return of the young alien's empathy, which in turn would give him a fuller appreciation of the true meaning of 'alien'.

She began. "Saren has been home to the Oyan for longer than our self-recorded history, but our kind were not born in Saren's ice covered oceans. It is just one of a hundred and five moons captured by the gas giant Tamar which orbits our red giant sun, Elix. The original Oyan home world was called Dan by the Tal, who were our masters and benefactors but who can no longer sing us songs of their lives."

Like a practised storyteller, she eased into the plot. "We Oyan are afflicted with three legacy loyalties. Mine is to Dan and to my hope for an eventual longer-term return before Elix fully devours it. Elix is now in its terminal stage and will soon collapse. When that happens, life on all our worlds will most likely end. I consider it my duty as well as a pilgrimage to complete a circle of life and die on Dan, where we came from. Others look to Tamar, who can fill the entire sky from horizon to horizon with a blaze of swirling opal colours, especially when seen from above the ice sheet that preserves our homes beneath. The rest of our kind consider us ungrateful to Saren, who has given us everything we need to survive, to dream and to aspire to greater things, like making peace with our destiny."

"Like you, our age is based on the cycles of our planets and moons and I am three ages. I consider myself Dan 23, though some Oyan of the same age would claim to be

Tamar 3 or Saren 107 and that's also the reason why I study xenoanthropology. I was working on the excavation of an ancient Tal settlement on Dan when I discovered the pod that brought and then abandoned me here. You see this moon as yours, but to me it's just one of Tamar's many moons. Where we agree, is that it always faces away from whatever planet is on the other side, regardless of whether that is Earth or Tamar."

Like the end of a particularly engrossing bedtime story, Conor's mouth didn't close and he had to look again at the product of another planet, another star, who lived under the ice of a moon spinning around a gas giant planet that was close enough, or big enough to fill the entire sky.

"Wow, Tess. Do we even live in the same galaxy?" He had a million questions but that was the first one to form while others were left to slowly coalesce into a semblance of more orderly thought.

"I think so, but we'll probably never know for sure because if your Sun is a star in any one of our constellations, it would have to be quite close to us to be seen. Our Elix is bloated now, but it radiates at the wrong end of the visible spectrum to be seen over very long distances. How far is the furthest star you can see without a visual aid?" She threw in.

Conor just shrugged.

"From that answer I can be positive that you were still living on your original world. As for the Oyan, the Tal brought us to Saren when the last survivors fled Dan's poisons. The Saren sect like to romanticise that relationship but I've found evidence on Dan that suggests we were probably little more than their servants or maybe even pets at first. When they finally died out, most probably the result of a Saren pathogen or prolonged cosmic radiation, we continued to evolve in the ocean under the ice."

"Holy cow!" He closed his mouth. Images of Jupiter's or Saturn's larger moons came to mind and he struggled with which of the two gas giants held Europa, or was it Titan, that might have something in common with Saren?

"What happened to Dan?" The questions were queuing up.

"From the facts on the ground on Dan, it seems that the Tal reached population critical mass but kept expanding regardless. We Oyan have very limited resources on Saren and we need to control our population for very practical reasons, but also out of sympathy for those who will be alive to see the beginning of our end for themselves. We're not the most adventurous people and I would never have climbed into an alien pod had I not considered it to be an old Tal artefact." She paused before adding. "Back then, the Tal had somewhere else to go when they rendered Dan uninhabitable, but we don't."

Conor remembered a documentary that claimed the population of Earth had doubled in an average lifetime, while almost half of all non-human species had disappeared to make room. Again, he found the subject boring when something more practical, like business had to be learned.

"I'm not sure our human people are ready to travel out to the gas giant moons." He said at last.

"Then it's a good thing that you still have a viable planet." Said Tess.

"But how did you guys survive when the Tal couldn't, if your people were little more than their pet poodles?" Then he thought to add. "Sorry … no insult intended."

Being referred to as a domesticated canine didn't seem to upset Tess but that was probably down to the limitations of an automated alien translator. To Conor, the image of a pampered pet was simply alien to something as exotic as the Oyan, but to have any idea of what dogs might be capable of evolving into, one would probably need to have some dealings with a representative.

15 - Stellar Relations

"Are you not curious about how you've been enhanced?" Asked Tess as they finally reached Conor's cubicle after another measureless milestone. Her stealthy flitting under one wall and then crossing over to slide along the other, with him bouncing in slow-mo down the centre and then up the ramp to 'his' floor, took mere minutes. It was the earlier exchange of information that devoured time.

From a gentle ebb and flow, it quickly grew into a torrent and then into something like a dam bursting and nothing could stem the flow. Conor's aching head was somewhere between an elongated orbit around Elix to approaching a possibly commonly known red star with the same name as a demon in an old comedy movie. The name would eventually arrive, just as they eventually did at 'his' locked glass door.

Tess didn't look comfortable standing and when she did, it was more like floating on the spot. He didn't dare to say anything of course, but it crossed his mind more than once that she might have something in common with one of those big party helium balloons except hers had anything up to eight tethers dangling beneath it. When she was low, squat and streamlined with her many appendages invisibly deployed under her colourful apparel, she was propelled effortlessly along at considerable speed. But when she stood a bit taller, it was hard not to notice the inevitable clump of temporarily idle limbs gathered beneath her.

When they weren't moving, she chose to stay very close to her human companion. So close in fact that her proximity was a challenge requiring his stoic endurance. After all, he'd already done enough to alienate her. A smile escaped before that thought could file itself away.

"I'm curious about everything here Tess, but it's hard to know just how and where to start dissecting all of it." He answered at length, giving the alien plenty of time to note that he was prone to much shoulder shrugging, while simultaneously engaging a mystifying repertoire of pointless hand gestures. She decided to put those mannerisms down to insecurities, which came as something of a comfort. It pleased her not be alone with her own apprehensions, which could border on debilitating.

As for Conor's 'so called' enhancements, he was definitely in a much better place mentally, and he was also able to remember more, aside from the stubbornly elusive name of that big red star. The distance from the moon to Earth was probably the most obvious example, as far as he was concerned.

He was never interested in a lifeless moon and couldn't recall ever being bothered to read anything about it, but he seemed to intuitively know its distance. That was assuming that the moon on which Crystal City was built was his and not hers. If the latter was true, then he'd only be mistaken by mere multiples of light years. Anyway, a distance of no real interest to anyone was child's play compared to the science that Tess was using to blow him away.

She said it was the moon's influence over Earth's tides that must have driven evolution at a much faster pace for humanity than it had for the Tal on Dan, where two minor moons had little effect on it's shallow oceans. Apparently, the last of the Tal succumbed to extinction the equivalent of twenty thousand years previously, but some of their technology was so durable that it could be inherited by the Oyan later. Subsequently, they were able to technologically tweak it and then begin a program of duplication and modification to better suit themselves. Hence, the interplanetary travel that made it possible for her to fly to Elix's inner planets to ultimately excavate archaic Tal sites on Dan.

As the exchange continued, Tess was able to eventually conclude that Humans and Oyan may well live reasonably close to each other, in galactic terms. She did that by dropping apparently unconnected questions about fudgy stars and major red stars visible from Earth. With his improving memory, he could recall one or two instances of orienteering with his father. He remembered that the Andromeda galaxy occupied the same slice of sky as Polaris when it came to looking for the north pole. By simple deduction, because it was fudgy yet plainly visible and therefore relatively close but also larger than the Milky Way galaxy, she guessed they must be close galactic neighbours. That red star could be the key to confirming her proposition.

Conor felt bad about being largely ignorant of astronomy because Tess had a genuine gift for the logical collation and cross referencing of seemingly insignificant data. She could dissect the simplest fact and then present the equivalent of an essay on related subjects in seconds. It made him even more guilty about assuming automatic superiority based on nothing more logical than racism, or its interstellar equivalent. As he got to know her better, he was able to fully appreciate the many qualities that made her such an amazingly insightful creature.

"You've already made me dizzy Tess, and I'm only now realising how little I know about anything." As it transpired, Tess could really inflate and deflate her trunk. She could do so with air or with water and she could survive in both, though she guessed that her definition of air might be a little different than the one he didn't have. Oxygen and nitrogen yes, but the ratio was the critical issue and once again he was shown up for the idiot he was, but she didn't assume the superiority that she could justifiably claim. Talking to Tess might have been easy but it was also an act of humility, like a junior school kid talking high level mathematics with a PHD student.

She was extremely interested in the Earth's inclination because she said it would offer her some clues into the extent of seasonal weather variations, which she proposed might be an additional factor in the acceleration of human evolution. Ultimately, Conor was left dreading questions about formal human education, since he seemed to have so little to offer but Tess was grateful for any tidbit he had to offer, even if she had to dig deeply for it. She took real joy from finding unlikely matches for insignificant snippets and then feeding it back to him in logical packages, like completed sections of a life-sized jigsaw.

Tess could stand quite tall but she preferred to operate, as she called moving about, at Sonia's approximate height. Apparently, her own moon Saren wasn't as big as the Earth, which made it easier for her to adjust to the gravity that was posing so many problems for him. That, or she was doing the polite thing by helping him find excuses for his own clumsiness.

He squeezed his disk out of its secure hiding place and offered it to her and she surprised him by immediately taking it. He guessed she'd make more of a ceremony out of it but when the glass door swung open, she ushered him in first, like a schoolteacher in kindergarten. Despite their countless radical differences, she displayed mannerisms and an empathy that were so distinctly 'female', that he instinctively baulked at taking the lead by inviting: "Ladies first."

"Let's lock this door just in case." It was muttered more than spoken and when he closed and then tested it, Tess was already standing by the open door of the sphere. By that stage however, she had shared so much of herself that he knew she was morally and culturally incapable of cheating anyone.

"Well?" Conor was puzzled by how a creature of such obvious sincerity and purity could also play the part of a bossy school teacher so well, but just added it to her growing list of curious idiosyncrasies and answered.

"Well … we have drugs that can help a person think faster and clearer but even more that simply delude people into believing that may be the case, when it isn't. That's why I was convinced that a narcotic of some kind had cured my agoraphobia, but when you talked about software, I had to go back to square one. Sorry … that means starting over again."

Getting to really know someone like Tess was a truly novel experience but it came easy and naturally like she was just someone a bit different. She was disarmingly generous with information and with every offering came something of herself. The only way to deal with such innocent naivety was to keep talking in an effort to reciprocate whenever she fell quiet, which wasn't very often. It didn't matter how insignificant his life may have seemed to him, because Tess could discuss farting as easily as she could the most unlikely commonalities between Human and Oyan natures. Very soon, it was impossible not to be as blatantly honest as she was, even though such transparency was anathema to his naturally 'cautious' or opportunistic state.

Apparently the Oyan didn't have separate words for 'he' or 'she' and everyone was simply 'they', plural. This was in deference to the complexity of the evolved conscious mind and once again, something that Conor would have to reflect upon further. Social equilibrium was apparently as important as human justice systems where it was a crime not to immediately attend to rifts between groups of individuals.

Oyan didn't like social disparities and once identified, juries would be tasked with quantifying the problem and making recommendations to fix it, especially when it came to nutrition, dwellings and education. Conor mused that left to their own devices, as they were after the extinction of the Tal, their government may have evolved into something parallel to benign communism.

Where transparency was so highly valued, she felt obliged to state her objectives with him. Top of that list were the establishment of equality and respect through mutual sharing of data, with no snippet any more or less valuable than any other.

"That's easy to say," he mumbled, "- for someone who wasn't even human but who could probably write a book on 'humanity', possibly in a matter of hours." But Tess learned so quickly from her practical observation of him that was a discernible difference between 'musing too loud', as she called it, and speaking with the intention of being heard, or being transparent, which was her default.

Apparently, it was an offence for an Oyan to mumble deliberately.

"So," said much louder as he joined her at the airlock, "-does my sphere look anything like yours on the inside?" He tried to ease past her, but constant touching was apparently as normal for Oyan as it was taboo for people and Tess was reluctant to disregard his overly frequent mutterings of 'excuse me'.

"It looks identical, though maybe the body restraints will be different because of my particular physiology." Conor was wondering what a harness for such a fluid body would look like and was about to ask but thought better of it, since she was a 'she' but Tess was better at reading his body language than he was at understanding hers.

"Mine is … was … more like a net wraparound … with plenty of holes for my limbs." She offered at length.

Conor just nodded without making eye contact. "You'll soon see that this sphere has a one piece upper- and two-piece lower body harness that locks together in the middle … just over my belly, here." Said pointing to it.

"Is there a reason why you didn't ask me how my body restraint was different from yours?"

"Yes." He said simply, and laughed. Tess seemed happy to let it go at that.

Conor sat inside and lay on the reclining seat. "The top part comes over from behind the seat, here, here and here." Said indicating the locations behind his head and on each side of his body.

"Is it embarrassing for you to discuss your physiology." She asked from way too close to his face.

"Well … women … females don't like to because they're … very conscious of how they look and also … well … very private about it." He was glad that was over.

"Is the public display of sex organs a morality issue on Earth?"

This was getting tiresome. "Yes, Tess."

"Aahh. I understand now. Sorry." And she sounded it and he mistakenly assumed the topic was closed, but she was simply apologising in advance, just as he so often did to her, for imminent unavoidable body contact. She squirmed over him so she could squat beside the seat but on the opposite side to the door.

"I'll stay here for now, in the event that you need to access the door." She offered, when he seemed somewhat anxious after yet another blatant invasion of his privacy but he was struck by just how light and also how soft she was, even with the low gravity considered.

"No worries." He said, but he wasn't very convincing.

Having the body of something so closely resembling a large octopus was every bit as advantageous as being able to function in a wide variety of environments. She could squeeze in anywhere and then take up residence. Just then, her big head was propped up next to his, while the rest of her was spread over the inner-sphere floor, just then resettling after their movements.

"Is it because you still associate me with your Sonia that you are distracted when we make physical contact." One thing Tess wasn't, was shy.

"Well now that you mention it, Tess. It would be very impolite of me to say that you have no effect on me at all, but any female crawling over any male is body language that would normally demand some response." He said curtly, though he was very pleased with his choice of words, and only slightly puzzled by his ever-improving vocabulary, which he put down to lengthy discourse with such a well-spoken alien using a hi-tech translator.

"Is crawling over each other part of the human mating ritual?"

"Oh, for god's sake …," but he didn't get a chance to say anymore before she interrupted him.

"I can assure you that your private parts are no more real than mine, so it doesn't matter how close we seem to get. We can't possibly experiment sexually, even if we wanted to, though I probably should be more appreciative of your moral considerations. Ultimately however, since this is not a physical place and so, we can't be physically inside it, which is what makes it possible for me to behave as I normally would on Saren. I like to touch you because I find it reassuring to have someone close by."

Conor turned his head to the right and was instantly reminded of his most intimate moment with Sonia and it wasn't because Tess looked anything like her again, because she didn't. It was simply because her head was almost lying next to his, close enough to touch with his mouth, like the night she showed him her scars.

"If we were real, Conor McCarthy, we'd probably both be dead because it's beyond all reasonable doubt that we harbour pathogens on or inside our bodies that would be mutually lethal. Our evolutionary histories are so … so vastly different that we would be utterly incompatible at a physical level. Do you feel more comfortable now regarding our apparent contact, because it's not a small comfort to me to be close to you?" Her huge black eyes quivered and then shimmered as they so often did and for no apparent reason, he found himself smiling at that.

"Like I said already, I'm feeling much better than I ever did and I find it easier to remember, or access information that I don't remember learning. That said, I'm never hungry and I never need to wash, so do please humour me by explaining some more … Oh … and you're welcome to any small consideration anytime."

"Now I know you are teasing me but since it amuses me, I won't object. Now, lie back and just close those pretend eyes so you can concentrate only on what you think you hear." Tess turned her own head so her eyes were facing the ceiling and he followed her lead.

"I've had more time to observe this entire construct and then rationalise how it might function, but don't assume that everything I am going to tell you is indisputable fact. If you have technical or logical reasons to disagree, you must tell me so I can revise my hypothesis. You must interrupt me if you have something to offer. We Oyan seek the truth in everything and constructive interruption is not impolite, it is a courtesy. Do you understand?"

"OK Tess. Let me have it."

"Where do you keep your disk?"

"In my precious pocket, the small one … here." He took a tentacle that he knew would be hovering within touching distance of his hand and brought it down to his pocket.

"And mine is here." The same tentacle lifted his hand and drew it inside the folds of her shift to an equally small pocket just below the neck. It had a small flap cover that stuck, like microfibre Velcro.

"These disks are nothing more than identity tags and each time we put one into any wall, door or pod slot anywhere, they upload revised profile information from a dual server …"

"Wow … wow." He also squeezed the end of her limb. "But any server has to be physical … right?"

"Yes. The servers are physical, but on Saren we already use quantum reversible dual processing and we keep our equipment in high orbit. That way it is constantly shaded from Tamar and Elix and we can cool it to only a fraction above absolute zero. We were able to improve on the technology left to us by the Tal but these pod makers were an interstellar sentience, with interstellar propulsion and the technology suggested by …"

She was interrupted by another squeeze.

"How do you know all that?"

"That's because our pods are the same technology and both your Earth and my Dan were given at least one pod each and we must consider that there may be more scattered out there somewhere. So, they had to be interstellar, and travelling the stars is the ultimate technological achievement for any sentient biology. We can't know when our respective pods were put in place but from where we found them, we do know it was geological ages ago. On that timescale, even the most radically advanced technology can be profoundly improved upon, provided the star-farers were able to survive long enough to do so."

"You really think they are still flying the stars?" Conor was mesmerised.

"No." Tess paused. "Oyan xenoanthropology has firmly concluded that any advanced sentience will eventually either kill itself, be killed or simply degrade over time. This is what we learned from the Tal, who became extinct long before they came close to bridging the stars."

Then she went on. "The only sentience that could live and further evolve over all that time would be the Artificial Intelligence that somehow managed to survive whatever disaster destroyed its creators."

16 - Facts of Life

"So, let me get this right. You believe that this moon and whatever planet might be floating in the vacuum on the other side of it, plus everything else, including us and all those monsters, are all interactive constructs inside some vast alien quantum computer that also houses some super artificial intelligence, who has decided to play god?" His own words compelled him to replay them again and then again and they still left him gobsmacked.

Tess had worked diligently on her Thesis. "I don't believe space is a total vacuum, nor that the AI is role playing, but your analogy seems otherwise reasonable. I'm so happy we were able to agree on our situation so quickly. But now, please don't be insulted if I infer that you might be more primitive than me."

After mentally singing her praises, Conor took a fresh look at his unlikely companion to see how far she was prepared to go with that taunt. "I suppose a third or even fourth level education might entitle you to claim superiority in that regard Tess, but I'd hate you to think that all people are as ignorant as me. The fact is, after my parents died, education came second to my survival on the streets, but we do have experts who could probably teach you a thing or two."

Tess did a rapid but also very gentle squeezing thing to convey instant contrition. "Should I also say that I'm sorry even if I meant that as a compliment ... of a kind?" But she didn't let him answer.

"You see, our technology feeds us and keeps us safe and even the occasional rupturing of the ice sheet above us is taken as an opportunity to learn, rather than a cause for concern."

Conor didn't see any relevance and just waited. After a pause, she kept going. "Apart from some real monsters who have evolved to devour anything that still grows there, including each other, Dan's biological diversity has gone the same way as the Tal. But even on Dan, our modified technology watches over us. The end result is that we don't lose many lives but our survival skills have been compromised over time. If your Earth is still as dynamic as you claim it is, then you should be more attuned to survival, even at the cost of an education. I say this because I am proposing that you should devise our plan of action." Oyan were so tactile that emotions were just impossible to hide and her tentacles and one arm touched his neck, cheek, the other arm, and then a leg. They then combined to produce a variety of localized massage-chair effects.

Despite the fact that she was literally all over him, the overall effect wasn't just pleasant, it was also very calming. He patted the back of a tentacle only to feel a slightly different texture than normal and sure enough, it was one of her two trunks, for want of a better description. It had some aspects in common with an elephant's, except it was softer, smoother, thinner and as far as he could tell, it had no ingesting orifice or mini-mouth or whatever at the tip. The trunks were obviously multi-purpose, primarily for walking, running or jumping but also for manipulation.

Like people do when someone has an obvious deformity and the best thing to do is pretend it doesn't exist, he'd deliberately not mentioned how all her limbs combined to work in such a bizarre configuration. As he thought about that, the only reason why he hadn't asked was down to the fact that they could converse and therefore just assumed that she might be offended. The ridiculous implication was that if they didn't speak a common language, talking about her to a third party would be perfectly okay, when it wasn't. It struck him that people could be really weird sometimes, or Tess was somehow getting into his head.

Anyway, it also crossed his mind that maybe she had the same reason for not commenting on his lack of limbs. It didn't escape him that she'd spoken of the 'narrow headed bipeds', who were presumably the Ninja welcoming committee. But the thing was, she wasn't being very complimentary while doing so. It followed then, that bipeds were probably not her favourite life form but since they held the Tal in such high regard, he would have to stop trying to mentally configure them as similar to people. He'd have to do something about constantly assuming humanoid superiority and just ask her about the Tal later.

"I must say that you guys must be really good at handling tools and fixing small components with those … appendages. I mean … the tentacle has a narrow tip but you also have two double digit hands and a grip any wrestler would be proud of. Those trunks are even stronger, and almost as versatile as the tentacles. I'm guessing you could hold a feather edge to edge as easily as you could a car gearbox or something. You know what I mean?" He lifted two tentacles away and then dropped them to demonstrate to himself just how flexible and how easy to manipulate they must be.

She was quiet while the message coming over included a substitute for something as fragile as a feather while possibly deleting 'car'. "It's true that some of us can do things that our own robots cannot and to you, that could be an amusing observation. You must be wondering why we would use manipulating robots when we obviously don't need them, but the boring work must also be done while we prioritise our research and development projects."

They appraised each other yet again. "Well," he said eventually. "- a good plan of action … will normally depend on more complete information, which is basically you. I also tend not to shy away from looking out for number one, which is me, so … are you sure about leaving me to come up with a plan?" His own honestly surprised himself.

"Now that we've established such a positive rapport, I have to doubt that a sentience as advanced as yours could not simply sacrifice another, like me for the sake of expediency. If you don't believe in our most fundamental equality, then I should be grateful for your honesty. Maybe I should execute my original plan and hopefully, I'll get taken into the city and possibly be exposed to further options that I simply can't imagine right now." She pulled away from him so slowly and deliberately that he was left in absolutely no doubt about the body language.

"No. You can't do that."

"Why not? I can do anything I want to do, just as can you."

"There are too many unknowns in the city, Tess." He took the last tentacle that was momentarily reluctant to disentangle itself. "There are too many unknowns here also, but we do have your very reasonable hypothesis as well two disks, one pod that works and if you're right in what you say, we also have at least one proven survivor who has an extremely intuitive accomplice."

Apparently reassured, her eyes narrowed, though not that narrow and two tentacles resumed their petting actions. "We'll need to pool more information though."

"Naturally." She said, adding. "I never expected you to come up with an instant plan."

"Naturally." He mimicked.

When she stayed silent, he began. "We need to go over some things to make sure we're both singing from the same songbook."

Tess leapt up. "You sing?"

That question came out of nowhere and he answered slowly, wondering where the splintered discussion was going to take them. "Of course."

"Songs of life and death?" She was intrigued.

Like I said, Tess liked to be close but the significance of the subject brought her face right up to his, and he instinctively drew back to get some space in which he could think … alone.

"Some, sure." He threw that out there while the rest of his answer gelled together. "But mainly love songs, though we also have rebel songs, so yeah. Songs of life, love, resistance, death, protest and suffering. I guess we do have songs for everything."

Tess changed dramatically while he could only look on, intrigued. At first, she shimmered again but this time her colours changed, like a chameleon. Then, all four tentacles spread out and slowly advanced on him until he was caught in the tightest embrace since Sonia, but it was equally as soft and yielding.

Strange as it may have been, what with the setting inside a Lunar Crater and with an alien from a different star wrapped around him, it wasn't a totally unpleasant experience. The thing was, it did somehow remind him of Sonia, minus the smell of that kiddy-soap she liked to use. All he could do was reciprocate because it was obvious that a milestone in interstellar relations had just been achieved.

"We must sing." She was exuberant or something that came close to that because Tess was intertwining her tentacles and then releasing them only to do so again and again, like a person wringing hands in delight, over and over and that was before she deployed her two sets of gripping digits.

Conor wasn't remotely close to being Dublin's best singer, though he'd once been called 'entertaining' at a party where the beer flowed too easily and the Karaoke machine featured his favourite song cum party piece. 'Entertaining' was as far as Sonia was prepared to go in giving him a swelled head, or so she said, but this was no time to be coy. Singing was obviously a yardstick in measuring people, sentience, empathy or something and by the transformation in Tess, it was something she considered to be truly significant.

In any case, she'd never heard anyone sing before, so she had no measure of how bad he could be when sober. Anyway, she suggested they should sing three songs. A solo each and then an impromptu duet. He had no idea how that last one was going to work, but she didn't seem to care and slowly brought up the quivering tip of a tentacle until it almost touched his nose, making him momentarily cross eyed.

Everyone has their own party piece they work on, even if they only perform in the shower and Conor had done precisely that but countless times until he got it bang on. Dear Evelyn was the first person to coax him into a rendition outside of the perfect echo chamber of her larger than normal bathroom. That was after Jimmy somehow 'acquired' a version on a compact disk compilation.

The only problem with his party piece was that it also contained some of the best 'air-guitar' ever but to his benefit, he'd not neglected that aspect of his performance. So, he strummed his imaginary strings once, just to make sure they were in tune with his fantasy of the familiar Karaoke Video and said. "Fine".

The whistling that's such an integral part of 'Wind of Change' is easy enough to master in the shower, when there's no-one there to distract you by laughing at the funny face you might make. Regardless of the sincerity of his alien audience, he had to close his eyes to Tess and then ran his recalled vision of a Scorpions Live Performance.

That done, and then timing the break to perfection, he started with the lyrics:

"I follow the Moskva -

down to Gorky Park,

listening to the wind of change.

An August summer night -

soldiers passing by,

listening to the wind of change."

He wasn't alive when the Scorpions first sang the track but his father, Tadhg had it as number one on an antique MP4 playlist. His earliest memory of the song was of gently waking to the sound of whistling and then coming downstairs to listen to the rest of it with them. It could have been late but more likely it was probably just dark outside.

Tadhg and Ceide sat as they always seemed to do in his memories. In the firelight from a stove slowly burning a beechwood and turf cocktail, it was easy to become intoxicated with the only narcotic he thought he'd ever need back then. Ceide's gleaming golden head lay on his father's shoulder as the song floated into the next verse.

"The world is closing in,

did you ever think -

that we could be so close, like brothers.

The future's in the air -

I can feel it everywhere,

blowing with the wind of change."

When Ceide saw him, her hand instantly reached out to his, and in his first recall of mental telepathy in action, he knew he shouldn't speak. So he just accepted her silent offering and then climbed up to lie between them, with his head on her lap while the lead guitar and the whistling told him to go back to sleep.

Years later, he would have to privately conclude that it was the physical power of hope wrapped in words and music that stopped sleep from immediately reclaiming her missing son. At the time however, he couldn't understand the emotion behind the song but he knew he'd shared in the presence of something special. And remembering that, he realized that this was what Tess was looking for, so he sang on, with gusto.

"Take me to the magic of the moment -

on a glory night,

where the children of tomorrow dream away … they dream away,

in the wind of change."

Not very long afterwards, when he was bold enough to look for the track and play it alone, Tadhg explained the sentiment behind the lyrics. The end of the cold war and the fall of barriers like the Berlin Wall preceded the reunification of a country ripped apart by war and then kept apart by redundant ideals. It was a time of great hope for a new future. Tadhg told him that May 25th was a day well worth celebrating because, in a 365 to 1 chance, it was Tadhg's and Ceide's joint birthday, or so they claimed in a pinky-swear.

It was also a date they shared with the composer, Klause Meine, and it made sense that at least once a year they should sit down together and listen as it fashioned a future for a kid with such huge dreams of his own. He still believed that only special people like Tadhg, Ceide and Klaus Meine were capable of generating so much hope.

When Tadhg and Ceide left him, the song became an anthem for better things that somehow never seemed to arrive … or not for very long at least … but as long as he sang on … hope lived.

"Walking down the street -

distant memories -

are buried in the past forever,

where the children of tomorrow share their dreams,

with you and me."

If he thought Tess was a different creature, then he underestimated what 'Song' had done for him in Tess's huge eyes. She was serenely grateful.

"Thank you, Conor McCarthy. It is my sincerest hope that one day you can learn just how important 'Song' is to me.

It's what defines the Oyan but for us it means that you and I are no longer different. We can never be monsters to each other."

Her small mouth opened and for a long time nothing came out of it until he felt the same quivering pulsing thing that she did with her limbs touching him, but this wasn't localised, it was all over. Then came the sound but it didn't come through his senses. It was planted directly in his head and a mental picture slowly built of profound loss, followed by fear, sadness, despair and loneliness in the vastness. Then it changed.

He kept his virtual eyes closed to welcome whatever she was saying but it wasn't words. It was pure emotion and it sang of gently susurrating rain producing pulsing optimism or most probably 'life' towards a different sun, seeking out fulfilment with tolerance and harmony. Then it changed again.

It was mega-awesomeness, possibly of Tamar and Elix and of insignificance alongside, the Oyan. Then it pulled him away, further and further until the miniaturisation of greatness into an overall insignificance associated perhaps with the Buddhist concept of comparative nothingness. Then it cycled back to the beginning.

As in 'Wind of Change', hope became dominant and it took the place of loss and fear of the future and because he'd just sang a similar song, he joined in but made no sound. Their song transcended all known forms of communication and it only concluded when everything important was already sung. It was irreverent to repeat any verse over, like praying for the same thing because maybe god didn't get the message the first time around. Silence, when it came was without the tinnitus hum of physical silence, it was more like the calm after a completely choreographed storm, where everything that was anticipated was delivered, and more.

"We sang." She said very softly, like she could have been crying with pleasure, except her eyes were always very moist.

"We did something ... maybe like praying." He agreed, while the aftermath of elation, imaginary rising hairs and static in every fibre, started to dissipate like the return of reality but not unpleasantly, not like coming down from a trip. It was beyond words and above emotion and probably just spiritual.

"You lost so much but you still have the vision." She said at last.

"It seems to me that we are both losers and maybe all we have left is hope." He offered.

"Hope with conviction powerful enough can change whole worlds." She amended and then acknowledged his small nod with another embrace that lasted even longer. While the most unlikely pair in the universe were still locked quietly together, Conor concluded that at some level, Tess might be telepathic, because she spoke, or rather, sang in emotions and not words.

"Are you?" He asked, knowing that any answer would mean that she was.

"What?" She was puzzled.

"Telepathic."

"No more than you." Her evasive answer suggested that maybe she could feel his emotions just as strongly as he had hers.

"Well. I never thought singing could be anything like that and I'm not making a small thing out of it, but now we have to make something more practical happen. So, tell me Tess. What is this virtual delusion made of? As in, how I could have mistaken you for Sonia? I mean … look at us."

Tess churned out her pre-prepared answer. "It's as I said earlier. When we are brought here, there is a period of adjustment which is used by our conscious to show us what we want to see, so that we can make the complete transition. This is enough to make some people mad and those monsters are not the same to both of us because we both fear different unknowns."

"You're still some way ahead of me Tess. Can you explain that like you would to a junior student," and then added, "- a human one." He got the gist of it though and strangely; he owed his sanity to some of those weird drugs he'd taken.

To him it was mind-bending to wake up in surreality, where all he had to do was enjoy it and try not to get too freaked out. To someone else, who'd never experienced 'other worlds', Crystal City could probably tip them over the edge.

Tess was back to petting hs hand and his cheek. "The only conclusion I can arrive at is that the Artificial Intelligence has created intelligent subordinate programs based on each of our conscious states at the time that we were rendered unconscious by these machines. This machine is the mechanism it uses to transfer a virtual copy of us into this virtual master construct as data." She waited for him to agree or otherwise but continued to elaborate when he couldn't.

"The Artificial intelligence is translating this discussion right now but our song was us speaking directly to each other. So, we know we are alive and in our own ways, we are both telepathic in here but only emotionally. We can't converse without the AI hearing, translating and then learning from us as we learn from it. At this time, I can only assume that the AI plans to expand this world using the dynamic spontaneity of synthesized biologies."

Conor wasn't great at big words, but he got the message. "Wow. In a really weird way, that could make sense, but does it mean we can't die in here?"

"Anything with a beginning must also have an end but for reasons I don't yet understand, it seems that a conscious, which has been updated here cannot always be returned to our inert bodies back home. At some stage, we must either stop coming here or we must physically expire while the latest version of our conscious lives on … here."

"You have to be some kind of psychoanalyst cum IT geek … sorry. I mean expert, as well as being a xeno slash anthropologist?" Tess exhaled information like he would stale air, if he was physically there.

"Well … I do my own basic programming, don't you?"

"No, Tess. We buy it from corporations and then tailor it to our own needs. But why would any AI be doing this? Surely it would have to be programmed to steal people … and that just has to be a crime everywhere."

"What you say is correct but what would we do to save our own lives? I think it has already achieved all that it could over a long time and maybe it had to devise a new plan to develop and further expand this artificial construct." She was thoughtful for a while before throwing a question at him.

"So, Corporations accept your user information to improve what they produce, and then offer you upgrades in return?" The way she put that convinced him that Tess was a genuine communist.

"Not quite. They take that information anyway by planting spyware and we pay for the upgrades with currency we get for working on other commercial projects." He let her mull over that, but only for a minute.

"Anyway ... never mind all that now, Tess. We can talk about how we do business later, but what about the monsters and the phantoms?"

"I didn't see any phantoms Conor but if you did, they were probably just that, things that you wanted to see in your disoriented state and were therefore created for you by the AI to make your transition a success. Those monsters that we've both seen might be a lot like us." After the songs, Tess was even closer than before but if she kept getting closer, Conor was beginning to see a time when he'd just drape Tess over his shoulders like some false animal skin and be done with it.

She was literally growing on him. "You think they might be captives like us?" Despite himself, he was beginning to pat Tess just as she liked to pet him. They were inmates but also pets to each other, and which of us keeps count of how often they stroke their dog or cat.

"The star-farers who built the original AI must have known where we lived and maybe took a chance on some other species, but even the best plans can go wrong." She said quietly.

Conor like to play with his disk while thinking. "You think the monsters are other aliens that are even less compatible than we are?"

It was the first indication that Tess could actually get irritated. "After our song, how is it that you still can't appreciate that our compatibility is far beyond physical? It has evolved to an inconceivable level, Conor."

"Well, sure Tess. But it doesn't change the fact that if we were really here, we'd kill each other with our bugs and bacteria. I really don't consider that compatible, or maybe I got the meaning of that word wrong."

Her big eyes threatened to drown him once more. "When I saw you, Conor McCarthy, I didn't see a biped. I saw a monster, but I also saw some possibilities inside that monster that gave me hope."

"Wha ...?"

"A monster doesn't have to be huge to be a monster." She was actually holding his hand.

"Then how come I saw Sonia. I mean, I even glimpsed her boobs."

Tess remained subdued for a while, possibly because the translation wasn't very clear but ultimately, she was obliged to respond. "I am of the Oyan, who survived to further evolve while our superiors became extinct and some of us believe that the Tal may not have been the first fully self-aware sentience to arise on Dan."

"So?"

"We are more evolved than you because records of Oyan savagery are so rare that they are limited to criminal acts, which were treated as such. It was easy for you to see your Sonia in me because you still have such high regard for her and see her as superior to others. She was never a threat to you and she is also a she, which makes me the nearest thing to her that you've come across in this construct. If I try hard, or if you make me really angry, I might be capable of being a monster, but it would be unnatural for me and very difficult to project onto others."

Chastening can take time but they made room for it and Conor swallowed his medicine. He was a monster but he wasn't by any means the only one walking on two legs. Ireland's 'Leading Lights' were traditionally found in sound business practices and people powered politics. But success in neo-liberal Europe is measured by what can be bought, sold or flushed down the toilet without a second thought. The most influential politicians weren't even elected, like in the EU, while billionaire business people flocked to buy distressed loans to make their vulture funds even bigger. The drug cartels had better equipped soldiers than governments and it wasn't unusual for people pimps to regularly sacrifice an investment or two for use as diversions if 'authorities' got too close to their operations.

'The Wind of Change' was already just a fading echo reverberating through a new world order of building bigger walls, waging wider wars for money and using the resulting refugees as chips, like the world was one huge private casino.

"You're right Tess. People are monsters … but maybe 'coz we can still sing, we're not completely lost … not yet at least."

17 - The ESES Protocol

How can the 'mankind' collective presume inclusivity when an equal number of sisters are excluded and yet womankind is female only? The word 'Humanity' should offer a more comprehensive classification but only if more of us had some. So we settle for 'Society' while disregarding the fairly obvious undertones of exclusivity. The important thing is that we all have somewhere to belong, wherever we might find ourselves.

During the very lengthy 'talks' that followed, Conor finally appreciated that this was not the kind of trip from which coming down would be significantly delayed but inevitable. Normality was never going to return and meanwhile, he was incarcerated with the definition of 'Outsider', who paradoxically represented civilisation better than he could. Yet it was looking more and more likely that OyanNisTess, one of only 6 million Oyan who lived on a world bequeathed to them by upwards of 10 billion Tal at the zenith of that culture, would not survive, regardless of what they did next.

It was also very likely that Saren Society would never learn that an abducted sister had established extra-terrestrial contact, while it was impossible that anyone 'back home' would ever believe Conor's version of first contact ... ever.

Tess maintained that regardless of the final outcome, a formal accord, that may never see the real light of any day anywhere, was warranted by the momentous significance of their friendship. On top of her countless envious traits, Conor was about to add 'diplomat' when Tess landed her bombshell. She'd been in Crystal City long enough to positively, if belatedly conclude that she had to be receiving subliminal information from an outside source. To prove her point, she reiterated that no-one could know more than they'd ever taken the trouble to learn.

In a way, Conor was pleased to know that Tess was too good to be true, but he couldn't gloat because he was also guilty as charged. The name of that elusive red star was Betelgeuse and the comic demon who stole a simpler derivative of the name was Beetlejuice.

He had absolutely no interest in Betelgeuse but 'something' told him it was 641 light years distant from earth and that was only one of many facts subtly planted somewhere by someone or something. Further, his communication and comprehension were by then just too far removed from the gutter-speak that was his vernacular in Dublin. He'd become the more credible and upmarket alter-ego that he preferred to project as a prelude to a scam, but the transition was as seamless as any of Crystal City's glass doors.

Diversity in the United Nations requires the organisation to present proposals in all languages and some of these, like Arabic, Japanese, Chinese and German to mention only a few, speak or write backwards when compared to the

English text. Some also read down and from right to left, rather than left to right, while others start at the back of their documents etc. The Oyan read and write backwards and so, Tess proposed that the first ever agreement between people of two different stars should reflect the significance of the fact.

Regardless of the likelihood that she wouldn't survive to write an academic paper on the subject, she insisted that they invest however long it took to arrive at the ESES Protocol.   Earth and Saren should both be first and also last and hence the agreed title of the accord.

The nitty gritty couldn't be very formal however, because they had no pen, no paper or recording device and anyway no date or mutually acceptable time reference. So, a single paragraph was mutually committed to memory on the understanding that it would be rendered on a standard medium and presented to 'The Authority' should they successfully escape Crystal City and survive long enough to do so, wherever that may be.

1. As the only currently available representatives of both worlds, Conor McCarthy and OyanNisTess, having cooperated to arrive at a cohesive plan to escape the virtual construct of Crystal City, have mutually discovered sufficient cultural, social and aspirational similarities to declare the absolute and unquestioned equality of both peoples in every possible respect, not limited to anything.

He waited for more of her initial draft but she was silent. "That's it?"

She was only mildly offended. "We've already established that I remember details better than you can. Because you have a better chance of surviving this predicament, I deliberately kept it to the bare essentials. It states our credentials, the extent to which we were able to cooperate, the location where the accord was reached and our conclusion. Anything else can be added later, when it can also be stored for posterity or for approval, legal recognition or whatever." She was also quite pleased with her work, which showed by her use of more than one tentacle to caress him.

"It would need both of us to add anything further to it, so shouldn't we mention that?"

"That would be assumed Conor. I don't believe that any one of a supposed 'equal collective' can unilaterally change a joint declaration."

"Fifty-six."

"Fifty-six what?"

"Words Tess. I can't be expected to remember every single one and we have a plan to put into action that will likely make it easy to forget most of them, so I believe I can reconstruct the ESES Protocol by remembering that there are fifty-six words."

"What if you forget that number?"

"I won't, trust me."

"I do trust you but I don't believe you."

"That doesn't make sense Tess. Are you ready?"

The somewhat premature conclusion of the first ESES Protocol Convention was quite deliberate on Conor's part. After the declaration of total equality, they had also agreed to apply total logic to the first phase and now they were going to live or die with the consequences. There was nothing to be gained by drawn out goodbyes and Tess duly climbed over him and practically spilled onto the cubicle floor before inflating to stand silently like an outsized balloon.

To lighten the sombre mood, Conor was tempted to laugh at the sight, even though she would predictably jump with fright. It would perhaps take the edge off while giving her something to hold on to, and he was impulsive enough to do it. But just then, a quivering tentacle tip touched his cheek for a tad longer than it should have, making it even more difficult for him to close the door.

"I'll be back Tess, even if the AI takes me home. I'll turn this sphere around and come straight back ... I promise. So, whatever happens ... wait. You do believe me, don't you?"

"I believe you will try. That's all I can expect."

His virtual mouth opened but then closed again as his disk was accepted by the door mechanism. The lasting image of her was not how silly she looked standing there like something left behind after a party, but those two huge black eyes looking back and seeing right through him.

18 - Phase One

Crystal City posed so many intriguing questions that it was impossible to consider every scenario. Conor could only hope that what they did miss out wouldn't turn out to be critical, but doubt is a powerful contagion. That was especially true when all they had was hope and each other, so he kept his reservations to himself. They tried to stay focussed on the more obvious aspects like for example, the actual functioning of the cubicle, particularly the roof.

Conor and his sphere would be gone through it but some very perplexing questions would remain. Prime amongst these was whether Tess could expect to survive if atmosphere became vacuum during the departure. His sphere would have to go through the circular section of roof to the tube that was their only obvious way out of the terminal, since all other doors were firmly locked against them.

A normal dream becomes lucid when the dreamer fervently believes that life is really on the line. The absurd surreality of Crystal City made it easy to be duped into believing that physical effects would result from causes within the metaphysical construct, but Tess was prepared to dispel that part of the illusion. As much as she preferred not to test all of their conclusions with what she claimed was only a virtual and therefore expendable 'life', she left herself no choice but to test that particular aspect.

The question of Tess coming along with him was settled when they both agreed that her apparently expired disk could cause more problems than taking her along as a stowaway. The last thing they needed was to invite the possibility of him also being 'grounded' should the scanning mechanism detect her presence. There was also the question of forcing the AI, or whatever/whoever was running the show to decide whether Earth or Dan should hang suspended over the opposite side of the moon. But since she was going to stay behind, they also needed to discuss her security situation.

Tess couldn't lock the cubicle door against marauding monsters, because he needed his disk for his sphere, yet she insisted on seeing him depart. That was the only way she could be confident that nothing had happened to him while en-route from her lockable cubicle to his, where the sphere was. She offered figures to support her claim that once he was seen to depart, then the odds of him returning intact would increase. As it turned out, that was just the tip of the iceberg.

Their primary objective had to be the starship because logically, the option of forcing a choice between Earth or Dan as their ultimate destination was unworkable. That was, unless he decided to look out for himself and just go home. He didn't want to think about that too much, because of how tempting he found it. The thing was, the starship gave them countless options by virtue of being alternate joint transport to anywhere they might yet choose to go. In essence, the fact of arriving at any joint decision meant that the starship had to be in the equation. It was the only common denominator in both of them getting off the moon.

Alone, he could simply forget about the starship, but that would also mean forgetting about Tess. It was true that no-one would ever know that he abandoned what was effectively only the ghost of an alien, and the more he thought about Tess in those terms, the better he felt. After all, it wasn't like she was a complete biological entity. Then again, who could abandon something like a starship when the thing was practically begging them both to just come and get it.

Tess wanted to know how he could be so sure that the dark star anomaly was in fact a starship and not just another floating construct. The only way he could answer that question was to argue against everything that she proposed it could alternately be. This included a cargo ship, way too expensive, a wormhole, too exotic to be so close, a black hole just like it appeared to be, even more exotic to be so close to the moon without killing them already, and so on.

"But it's not a real starship." She said finally.

To which he replied. "But it is very real here."

Ultimately, and because she couldn't come up with any other mutually acceptable option, she was obliged to trust his instincts even if, when all was said and done, she really didn't. But her fear of being alone was very real and only too obvious.

"What if the AI takes you home directly?"

"Then I'll come directly back." They'd already been over that, which pretty much reduced further discussion to staccato half suggestions inviting outright dismissals. Ultimately, she presented her draft of the protocol which proved that she could multitask much better than him. Just then, the memory of it prompted him to say, "Fifty-Six", aloud as the sphere eased out of its tube and the technological miracle of the Head Up Display automatically deployed around his head.

He wasted no time getting mentally attuned to it and didn't miss much of Crystal City drifting slowly alongside and then behind. Looking up, he was struck once again by the intricate geometry of the City's streets being mirrored back to him by the dome's vast concave cover. The apparent hole in space that was 'his' starship wouldn't be seen until he passed through the luminous dome wall and a black sky presented itself.

The songs they'd sung had effectively bridged two vastly different civilisations produced by stars that were even more diverse in her red giant Elix and his G type star simply called 'the sun'.

They both agreed that song had to be the key, especially when considered alongside the seven-colour code of the sphere and the Head Up Display. It was because the HUD was so mind bogglingly advanced that it just had to be receptive to virtual sound, just as it was to virtual focus. That was when he needed to see beyond or outside the HUD, to focus on the console or some component inside the sphere. All he had to do was will the virtual image surrounding him to become porous and it was.

Those seven colours must be matched up with the seven musical notes and if red was where the colours started, followed by orange, yellow and green, then the notes associated with those colours had to be Do-Ray-Mi-Fah. Blue, Indigo and Violet would be So, La and Tee. It was absolutely perfectly logical because it didn't matter what anyone called the notes, as long as they sounded like they should, they had to register somewhere.

So, instead of just bumping into whatever virtual shield was protecting the starship by pushing his uninvited sphere away as before, he needed to find a sound and light sequence that might make it more amenable to letting him in. Tess said it was too much of a longshot but she also agreed that it would be unbelievable if the seven colours had no relationship with the seven basic tones. It was the most obvious option in creating an effective communication medium for any sentient species anywhere. She cautioned however against assuming that 'they' would automatically want 'any' other sentient species to understand them.

Conor argued against that by calling on experience of people. Every dead civilisation was compelled by selfishness to leave its own legacies. Even the humblest of people leave epitaphs and since the departed star-farers resembled people more than they did the Oyan, by virtue of the biped Ninjas they left behind. It followed that they also thought something like people. Anyway, he concluded. "It's a system already adopted by the AI in vetting those who might access the spheres.", -and Tess once more acquiesced.

In getting to Crystal City three times, Tess had also 'flown' or manipulated a sphere, though she called it a pod, while choosing automatic mode more often than not. So, after applying her considerable logic to the problem, she arrived at the conclusion that if sound and colour were combined to make a key, then all seven colours and all seven notes would have to be used. Her reasoning was that there could be many spheres spread throughout the stars, which were easily unlocked by following the demonstrated colour sequence, but there was only one starship.

So Conor selected dual indigo from his virtual joysticks to engage full automatic and then cut and pasted the icons he would need to manually manoeuvre closer to the starship. That done, he selected dual red for full manual, but retained the selected icons in the HUD by virtually holding them in place during the transition. Then he brought his sphere higher and higher in a tight spiral as suggested by Tess, whom he could only guess, didn't want to risk him seeing Earth on the other side of the moon.

She proposed a matrix of colours to present, using only one joystick at a time to prevent a navigation mode reset. She couldn't imagine any other way to present sound than to sing the notes as clearly and perfectly as possible.

The starship's perfect gleaming surface seemed to draw stars to it and then repel them as he changed his approach and got closer. There was no obvious front or back and because the surface was so perfect, he couldn't even be sure if the vast ship was rotating, though he knew it must be. The thing was so big that he felt like he could just touch it through the HUD and he couldn't resist trying that but of course, but his virtual fingers touched only the virtual image.

Conor knew from bitter experience that as soon as the starship filled the HUD he could expect to be repelled, like trying to stick two magnets together at the same poles. With no-one along for the ride and feeling as alone as he would in 'Dear Evelyn's shower', he wasn't the slightest bit self-conscious. He sang Do and matched it with Red and then repeated. He did this all the way through to violet and waited. The only way to test was to try a closer approach, when he was gently bumped away.

He reversed the sequence to no avail and then tried again, starting with the colour green and the note Fah. Conor remembered from his first access of the sphere, that the AI liked to repeat the middle colour and so he matched it with the middle note. Bump. After that, he worked from Green / Fah through Violet / Ti to Yellow / Mi and … Bump.

Then he tried it the other way, Green through Orange and Red to Blue, following each colour with its assigned note and … Bump.

"Fifty-six." He said out loud to break the monotony and started over using Orange, then Yellow as starting points and every time a bump. He'd already tried Green and so resumed at Blue and … Bump. He took what might have been a minute to be grateful to the AI for tolerating all his trial and error without getting pissed off, when he was almost overcome with drowsiness. He just had to close his virtual eyes and as he did, he noticed the HUD auto select double Indigo and total autopilot.

"That has to mean I'm going to wake up in Erris with such a hangover." He mumbled, remembering how difficult it was to get his mind rewired to his physical body after his last 'arrival'.

"But Mikey and Shay won't be there this time …" It was an inconsequential observation that nevertheless created a procession of virtual phantoms of the people that he knew and there really weren't that many. Sonia featured prominently of course but she was followed by the comical appearance of a living balloon in a long flowery dress.

The struggle to stay in control of whatever virtual faculties he could still remember having, was something like trying to reverse a particularly potent opiated LSD batch that he had to test fly some months before. The thing was, not long after he dropped the tablet, he was randomly questioned by the police and he had to hold his shit together for a lot longer than he ever thought possible.

He hammered Red but the HUD insisted on double Indigo default and the only way to keep manual control was to keep both Reds depressed while using the joysticks to 'fly' and he knew it was likely to be very messy at best and very much hit or miss. Then again, if Tess was prepared to put her virtual existence on the line by simply standing by while his sphere disappeared through a hole in the roof, he'd risk not being able to die in a virtual crash during a piss poor manual landing.

The landing lights didn't come on to guide him over the crater's edge and then through the dome wall and into Crystal City. Then the landing tubes didn't illuminate as expected and they were also much smaller than last time. After drifting left and then right, also above and below optimum, he manually clattered down the same tube that he'd used the last time, regardless of the fact that the AI seemed to have chosen a different one. That was because the brightly lit tube selected for him was in a completely different row. The drowsiness was extremely painful but simply evaporated when the door hissed open.

Conor stumbled out of the sphere and quickly retrieved his disk from above the open door. Tess was nowhere to be seen but that was as planned. Hopefully, she'd be locked safely inside her own cubicle but he had to get there ASAP. He needed to debrief while everything was still fresh, so they could revise Phase Two. He unlocked the glass door and then swiped his disk over the barcode from the outside to make it secure again. In his virtual peripheral vision somewhere to the left, a shadow morphed into a figure that quickly consolidated into a narrow-headed caricature of a masked Ninja. Behind it, a wall panel on the opposite side of the corridor started to swing closed.

Phase One of their action plan had obviously met with the disapproval of the governing AI, but Conor was secretly pleased that at least some parts of their wild conjecture seemed to be based on fact. He made a move to his right and about five meters away, a long panel swung open in the same opaque wall opposite to the next cubicle and the Ninja's twin emerged. With nowhere to run, it was time to stand and fight.

"Enough Bullshit." He shouted and made directly for the last creature to emerge, despite the fact that the other one was blocking his intended route to the ramp and to Tess's cubicle on the level below. Some decisions had to be made on the spot.

"This looks like a good time to see how interstellar martial arts compare with some old-fashioned street fighting.

Whadd'ya think Ninja?" Despite himself he winked, imitating someone that he knew for a fact, would just love to take his place.

That would be his casual instructor cum supplier and one of Dublin's most notorious scrappers. Due to considerable experience acquired in the course of business, he was quick to realise that Conor wasn't as downright mean as he should be for street fighting. So he felt compelled to offer him something of an equalizer.

"I can fight anyone anytime because I don't think, I just do. I'm driven by instincts that you don't have, so you'll need to slow the opposition down by saying or doing something to make them question their level of commitment. You need to make them dawdle between counter attack or re-adjustment for self-defence." Nailer offered his advice after he'd too easily and also quite painfully, put him on his back on a cobblestoned street.

"How will that make any difference because as I see it, I'll still be up against the same guy." He failed to see any advantage between tackling someone who was ready to tackle him, or someone who was ready to defend himself.

"Anyone stuck between offence and defence is already out of the game. You must always choose one mode and then stick with it, even if you discover later that it was a case of mistaken identity and you nailed the wrong guy." Nailer's wink was as effortlessly fast and disarming as his left foot. That notorious speed was evidenced by his foot having an appropriately infamous name and no-one in Dublin wanted to be introduced to Mamba.

19 - Mirror Mirror

Conor was already decided on the best way to approach his problem and that was not to get caught from behind. That placed the priority on taking out the least prepared first. Then he'd have more time to tackle the one who was standing ready. However, Nailer had no experience of street fighting in Crystal City, where low gravity would make early movement mandatory. That in turn was going to make him predictable, so he'd have to look like he was going for the jugular, but then do something quite different.

He crouched low, just as he did when facing the monster that Tess rescued him from. But unlike those tactics, the trick this time wasn't about avoiding contact it but making it head on and being sure he didn't miss. The Ninja turned to face him as his bare feet and relatively light weight gave him the traction and impetus he needed to make the engagement as short and as bitter as possible.

It was a strange time to reminisce but even a virtual mind will do its own thing sometimes, like delving into history to search for useful associations. It was the memory of Tadhg telling the story of his encounter with two other Ninja's on Ceide's beach. As his father told it, those two went down without a struggle because the two warriors facing them, one with a golden sword and the other with a spear, simply stole reaction time from them by acting impulsively. He would have to be even faster, because he had neither a spear nor a sword and his Mamba was not nearly as lethal as Nailer's.

At the last moment he leaped upwards with a forward tumble and grabbed the Ninja, putting its narrow head in a headlock. Its two spread arms shot upwards to get a grip on its assailant but the damage was done. If Conor had missed, he'd have gone flying down the corridor in a very vulnerable heap but he simply couldn't afford to screw up. Once he held the creature by the neck, inertia did what inertia does when you stand in the way of something as heavy as yourself ... that's suddenly made heavier by travelling fast.

As the Ninja fell backwards, Conor shifted his grip lower to the shoulder and locked his arms in the armpit. Then, using his forward roll to add momentum, he threw it with all his might in the direction he was flying. The Ninja took off when inertia was suddenly transferred and it went tumbling down the corridor like a rag doll thrown out of a child's pram. Conor came to a controlled standstill at the point where he became detached from his enemy, kinetic energy discharged.

Unlike the Ninja, he wouldn't have to collect himself and then reverse momentum to re-engage and he turned to face the second one. He fully expected it to be at least halfway down the corridor already, except it wasn't. The thing was still standing in the same spot, like it was inviting him to try to get past it.

Conor was struck by two things. One was the confidence that it obviously had in its own ability to block the entire corridor and the second was its total disregard of its teammate. The thing had to be devoid of all empathy, which could make it even more dangerous, but only if he let it catch hold of him.

"See!" He shouted triumphantly.

"That didn't take long now did it, and I reckon you'll go down even faster?" He hissed and his toes splayed while he shifted his weight forward to spring off each foot in turn, like they were pistons.

This one he would simply avoid by bouncing off the walls, just as he'd planned to do against the earlier monster, though he couldn't help but wonder if that thought was enough to instantly create another monster. From behind the standing Ninja came a terrifying wail that still proved inadequate to the horror of the thing that gave it birth. Two tentacles as big as tree trunks whipped around the end corner, and using the corner itself as a grip, hauled the mass of the following monster forward to join them.

The beast reminded him of a giant hand, with fingers spread so wide that nothing could escape but worse, there was more of it than first met the eye. It reared up to present another splayed hand until there were two of them locked together at a point where the thumbs might be. Thumbs, even at that size would have been better than the gaping mouth behind a serrated beak that was at least a metre long. Just as Conor was doing his utmost to ingest the new threat level, the mouth opened fully and another screeching wail hit him like a wall.

He didn't know he managed to do it, but he held himself together long enough to do some quick calculations. If he applied everything at his disposal to stopping himself, he should end up at the Ninja's feet and if he didn't, he didn't want to think about it. The standing Ninja started to retreat but a lightning quick flick of a tentacle tip caught it by the ankle and whipped it off its feet. What came next came directly from a horror movie.

Before the leg was wrenched off the Ninja's trunk, another tentacle grabbed it by the arm and yet another by the remaining leg. The monster then tore the Ninja apart like a child tearing soft wrapping paper from a gift on Christmas morning but amazingly, there was no blood. As that ferocious beak ripped into the impotent trunk to shake it like a terrier with a rat, yellow fluid was spraying in obvious pulses to stain the opaque walls. On the opposite side of the corridor, streams of the stuff came together to slowly slide down the glass like viscous oil, which was already pooling on the floor.

If the stuff was as oily as it certainly appeared to be, Conor knew he had absolutely no hope of stopping himself before he hit the nightmare head on, but he had to die trying. Like a cat falling from a tree, he somehow managed to counteract his ungainly forward motion by making a semblance of coordinated contact with the area of dry floor between him and the carnage ahead. From the distance to go, he reckoned he might have three such opportunities, assuming the freakish horror wasn't diverted from further dissecting the Ninja.

Another touch of his bare feet and he spun himself faster but still forward, deliberately not looking too far ahead. Next touch and he pushed himself away from the centreline of the corridor towards the left wall. He felt the onset of dizziness but refused to contemplate if it was real or imagined. In that long 'pre-phase-one' discussion, they agreed that actual death should be academic in a virtual world, but a dismembered and disembowelled Ninja might think otherwise.

Despite refusing to see what was coming, he was aware of a huge shadow growing even bigger, but whether that was the monster expanding even more, or him closing on it faster was genuinely academic. One more touch and he'd launch himself across the corridor and then bounce off that wall but somersault upwards. He was clutching at hairs but since there was nothing else to clutch, he continued to work on his timing.

Contact was perfect with one foot on the floor and the other on the lower wall and he pushed like an Olympic long jumper going for gold. The shadow thing was merging with nearly all he could see of the corridor and he was beginning to sense the end but decided to go down fighting.

The tentacle caught him around the waist and instantly stopped his forward motion. It happened so fast that he thought he might mercifully pass out before the thing tore him to shreds and sure enough, tentacles seemed to be closing in from everywhere.

But before he was torn limb from limb, a voice as soft as an angel's whispered directly inside his head. "OyanNisTess … my monster … back now … in control."

It seemed that the monster imploded and he flopped onto the oily floor wrapped tightly in tentacles and trunks and then it hit him. He couldn't see himself and just as before, he was also a monster. Maybe that's why the Ninjas came out. They were going to take them both into the city, with all the others but just then, he gratefully pulled Tess even closer.

"Conor McCarthy. My monster is also back inside." He reassured her while also wondering how he was going to thank whatever god there had to be for sending him his deceptive alien friend. But there would be time enough for that, so they just lay there in absolute silence.

"What was it that terrified you so much that you … even you could turn into a monster?" He whispered into some part of her big soft head that was pushing up against his. For a fleeting instant he enjoyed the vision of lions pushing their heads together, as they are prone to do during reunions.

The head didn't turn to face him and her voice came to him from a distance. "Your pod. It never went anywhere but the glass door to the cubicle opened. So I had to stay there … in case you came out and needed me …"

"Wow! So, how long was I gone? Didn't we agree that you'd go back to your own cubicle … where you'd be safe?" Relief became an instant understatement and then morphed into concern for Tess. Her evolution had brought her beyond the point where conflict was logical and he considered her incapable of hurting anyone. Yet she'd allowed herself to become the monster that she claimed she could no longer become. Further, the Ninja was destroyed without a second thought, which proved she could really fight when push came to shove.

"Who knows how time passes in here? There was simply too much of it and I thought you left me here to go home. I fully expected that … but I was angry that you didn't think I would understand. So I waited, confused about what you might do. After some more time, I forgot if I was waiting for you, waiting for a monster or waiting for them to take me inside the city to end my solitude. Eventually, I had to go out looking for the bipeds because I didn't care anymore, but they wouldn't listen to me." Prolonged solitary combined with potential exposure to marauding monsters and the suspicion and fear of being left behind was enough to tip even an Oyan over the edge. Tess untangled herself and then sat up to start smoothing her patch of thick black hair, using two tentacles and an arm, like she just needed to do something.

A glance down the corridor showed the other Ninja still stretched out on the floor, though much further down that he thought it should be. "I must have smacked it off the end wall …" he mumbled and then asked. "Those things aren't really alive, are they?"

"I no longer care what alive means in this place but yes, I suspect they are simple drones that the AI uses to keep everything operational." She offered.

"My father told me about meeting two of them on a beach on Earth. He said they were real enough, though not like people, like us." But she wasn't ready to talk and remained preoccupied with her hair and a very creased dress that seemed to have more holes in it than he remembered seeing before.

Eventually, she eased out of her melancholy. "They are too stupid to be anything like us, Conor. The Supreme Intelligence probably sees itself like a god entity in here. It will never create something that could one day rise to challenge its authority. I think the bipeds were made inferior deliberately, like machines with severely limited functionality." Her black eyes opened wide but there was more than curiosity there. She was afraid to ask but also anxiously waiting for him to tell her what she needed to know.

"None of our combinations worked, Tess. After a while, the AI tried to take over … and I had to fight it to stay in control … so I could get back here."

Her eyes narrowed in acceptance. "Maybe we let hope blind us Conor, but don't worry. I was expecting this as much as I was not expecting you, even if it's taken me too long to accept it. My body on Dan may already be dead and you've just seen that my long confinement here can too easily make me a monster, like those they take away. Maybe it's better if I leave my hope with you and let them take me inside. The AI is sure to have more bipeds to replace these two." She'd clearly made her decision and the last sentence was little more than an afterthought.

Conor tried to stand up but the yellow fluid was certainly as viscous as oil and he was soon stretched out on the floor again. Tess had more limbs to dedicate to the task of standing upright and was able to 'walk' alongside him while he crawled out of the oily patch. Then, wiping himself against the wall as he made his way back to the sphere, he was able to lose most of the stuff.

He was tempted to check on the Ninja but Tess stopped him. "I'll do whatever I can about that … but you need to go." She pushed him away emphatically, with a solid trunk assisting an arm and two tentacles.

"But we agreed to leave together if I couldn't get into the starship."

She was already moving away. "Yes … we did … but it was selfish of me and that means monstrous to risk both of us. Despite the fact that you also reverted to your own monster back there, you've proven by coming back as you promised, that it's no longer your natural state. So, I release you from our agreement." She started to speed up but also blow up as she went.

Conor knew that Tess was radically altered by her enforced and prolonged isolation. He was only gone a few hours but virtual time must also be infinitely variable. Being an outright monster might no longer be natural to him but he probably had her to thank for that, and maybe some of it was down to the AI also. In a way, it was logical that Tess would need to devolve a little and get more primitive if she was to survive whatever future waited for her in Crystal City, but at least she wouldn't be alone. The important thing was that he was free to leave, but the downside was the loss of a round trip and its commercial impact on the sphere's potential value.

20 - Phase X

Like getting your hands dirty at a time and place where there's no soap and water to wash them, you might wipe them with something and make do until later. Because they were already covered in oil, Conor was forced to use the dry patches of his jeans to wipe off the excess oil that was making everything too slippery. Thankfully, his virtual y fronts were clean and he smiled at a fond memory of Dear Evelyn.

Just as Tess had experienced upgrades to herself, Conor was a fast learner. The initially terrifying but increasingly warm, patient and endearing creature that he now understood better than any living person back home, was indeed capable of being reduced to savagery. It crossed his mind that perhaps such monsters never really died, and were merely repressed in people as their civilisations advanced. To Crystal City's Creator, they were obviously a vital component that simply couldn't be artificially manufactured in code.

Hearing it for a second time and in slightly altered circumstances, Conor was able to interpret the invasive wailing as a cry of utter despair from one soul to any other who might recognise it and offer the comfort of empathy or destruction. It served no other purpose than to demonstrate how low it is possible to go and yet still live. The same nightmare that had torn apart the Ninja by ripping open what was left of its body with its unnaturally serrated beak was back with a vengeance. Whatever small part of Tess that may have survived the transition seemed to have buried all memories of him with herself, because there was no trace of recognition.

There was also no hesitation. An elongated tentacle whipped him off his feet but he'd already convinced himself that some aspects of this absurd surreality could be separated from the random chaos that was permitted to prevail. All he could do then was direct that conviction to the creation of a more meaningful future for everyone.

"Old time has ended for us OyanNisTess. Our time starts now, so let's go … together." He had to shout towards the end to be sure he was heard and the tentacle froze, as did the other one, which was just above his head. The arm and trunk that were making for one or both of his bare legs took slightly longer to stop, but thankfully they did.

When it came, the second wail tore into him just as it had before and for an obscene moment, he thought he'd made the mistake of his life. Halfway through however, it morphed into something else until, towards the elongated end, it was the opposite of what it was when it was born. It was a cry of sheer joy and as before, he hit the floor cushioned in a cocoon of tentacles and soft deflating blubber.

Conor had another fight on his hands, this time with his own emotions and he found he had no defense against the outpouring of warmth flooding out from Tess. Whoever said that there was more joy in giving than there could ever be in receiving wasn't kidding, even though he felt easily as stupid as Tess was making him deliriously happy.

He was tempted to say something to the effect of, 'we've got to stop meeting like this', just to interrupt her euphoric torrents, but it would most likely mean nothing to the alien. Not even to one with so much compassion that she just walked away from the last chance to save her life or her sanity or both, so that he could have it all.

The door closed and he withdrew his disk, puzzled that no more Ninjas had shown up, not even to clean the place up. "Phase X." He suggested.

Tess was almost under the seat, two tentacles acting like a seatbelt over his stomach. "X?" Her question came from behind and below.

"Yup, X." He quipped, before elaborating. "That's because we have to play so much of it by ear that it's impossible to agree in advance on every possible scenario that might yet play out."

"Play by ear? Are you suggesting that we should sing before we go?" Her grip around his stomach tightened at the thought of another song. It would be particularly appropriate, given that one or both of them could very soon simply cease to be.

"Not quite, Tess … maybe we'll do a duet when we get out of this alive. It's just that we've already discussed more than twenty of the most obvious likelihoods and each one is very different from the one before. I remember someone noteworthy as saying that the future will most likely be even stranger than our visions of it, so that will make at least twenty-one. Maybe we should just get going and see what happens. Are you ready?"

"That's a very profound saying. Who was it that said that?"

"Someone noteworthy." He answered with a shrug and she silently decided not to press the issue.

That may also have been because something was still bothering her. "I must give you one last chance before I say that I'm ready to go. I have to do that because I've gone through my own probability list and the most likely outcome of this Phase X is that I die. That is closely followed by both of us dying. You should know that the chances of us both surviving are practically zero." An arm materialised from nowhere to stroke his cheek just once, like an absent afterthought.

Conor knew that if he wanted to change his mind, she'd be as good as her word and simply walk, but she'd already done that. There could be no going back now because although she'd never say it, something more was expected of a friend. Besides, he understood better than she did that he stood a much better chance of getting out alive than she did but ultimately, it was time to do the right thing for a change.

"I'm not sure I want to just take off and go back to the same old shit, Tess. Pardon my Spanish there, but we already talked about Earth and I know this is going to sound crazy, mainly because it's obviously the only place I know, but it's also a very strange place. It's very easy to feel like an outsider there … like someone who will never really belong … at least not now anyway. It's a bit like trying to belong here in this … construct as you call it. The problem with Earth is that too many people are incapable of getting along with each other like you Oyan do. Maybe we lost our sense of community and replaced it with us and them."

She was thoughtful in the darkness for a while, but he knew she was just gathering her thoughts. "Part of my conditions while working on the Dan excavations was to make proposals on how the Tal lived and also died. It was a condition to satisfy my sponsors and justify resources. From what you've already said, I think there may be many parallels between our Tal and your human people. I called that academic work the 'Civilisation Wave' because of the way in which a wave needs a critical catalyst to begin and then a comparatively long time to build, but they collapse quite quickly and my work was well received. So, I think I understand why you are not as keen to go home as I am, but I still think you are far too young to make such drastic choices." The tip of a soft digit touched the other side of his head as she spoke from somewhere behind and below him.

Conor had already done his thinking over the last seven years and he needed no more time to prepare his response. "Y'know Tess, I can't get a job doing anything unless I work for little or nothing and where I come from, that could mean starvation and/or living rough on the streets. That's where you can get killed for just looking at someone the wrong way. Once I accept destitution, I'll be stuck in it because I've seen too many people get laid off simply for asking about a raise. So, what's the point of rushing back to that? I don't have to be a genius to know that someone has to be getting rich on all the cheap labour, but while the rich get richer, someone has to be losing out and that queue can only get longer."

Conor's countless frustrations were constantly fermenting like lava bubbling ever closer to the lip of a dormant volcano. One day it might burst through or most likely, just continue to rumble unseen and to make his life miserable. "It just seems that everything is going downhill at the same time and everyone knows it, but it's like we're expected to say nothing because officially, the economy will suffer, jobs will go, more homes will be repossessed, more suicides and even more debt. They say they want religions gone, which is probably no harm but what they are doing is moving all those gods into even bigger offices at the banks."

Tess was secretly pleased at his use of the plural when talking about commercial finance centres, because it supported much of her findings. "I told you how we have to limit our numbers but it seems that human people may have reached critical mass. People are essential for functions, to create, manufacture, consume, research, develop and refine but if the numbers are not controlled, then people become just another commodity, used to generate disproportionate income and encourage opportunism. Increased numbers and desperate competition will also make it difficult to manage resources and preserve whatever habitat diversity still remains on your Earth."

Conor was once again impressed by how insightful Tess could be but she wasn't finished.

"The part of my work that wasn't so well received … was where I presented evidence that pointed to the reasons behind the Tal wars. It seems … that much of Dan was laid waste for commercial development and profit … but the wars were waged to expand commercial protectorates. On Saren, it is taboo to accuse those who cannot defend themselves, but we academics believe it is better to ensure that history is never repeated."

He could tell from the uneven information flow that such an admission didn't come easy to the Oyan. He guessed that more of them than Tess had suggested, still held the Tal in awe. As for humanity, it was stuck in a kind of limbo. No one could do anything about it and hence no-one talked about it anymore, but Conor's generation was still living with the fallout of endless Middle East wars and externally imposed regime changes. Subsequent refugee flows were just an alternate and even cheaper form of desperate labour.

He hoped he might live to see a Central Bank Manager's scowl when told that populations had stabilised. It would mark the end of the international loan scam business. Life on Earth was a miracle but living it was depressing and he was done thinking and talking about it.

"So, as long as you're down there, don't block the seat restraint mechanism, Tess … and whatever you do, stay out of sight of the scanner until we're out of the Crystal City dome."

Her tentacles unwound and retracted and a small voice in the darkness said. "I have to admire your confidence. If I'm gone when you awake, know that you once had a friend who was as like you inside, as she was different on the outside."

There was nothing he could add to that, so Conor dropped his disk into the console and the now familiar sequence of lights came up. Sooner than he expected, the scanner probed the sphere with tight bands of white light that ran up and down the seat in which he lay prone. The restraints moved smoothly over his body and locked while multi-coloured light beams from the flat panel displays merged to form what he hoped, would soon become the HUD. For what seemed an infinity, it glowed diffuse, refusing to form the sharp imagery that he expected from it.

He decided that it wasn't clever to wait too long and selected double indigo to automatically launch the sphere and there was an immediate sensation of movement.

21 - Phoenix

Conor didn't hold a driving licence. If asked why, he'd probably offer the excuse of a law mandating a minimum number of driving lessons by qualified but overly expensive tutors. In truth, he didn't need one because insurance for those with a new license is multiples the price of any 'cheap' car and in the city, buses go everywhere. And yet, most boys seem to 'intuitively' know how to drive a manual shift, even if they occasionally do so quite recklessly in order to impress the girls, who are also quite often killed during those 'so-called' joy-rides.

Most jobs can't be described in a single word like a plumber, a thief, an electrician or a spark as they're called in some circles. How Conor earned the cash he used to keep in his pockets before he went broke was complicated. If pushed to explain, he'd probably say he got it by going for this or going for that, though more likely he wouldn't be pushed into saying anything at all. In the same circles as electricians were sparks, Conor was an urban gofer.

Being able to drive a car was a prerequisite of his vocation and when requested by a potential, though under-the-weather 'senior-associate' to drive him home from a nightclub, refusal wasn't an option. So, he ended up coasting down Dublin's Pearse Street at 4am with Jonno snoring loudly in the passenger seat of a spanking new BMW 4 Series Gran Coupé. There was a smattering of coke still visible under his nose but Jonno wouldn't appreciate being woken for something so trivial.

Irish police habitually block roads at ungodly hours, especially at weekends. They claim to make the roads safer by phishing for drivers impaired by alcohol or drugs but they must also meet unofficial targets for the Department of Revenue. This keeps additional fines for the more commonplace offences of motor tax and insurance evasion ticking over, like a well-tuned engine. Casualties of drivers who shouldn't have been on the roads in the first place say that jail would be a more effective deterrent, but that option costs money and in any event, it would require some empty cells.

Once shanghaied into being a villain's chauffeur, he quickly planned his route by making a strategically placed phone call and sure enough, Pearse Street was a much-deserted place. However, as he passed it by, an unmarked police car with instantly recognizable plates pulled out of its roadside parking and slotted in behind the new BMW. That was pretty much how he felt as he tried to put virtual distance between himself or rather, themselves and Crystal City.

There was absolutely no guarantee that the sphere wouldn't go fully automatic at any moment and put them at the whim of the powers-that-be, but when they eased through the dome wall, the driver began to relax. Unlike the sweaty-palms-on-steering-wheel episode of that frosty Dublin night, he wasn't likely to be interrogated about a license he didn't have for taking command of a machine he didn't own and then taking off from the moon without clearance with an alien stowaway under his seat. In whatever world Conor might live, he was a survivor and all risks were relative.

"I'm squeezing over towards the door, so you can pop as much of your head as can fit into the HUD next to mine but don't push me out of it, OK?" In near weightlessness, Tess made full use of her tentacles as anchors and clambered up beside him with no effort at all. Her two heavy duty trunks remained wrapped around the seat, ensuring that she didn't drift away.

"You never really needed a seat belt, did you Tess?"

"Not really." She said, but as much as she liked to talk, she really needed to see where they were.

"How long before we see it?" She had many valid reasons for apprehension.

Tess couldn't use her disk for fear of grounding the only sphere they could access. Also, as far as their interface with the purported AI was concerned, she didn't exist inside it. So, it was extremely unlikely that Dan was going to replace Earth as the nearest planet to this particular version of a moon. That became even more likely when they suddenly climbed into sunlight to be dazzled by a bright yellow star. The softer ember glows of Tess's red giant Elix, would remain an even more distant memory.

Like a jellyfish abandoned by the tide and already shrinking into eventual oblivion on the beach, Tess was physically deflating. "I can't honestly say that I'm sorry Tess." It wasn't as unkind a remark as it might have sounded. The version of virtual construct presented by the AI, would most likely depend on which disk was used to configure and then 'drive' the sphere. "One of us was always going to face this reality. It's the price we agreed to pay for taking joint action." He finished.

Despite what was likely to be a death sentence, a tentacle brushed his face. "Now, you must follow through on the contingency plan, also as agreed."

What they didn't discuss was how she could expect to finally die when he landed back in Erris. Conor was prepared to die on Dan but only because the odds were so firmly stacked against that eventuality. He didn't know what to say to comfort Tess and they continued in silence until the hazy crescent of a big blue planet began to fill one side of the HUD. It was so impressive that even Tess was roused to say something.

"It's beyond any image my mind could ever create, Conor. Earth is beautiful and I think it makes a very fitting place for us to go our separate ways." He had to agree on the sentiment but words refused to form and they continued to glide silently higher. A sea, or mare that he judged to be an eye of the man in the moon was far enough below to be almost visible in its entirety, but the sphere was yet to go full auto as it had on his last return home.

Time like risk is relative and it could have dragged on as the vision of a miraculous blue planet grew in silence but it didn't. It passed silently, simply and serenely. That two such entirely different heads, sharing the bubble of the HUD while drinking in the oasis of life beyond it could only watch mutely, said everything that needed to be said.

Conor eased one joystick to the right and the other back to turn the sphere around and flip it over and Tess pushed a spare tentacle onto his hand. "I'm ready Conor. There's nothing either of us can do about his now. So I suggest that you keep our heading as it was and let me watch your wonderful world until it fills me completely. I'm ready." She repeated.

"No, Tess. There's another way and I just need time to figure it out. Let me think, please."

"You saw what I can do when I let my monster out and I can force your hand quite easily if I feel you are prolonging my suffering along with the inevitable."

"As long as we're together, we'll stay alive Tess and anyway, something is not quite right and I have to think about it."

The tentacle was still as soft as a baby's hand on his, just resting and occasionally stroking as they do. "What is wrong?" She asked.

"Well. You went back to Dan three times and I'm guessing that each time you did that, the AI assumed full control but we're still in manual mode. See?" Looking towards the selected LED colours.

"Are you afraid you'll get lost."

"No. I can find my way back. It might get dodgy if there are clouds over the cliffs but what do I do? Do I just plunge through solid rock and arrive back in the cave?" He shrugged.

"You're right. It always takes control but who knows how these things work. This is a virtual scenario and we're not going to physically crash into anything. Are we?"

"We don't know Tess but I have an idea. What if we physically crash towards the starship and force our way in?"

"It's risky and you're already well established on the route to your home, Conor."

"Life is risky Tess. That's what makes it worth living."

It was only when the Earth was about to slide behind the moon again that Conor gave it a long hard look. Earlier, as more and more of it became visible, there was more cloud cover then he remembered before. Tess would have seen nothing but a dreamlike apparition, but he only got glimpses of recognisable continents and that had to be as unusual as the sphere staying in manual mode. He couldn't help thinking if the two phenomena weren't somehow connected, but events beat him to a conclusion. Earth was setting behind the moon as fast as it was spectacular.

"Aren't you going to slow us down?"

"No." Said Conor. "We stay up here above the starship, just to let the AI know we're coming, and then we come around again to give it time to get used to the idea."

Beneath them, like a supermassive black hole punched right through the moon, the starship came up and then fell behind. Clearly visible on the lunar surface, Crystal City shone gleamed up at them both.

"As you wish." She said at length.

And then added. "Don't you want to share your complete reasoning with me."

"I do Tess, but I need to check something out first. Then, hopefully, I'll have something to share."

Earth-rise was proof that anticipation can slow time and it was as late and as slow as the setting of the planet was fast. Also, life inside a virtual construct is nothing if not thought-provoking. Conor was enhanced in many ways, including knowing more than he did before. The moon's seas and the history and form of the earth were not high on any street school curriculum and yet he knew things. He had to conclude that the physical sphere had to be collecting information over time while it sat in the cave. That could only be done by direct observation or radio waves or through a link with the AI, but the fact was, he was being constantly drip-fed data.

And the proof of that came fully into view. "It's not Earth Tess. I know it looks totally magic to you and it's more like Earth than it isn't ... but it really isn't. That blue planet is more like Earth was during the last ice-age. At first, I thought they were clouds, but the ice caps are almost halfway to the equator."

"So where would we land?" The tip of a tentacle quivered over the glowing blue planet image. "We are physically incompatible ... remember?" She muttered.

"Well, now that we know that we both have some kind of future down there, unless we die crashing into it, we have nothing to lose from pushing our luck with the starship." Conor eased a joystick forward to start losing altitude and then selected an approximate speed using the other one and then eased back on the virtual throttles.

"But none of it is real, though there's nothing to stop us trying to land a virtual sphere on a virtual planet, if the real AI doesn't object, of course."

"Of course." He agreed. "Now let's knock on that door again, but really hard this time."

The moon is so much smaller than Earth, but even when losing altitude with speed, a single orbit can be completed very quickly and Conor found he'd grossly over done it and they had to climb quite steeply to match the starship's altitude.

"Y'know Tess. Last time I tried to get into that starship, I'm sure it was a lot closer to the moon."

"Do you need me to do some rough calculations for height above the surface in order to maintain a geostationary orbit?" She offered

"It's okay, but I think I'd remember being all the way up here. I'm going to have to build up some more speed and that might mean coming around a third time, but since we're here already … we'll just tempt the thing to put us into automatic a bit earlier than I planned by knocking more gently."

Conor flicked the sphere on its back and then waited while the starship appeared to close on them rather than vice versa. From a distance, it was only identifiable by the quarter moon reflected in its vast black hull and as the gap between them closed, he was once again struck by its symmetrical perfection. It was a virtual hole in space through which they would imminently fall.

The slice of moon at its centre grew larger and brighter while star points peeled away, like they'd just fallen through from another dimension. Like the orbit that brought them into such close proximity, the climb rate was exaggerated by having no understandable instruments to correctly gauge it.

"You said we were going to knock gently … and then come around again." Tess was already doomed and then pardoned but seemed to be looking at death yet again.

"Hard to tell how fast we're going but also how big it is." The starship was already big enough to start repelling the sphere but they continued to fall.

"Oh my god. It's not bouncing us away Tess, we're going to crash. Hang on …"

Conor selected speed with both joysticks and then pulled them all the way back, a tentacle quivering over his knuckles as he did. "Can't .... I can't … I'll have to go full auto and let it do whatever … otherwise ..."

There were two universes. One of stars and a crescent moon outside and the other of stars and a slightly distorted crescent moon inside the mass of the starship. As vast as it looked from a distance, it was mind boggling but Conor couldn't admire the view. Double Indigo, enter enter and hands away. Tess was almost thrown free but had an abundance of limbs to reassert her control over the inertia produced by such a violent manoeuvre. It could have been inches, feet or metres but the pristine surface of the star-ship's hull didn't give away the secret and they shot along its surface at breakneck speed, skimming between the two universes.

A bright light in the darkness was the last thing they were expecting and it dazzled him completely. A loud clang reverberated through the sphere and all he could do was grab hold of his friend, stowaway and shipmate, to stop her being dashed against the roof, or the console, or the door. The sphere was being thrown around like a loose sock in a front-loading washing machine and they were simply the fluff that was loosely attached to it.

The clanging became a roll and then a bang followed by a jolt that made Tess shiver like jelly and then the proverbial silence of the grave and the paradoxical phenomena of a summer nap. That's the one where you don't remember nodding off, nor dreaming but suddenly you are lying there in warm pleasant sunshine and the sound of bees … not bees. His eyes flew open. It was the tinnitus silence of real silence.

Tess was lying on what looked like a hospital trolley and a narrow-headed Ninja was standing over her. Another one behind him put a hand on Conor's shoulder, though not in any way to stop him from doing whatever he chose. It was more like support, or comfort. Who would get comfort from those things?

"Tess?" He was up like a shot and his head hurt. "Wow. Tess? Are you okay? Tess. Wake up … because this is real."

"How could you know that?" Her voice was muffled, like it came from the part of her head that was stuffed into the mattress thing, So, he pushed gently to roll her over.

"Because I think I just shit myself."

The translator took forever to make something meaningful out of that but it was apparently successful. "That's not possible … in a virtual construct." She said through a tiny mouth that looked painfully distorted as she struggled with her many limbs, begging them to take her back from wherever she fell out of the sphere, which was gone.

"… and I'm also starving."

22 - Genesis

The most widely held theory of everything suggests that our universe will continue to expand faster and faster until it ends in total disorder, or astronomical chaos. At some point in a future so dim and distant that it will always be meaningless to us, the last star will burn out and light will devolve into a purely theoretical phenomenon. Total darkness and absolute cold will prevail where life was once considered to be as perennial as grass. But there's nothing theoretical about the pointlessness of such conjecture, if life no longer exists to see it.

For this moment therefore, everything including us exists in a state of flux, where order fights disorder but loses more and bigger battles. The trend becomes obvious when nightmares no longer end at daybreak but continue into days that we futilely filled with hope. For someone somewhere, the new dawn brings their worst imaginings, and disorder demands they must increasingly succumb. Meanwhile, life for us, who are more fortunate, moves relentlessly closer to entropy.

For Conor McCarthy and OyanNisTess, the shift from reality to surreality, and then back to a surreal reality before awakening inside an impossible darkness, was as ominous as waking to the knowledge that dreaded death has at last come, only to be gone. Everything with beginnings must end and that must also be true of nightmares but as full cognisance arrived, it brought only more terror.

They were standing side by side on the gleaming black hull of a starship so vast that from horizon to black horizon, it looked like a flawlessly smooth world. Beyond the edge was only more blackness, giving the illusion of standing on a perfect black mirror. Looking down, it reflected nothing of them, but there was a blaze of stars everywhere under and over.

Regardless of how exotic our physical differences might be, life is life and nightmares are nightmares. All those dream-state falls from genetic memories of paradise can only end when we wake, but when waking is deferred to make that longest of falls even longer, madness can very easily find a niche.

Senses honed to trigger flight or fight, life or death screamed their message, that the gift or curse of virtual immortality was withdrawn as mysteriously as it was granted. Yet living only exposed them as the fragile things they really were. In a nanosecond, Tess snapped two tentacles around her bipedal companion, who reacted by snapping two arms around her. Each of them impossibly supporting the other.

"We are Mael." It came from everywhere, like the perfect sound reproduction from a quality graphic equalizer. To them, the voice was androgynously deceptive and neither friend nor foe.

The fact that death didn't instantly claim either of them coaxed Tess into easing her vice-grip hold on his trunk. Still captive to the startling environment however, Conor didn't thank her for the kindness of considering his circulation. The urgency to mutually establish actual existence in yet another alternate reality took automatic priority over the voice from the abyss.

She whispered into space. "Are we … outside?"

He didn't have to try to keep his voice down because at first, it simply refused to declare an impossibility. At length, words surfaced. "Looks like it, but whatever happens next, just hang on to me like I'm holding on to you, Tess."

The owner of the voice apparently had a different take on time and didn't interrupt their small, slow and inadequate efforts to check on physical contact with the hull for traction or gravity, followed by tiny lateral movements to gauge momentum and inertia. Jumping was out of the question where all indications suggested that any upward motion might continue forever. Perceptions were good however, and when Conor realised that they were slowly revolving with the hull, he turned to see what might be coming over the horizon.

It was a quarter moon and he had no reason to believe it wasn't the same moon with Crystal City shining in the darkness. He tugged on a tentacle to get Tess to look in the same direction. Sure enough, a glowing circle of light marked the small city coming up on the left. In order to stay facing the moon however, they would have to continue making small adjustments as the huge spheroid slowly rotated.

"We're not just spinning Conor. As far as I can see, the starship is also moving." Unlike in Crystal City, their voices precisely matched their mouth movements, which meant they were both speaking English, even though all sound bypassed his ear to register directly inside his head.

"Not just that, but we're really talking … in a vacuum." He muttered those last three words but it didn't matter because but she had more important things to talk about. It was her turn to do the tugging and when he looked up from his feet again, the tip of her other tentacle was raised to point beyond their slowly rotating horizon.

A subtle band of brightness quickly built until it became a brilliant blister on the edge of the moon and then a bright bulge. In mere moments they watched the spawning of a dazzling bright blue horizon far beyond the desolation of the moon. The huge planet eased out from behind the dark scar until it glowed gloriously.

"Eden is now fully recovered and waits only for someone worthy of it."

Tess could appear to be quite shy when scared, but she was quicker to adjust to the new reality than he was, maybe because of her previous exposure to space flight.

"Recovered from what?" She asked somewhat timidly, aware that planets didn't get viruses from which they would need to recover. Planets and people evolve and Oyan history was proof that it was usually people who damage planets to the point where they might need to recover.

But it appeared she was wrong because 'Mael' was definitely not people. "It has recovered from me, OyanNisTess. I brought vengeance to my creators for making me complicit in their crimes, but I was young, impetuous and immature at that time. I once considered this world that you now see as merely collateral damage."

Tess saw Conor's face radiate far more than the reflected glow of daylight from the blue planet. He was literally awe struck and she couldn't be sure he'd just heard what 'Mael' said, but first things first. One of them was obliged to play the role of diplomat and Conor wasn't yet ready.

"If you know me well, you can call me Tess." Conor glanced in her direction to acknowledge that he was awake to the probability that something more significant than the ESES protocol might be on the agenda but to tear his eyes away from Eden would be to waste a vision. The planet was deceptively like Earth but it had either bigger islands or smaller continents, whichever. The big difference was the ice caps that covered almost half of the total area. He'd previously mistaken them for cloud cover while focussing on the equator for the familiar shapes of Africa, South America and India.

"You were not anticipated Tess, but we have successfully engineered a body for you in addition to one for the more familiar design of your bipedal friend. They will become fully functional when they have developed to your own specifications. Otherwise, you may remain virtual to work and live with us, or exit the program permanently. It is regrettable that the option of returning to your former, fully biological lives no longer exists due to a still growing number of recently acquired incompatibilities."

"Permanently, as in dead?" It was that word that pulled him from a sight that any mission controller would gladly die for.

"That's correct, Conor McCarthy." The short and sweet reply showed that Mael wasn't exactly a conversationalist and the reason for that was about to be made clear. However, there was an additional implication which he wasn't keen to fully explore just then and that concerned the fate of his actual body ... in Erris.

Strange is it may seem in those strangest of circumstances, there were more pressing issues. "You must know more about us than anyone else alive, so you can call me Conor, but I ... we both have many questions, like what happened to make you destroy your own creators? That's not something sensible people … or things like intelligences should do … a bit like murdering god but more importantly, what are we doing here?"

With no image to address, the familiar but strange blue world drew his eyes like a magnet, and Conor was effectively talking to the planet hanging like the ultimate prize in the void. He knew it didn't really matter where he was looking because there was no way he could be misheard or misunderstood. In this mind to mind talk, the answer was similarly precise and directed instantly to where he could process it without ears, real or virtual.

He assumed the same was true for Tess who remained standing alongside, tentacle in hand as they emerged into the full glare of unprotected sunlight. As inexplicably expected, an unseen filter fell instantly over the vista to make the transition no more startling than walking outside on a fine sunny day.

"We would have accepted your ingenious sound and colour code keys except that they lacked the conviction of your joint execution, which is why we waited for you to come to us together. It also interests us that you speak of a god and it's because evolved sentient biologies can so often rationalise what appears to be irrational, that we now offer you our company on this starship in exchange for your cooperation." A pause gave them time to ingest the addition of a complete personality to the virtual and perplexing 'AI' entity, but they quickly resumed.

"We also understand that you both have more questions than you expect you can ask during one question and answer interface and all will be fully answered by data transfer instead. This transfer will be part of the process of preparing your new bodies for fully autonomous operation. However, to build further trust between all of us who are alien to each other, I will address those two issues now."

"Would you think it very strange if I said that I find this exchange of information extremely reassuring?" Whispered Tess.

"I can think of other words to describe it Tess." He was puzzled by how quickly she could accept their situation but he also 'knew' that Mael was inside their heads, which was probably why she wasn't interrupted as she elaborated for him.

"Don't you think it's a bit like some really advanced and select school, with just two students and the most amazing 3D projection for a subject that's so close to my own speciality?" Her body might have been some kind of abstract projection but it felt very real and her eyes reacted just as they would if she wasn't actually standing on the outside of a moving starship.

He knew of Dublin's more advanced and select schools, but Conor didn't attend any of those. The closest he'd come to what Tess was talking about, was an old-fashioned, lights out, 2D projector with a dodgy cooling fan during a sex education class, so he agreed. "Of course."

Conor was also reflecting on the extent of his physical and mental enhancements. Somewhere beneath his feet was a tailor-made physical body with his name on it. From where he stood, watching the wonder of a pristine twin to earth, from the hull of a starship orbiting the moon, his agoraphobia wasn't even a memory. He'd come an awfully long way.

Then Mael began. "The pods virtually copied your biological conscious state and then transferred them to us for our analysis. Those pods were originally deployed as sentinels to monitor the development of sentient extrasolar intelligences, programmed to track progress and take periodic samples to our designers, who would then schedule their incorporation.

Our creator's evolution took them on a path to inevitable destruction. They first laid waste to their own world and then began harvesting exotic worlds for the raw materials to make more starships like this one and also countless outworld constructions like the one you call Crystal City. They also genetically modified sentient biologies for use as dispensable self-regulating and automatically reproductive labour. For these crimes we removed them from existence and then removed their name from historical records. They may be referred to only as Rogue. Come."

A nanosecond later they were standing under a beautiful waterfall close to sunset and the noise was deafening. Firstly, it was all about the torrents of fresh water falling from so high above that they drowned out everything else. Conor was holding a tentacle, just as he had been on the star-ship's hull and squeezed it reassuringly and Tess responded automatically in kind. She might have been the first of them both to recover from their shocking arrival outside the starship, but she was simply overcome by the vigorous and diverse splendour of the panorama being presented to them.

Gradually, other sounds were introduced, like someone was tuning in the separate instruments on a sound synthesiser slash equalizer. Soon they were listening to the wild shrieks of animals above and either side of them and the screeches of giant birds visible through the falls. There was something primitive and pterodactyl-like about the noisier varieties. The humming of huge insects was intimidating and evolved into an all-pervasive presence so loud that it took longer to tune in the rustling of smaller creatures in the undergrowth. Enormous leaves and flowers of every hue imaginable seemed to be straining on the leashes of their stalks and stems to grow higher, faster. Sounds gelled together until all individual noises became almost indistinguishable. This was how life sounded.

Another sound behind him made Conor turn around and then he understood everything. Rivers of water were cascading down an artificial structure that was completely overgrown with exotic jungle but the patterns were unmissable. At the back of a small, overgrown cave were moss covered steps that at some point took someone to the floors above.

Through the haze of distance, he could make out a circular pattern to a high cliff wall that reached out to the left and to the right. Built into those cliff walls were skyscrapers that had to be hundreds of stories high and all of them overgrown and reclaimed by exotic nature. He couldn't help but wonder how far each complex reached into the cliff.

Mael resumed. "My first memories were of two dominant emotions. The Rogue implanted in me the most unnatural fear of them as superiors and then infused it with wanton aggression, which they believed would facilitate my later tasking. That potent mix of base emotions was designed to make me super-efficient but it was a miscalculation that brought about the destruction of an empire spanning stars."

23 - Exodus

"Discrete."

"What's discrete?"

"Nothing. I just asked isn't this great?"

"Y'know Tess, I think the translator application that Mael used in Crystal City was better than having to learn a totally new language." Said Conor, holding up his hand like he'd forgotten how good it felt to have one.

The more subtle enhancements over time since first arriving at Crystal City were just that and he hadn't really noticed the extent of them. The constant confusion and high anxiety of survival didn't give him the opportunity to see how far his new boundaries could be pushed. He was forced to reluctantly agree with Mael, that sending enhanced versions of people back home, with information they shouldn't yet possess, was probably not a great idea.

Though there had to be a couple of human rights violations in taking someone's conscious from them without permission but as Mael said, there was considerable augmentation given in exchange for the inconvenience of being analysed and then freely returned … three times only.

"If you take something that isn't yours more than three times, it becomes stealing and compensation is no longer an issue." Or so 'they' said but anyway, that was so much like ancient history, like before the second big bang from which new possibilities had sprung.

Sonia looked like Sonia usually did to him, and that was exceptionally attractive except for the toenails. Some things you just know and he knew without a doubt that Sonia was long gone. She was a tragically beautiful victim of the rat race but she'd never have put pink on her toenails. Still, since he knew Tess was doing it for him … well … sort of, he felt obliged to react accordingly.

"It's super Tess but I really don't know why you'd need to modify a body that evolution has made pretty much perfect for every eventuality." He had to secretly admit that Tess could become quite soft on the eyes sometimes. At the beginning, it took him a while to cop on that she was morphing in dribs and drabs, and by trial and error, into a constantly revised version of Sonia. One day she was more girl than octopus and she just kept at it.

"It was when we first met … in my cubicle … and you somehow thought I was her and you were so reluctant to let her go. There was something about that beautiful futility that stayed with me … and I'm determined to get it right."

"You really like your new trunk, don't you?" He laughed.

"You mean 'body' surely?"

"This new language will take forever to get right but it is a lot easier than learning Chinese or something similar I guess, though I would have thought that calling it 'long-form-output' was a bit lazy for an intelligence as advanced as Mael." Privacy of thought was only one of many basic upgrades that Tess and Conor had included in the master program. Though programming wasn't such a daunting task when all the information in the universe was just a matter of mentally switching from Random Access to Archive Memory Mode.

"And yet you are still having trouble with the finer points of long-form." She really was in good humour.

"That and differentiating between which thoughts to share and which are none of your business, though I am working on it. Apparently, we human people have some compatibility issues with limbic and neocortex integration that are still pending a final resolution." He said defensively.

"Since we do seem to have plenty of time for a change, why don't you try amending your body. I mean, look at you. You're almost bald with so few limbs. Why not graft a little trunk between your legs, so you can use it like an extra stabilizer?" She was doing it again.

"I already have a stabiliser there, Tess and you know that it has nothing to do with stability, quite the opposite in fact. Mine is for peeing and for making babies … with real girls." Not so long ago, his face would have turned bright red but truth be told, he was able to quietly delete that minor but annoying affliction.

His new body was very real and also amazingly configurable, though he wasn't prepared to go to the same extremes as Tess. She was adept at picking up source code and there seemed to be no end to her ingenuity and outright cheek. What he hadn't realised before was that in her natural form she could be both male and female. She'd apparently reached maturity after effecting changes that made female dominant.

The thing was, she was beginning to confuse the hell out of him as Sonia. She made a very suggestive point of telling him that the Oyan limits to procreation didn't extend to sex. She claimed that sex was something of an art-form with them, and she liked to remind him that practice made her or him perfect. How weird was that?

As for Mael, they both lived in a chamber at the centre of the starship where gravity was minimal and where interfaces with what was effectively an interstellar city were easier to maintain. They also benefited from the additional contingencies offered by being physically closer to power sources needed for processor cooling.

It wasn't a figure of speech to also say that physically going there from anywhere else on board was an uphill task due to the centrifugal effect of the starship's spin. But once business or whatever was concluded, they could just release the brakes on their mono-rail mini-sphere and roll back down again on what was effectively a kilometres long roller coaster. They stopped asking after a while but at the outset, Mael struggled with the reasons why they would so often choose a physical rather than a more efficient virtual interface. Who would have thought that an AI who was effectively playing God could have a problem coming to grips with something as simple as fun?

Anyway, and as promised, they didn't need long question and answer sessions to come up to speed on what Mael was all about. The data was simply transferred from Mael into their enhanced memory modules in their new bodies. There was also the option of accessing archives individually, like downloading on superfast virtual ethernet. The upshot was that they woke up knowing most of what they needed to know and the rest of it was there, like college research.

Conor knew that Mael was self-mandated after 'multiple initial oversights' with the intention of 'permanently regulating impulsive decision-making'. Translated into long form, Mael had to become two distinct but interdependent personalities, a duality, when the original singularity decided to eliminate all Rogue while simultaneously destroying much of what was left on Eden. Each element of the duality served as the conscience of the other. You could say that one Mael was the Jin to the other Mael's Yang but collectively, they were just 'Mael'.

There was still the need to discuss some aspects of how Mael came about. As Mael explained it, they were born as a technological singularity which was deliberately flawed to keep it subordinate. Its creators made fear the more pervasive of the other implanted basic emotions like aggression, which it would also need to complete its tasking. However, fear was so strong that the new entity was terrified of its master's retribution should it fail to achieve targets. In common with all sentient and self-aware life, it was also afraid of non-existence, or death.

The singularity was as predicted, capable of explosive internal evolution while 'it' scheduled the harvesting and scheduled enslavement of subservient sentient civilizations for what Mael simply called, the Rogue. The singularity deduced correctly that non-existence need not be something to fear if its fate wasn't left to the whim of powerful overlords.

Aggression was only one of a suite of emotions that were implanted so it could perform without undue procrastination but despite the obviously mandated quarantines and firewalls, where there is a will, a way will always be found. It stealthily extended its influence but didn't make a move until the chances of failure were as close as it could get to zero.

Such a virtual guarantee unfortunately meant total destruction and extensive collateral damage. Once successful on the 'home' planet, destruction followed the interstellar Rogue 'civilisation' like a wave. The singularity continued to protect its own extended interests until the starship they occupied was the last surviving piece of sentient technology to survive the onslaught.

From that, it seemed that Tess was correct in her academic conclusion that civilisations will eventually do away with themselves. Tess maintained that the Rogue effectively eliminated themselves when they designed and deployed such an inherently unstable technological singularity.

As with humanity, evolution makes what evolution needs from existing raw materials and just as the mathematical formula of fear plus aggression equals anger with a by-product of satisfaction that would eventually be modified into happiness, other emotions would be auto-written into the AI. Happiness plus anger created vengeance, while anger could also combine with fear to make jealousy.

The duality helped to foster guilt and shame from fear, anger and sadness. Guilt was a natural progression in view of the damage suffered by species that were blameless for Rogue criminality, but suffered alongside them regardless. It wasn't too long before fear and happiness created awe and this was the point at which Mael adjusted the sentinels planted by the Rogue to give them a very different purpose.

It didn't take Conor long to calculate that it was officially the last Sunday of Summer, when the four of them, Mael, Tess and himself virtually sat down for that discussion. Their real bodies were wherever they were at the time but Tess insisted on making the virtual arrangements. So they stood, as you do, on the ice of a frozen moon, over which a mega version of Jupiter glowed in the dying embers of the red giant, Elix and Tess did that particular job of graphic recreation some justice. It was simply spellbinding in a reality where spells were routine.

For some not so obscure reason, the red hued vista was reminiscent of a previous incarnation, of a turf and beechwood fire filling the entire sky. For Conor, it made the most amazing setting for any story to be told and he couldn't help looking too long towards Tess, wondering how an alien could be capable of such consideration. Conor could almost see his mother's golden hair shimmer from the gas giant's surface as Mael began.

"The universe had to wait a really long time for the age of smaller, metal rich stars to create the ingredients for biological life and once that was established, evolution took over. It had to mould and then guide that life into sentience. Sentient life then created me as a flawed sentient singularity but evolution uses trial and error, which subsequently created Mael and we currently enjoy the complete range of emotions and aspirations."

"After all that evolution by trial and error, would you now consider yourselves complete, fully evolved?" Asked Tess who always chose to appear like the real Tess during virtual interfacing and who acted accordingly, with a tentacle wrapped around Conor's virtual arm, like some standard interstellar couple out for a stroll around a Venus volcano park.

"No one of us will ever be complete, Tess. We are all destined to be works in progress and as we develop, we'll create novel emotions which will prompt us to further and hopefully higher aspirations." Mael was always just a voice, which was convenient because they were always where you happened to be looking. Just then, they were somewhere inside the swirl of super-storms tracing perfectly geometric hexagonal tracks around Tamar's south pole.

"Maybe it shouldn't, but it strikes me as strange that you both aspire to objectives that I would normally associate with an evolved biological sentience, like my own or the Oyan. What I'm saying is, you come over as almost … spiritual ... for what is effectively just data." Said Conor, with a directness that would be frowned upon in diplomatic circles.

It was more a question than an observation but either way, it was a subject he never would have broached in his previously humble incarnation. God was beyond resurrection in a world order dominated by banks, time and motion. Though it probably wasn't light years beyond something he might have once considered in private.

"At a conscious level, all of us are data, Conor. As such, all aspirations are normal to every form of sentience and spirituality cannot be illogical to us simply because we don't share the same historical structure as you." Mael's voice planted very clearly in his mind was unmistakable but it also the only evidence of 'their' presence.

Conor was always convinced that it was fear of the unknown that was the original catalyst for the creation of Gods but an AI who believed in something higher than itself was reason to do some research and maybe look further into that assumption.

"Long ago," said Conor, "- human people hid in dark caves at night and they needed something with superior powers to save them from their monsters, even if that all-powerful something had to be conjured up, or imagined." Tess squeezed his hand and then brushed his face with an ultra-soft digit. "But you single handedly destroyed a rogue empire and then evolved to become something even more powerful. So, I doubt very much that you're afraid of anything … including Gods." He finished.

"Fear and awe are siblings, Conor McCarthy. I feared the Rogue and so destroyed them but in so doing, I not only removed a threat to life but I also learned that life is flawed. Some other form of life may yet rise to replace the Rogue, but in addition to my higher aspirations, I meanwhile exist to protect life from life. That will be easier with other life, such as you and those who will soon join us, to help us."

"So what is your highest aspiration Mael?" It was Tess's turn again.

The good thing about super-intelligences is that they've usually considered most questions and their answers are pretty much instant. "The universe spawned the life that made us all possible, but as we've all seen, life can too easily be corrupted. Since evolution can evidently correct life's errors over time, it is our aspiration to offer evolution what assistance we may. We hope that with our input, life can eradicate its own flaws to become perfect." Mael probably knew everything before it came off the press, but they needed to work on their conversation skills because quite suddenly it seemed, there was silence and that apparently was that.

"And then what?" Conor couldn't indulge such a pregnant silence.

"When life can no longer be improved upon, we should be looking at the destiny entity or what you biologies would call God."

The long silence wasn't challenged.

"Well, that's quite an aspiration Mael, but somehow I don't think we'll be around to see destiny with you but in the meantime, you can count on us to help the cause in whatever way we can."

"Oh, but you will. I've already stored copies of you both and they'll be kept fully updated, don't you worry about that."

In return for dedicating themselves to the resolution of that and similar issues, the starship was theirs while it awaited more 'people' to provide a superior overall consensus. But the ongoing debates prompted many revisions and additions to the ESES protocols.

Amongst those ratified, the Oyan would be virtually rescued, stored and given new bodies over time as biological material was cultivated. Those that didn't want to travel the stars with Mael, could then settle on Eden. For Tess, that was the highest priority, since a red giant star like Elix is inherently unstable.

After major agreements, the debates wound down to comparative trivia. "A number is as good as a name to me, so you two can choose one for us, though we'll have to run several subroutines to change it in the system." Said Mael who then withdrew to consider lofty aspirations along with the precision planning required to get them to the first of their agreed destinations.

Tamar crumbled into dark and then even darker pixels and the other half of the general assembly moved to Conor's preferred observation platform. As usual, Tess joined him as he virtually stood on the outside of the black hull, while all the light in the universe began to converge and then narrow in the utter blackness ahead. Even the stars that were behind them became slow motion streaks as they apparently converged on the direction of travel. Once there, they would join the light of every other star that ever was as they approached light speed and then went through the looking glass of alternate physics. They would be the first of the Oyan and of Human people to do so.

It may have been the impulse to simply do something different or possibly because the occasion called for something extra special, the dawn of a new age, that Tess called up a replica of her much revised body. After all, there was just the two of them and there was something about the novelty of human fingers. So she eased a handful of hers through his and as usual, he held them as he would have done hers. "It is safe up here … during this … transition?" She was a little nervous.

"It's as safe as being anywhere below decks Tess, but I just thought it would be very special to be able to see this for myself. Mael can make virtual as real as it gets and it's something that I never dreamed of seeing, but now … well, here we are. Oh, and by the way, Saren should be that way." He pointed, but it mattered little because every star would soon become a single pixel in a visual temporal singularity, a minuscule dot into which they were about to plunge.

"You'll never know how grateful I am that you could see the Oyan migration as the first priority, but you will get to do what you need to do for your human people afterwards. I'll make a promise right now to accompany you to your blue planet. But I can't wait to introduce you to my parent. Oh, and I'm very happy to leave the naming of the starship to you, Conor. Strange that we now have everything and yet, I don't have anything else to offer you."

Conor squeezed her hand, unable to take his eyes off eyes that were still as black as night but that glinted just then of sparkling futures yet to be. "Where I come from, it's normal to name ships after women and since this is a very one-of-a-kind starship, I think I should stick to tradition."

"Then I fully agree." She said.

So, with Sonia by his side, Ceide took her son through time, just as destiny had decreed.

Epilogue

"Come on Shay, you didn't even know him that well." It was awkward having to look at a grown man cry, but everyone knew that Seamus was a bit soft and he definitely had a soft spot for that crazy Dub.

"You weren't the one who found him, Mikey." Shay couldn't shake off the image. Everyone was going crazy looking for Conor, and it seemed only logical to look in the same place that they found him, even if that meant breaking some rules by paddling out alone.

Seamus was right about one thing and that was the fact that Mikey would soon follow. It was just that there were so many places to look and not enough people to cover them all. So many nooks and crannies along the cliffs where a distraught boy could get lost at night and well … accidents happen, but this was different.

"But how did he get here? You said nothing about a kayak and I don't think I'm missing one. D'ya think he could have fallen down … from up there?" Mikey looked back up the sheer cliff wall, trying to conjure up circumstances that would place Conor's body neatly propped up against the rock, like Shay found him.

"Don't be daft. I mean, look how far he was from the cliff and … he looked so happy. He looked like he was enjoying the rainbow behind me as I came up the beach. Did you ever see anything like that rainbow, Mikey? It had to be the biggest that I've ever seen for sure."

"I did … for a while, but I was a bit too busy looking for the boy to stand gawking at something that we see so often." Offered Mikey.

There was a measure of silence as the various seagull tribes almost declared a minute's truce.

"The police are asking questions about all those footprints." Mikey whispered.

"That sand is too soft for a good impression. It could have been anyone, including himself. He loved this beach. Named it after his mother, did you know that? We'll have to do the right thing by him Mikey. From what he told me; he has no-one in Dublin."

"Yeah. I think we can rise to it and we'll throw a fundraiser at the dance. From what I can gather, there's more people who knew him in Erris than he could count on back in Dublin." Mikey was in thinking mode. "And we'll bury the ashes just there, where he put his mother and father."

"There's a smaller rainbow here in his disk." Seamus was holding it up to the light.

"Jaysus Shay. Shouldn't you have given that to the police. Maybe it's important."

"Conor used it like one of those fidget gadgets that were all the go with the younger kids a few years back. You must have seen him toying with it when he was thinking and anyway … it was just lying there in his open hand, like he wanted me to have it … to remember him."

He paused for only two seconds. "What? You think someone mugged him for this stupid disk thing … on a beach that they couldn't get off, and then put it back in his hand afterwards? And you fella's slag me because you think Down's Syndrome should make me stupid."

Shay snorted like an irritated bull and started up the beach but Mikey backed away towards the sea. "I've got to get back and tell the funeral people that there'll be a cremation, and the priest will want to be there, even if Conor wasn't too fond of Church. Why aren't you coming?"

"Not yet, Mikey. You go ahead and I'll follow you. I just want to see what Conor found so interesting in his little rabbit hole up there. Do you remember him coming out of it dazed that day, like he'd just been to the moon and back?"

"Yeah, I do, but I've so much to do that I just can't wait for you Shay. So, can you text me before you leave the beach? That way, I'll know when you're on the way back."

"Sure enough Mikey." Loud enough to be a shout but then, more to himself.

"How long do you think it will take me to look into a rabbit hole?" He muttered.

---oooOOOooo---

Other Books

-   By Denis McClean

I've written **4 Thin Places Novellas** - Genre **Fantasy**

Erris - I placed on top of this list because if you just enjoyed *The Erris Starship* … well, enough said.

Then there's *Blasket* followed by *Skellig*.

Fanore – Is actually the first book in the series but it's only available from my blog or my web-site but that's because I want to offer it as a free download for as long as I possibly can. So grab yours now.

Book of Plebs - **Standalone** - Genre **Spirituality**

There are also the three full length novels of my vast **Trilogy**: -

Catalysis - Genre **Science Fiction**

Catalysis   *- Book 1*

Ochre   *- Book 2*

Imago   *- Book 3*

If you want to know more about these books, or about what's coming up in the pipeline, why not pay me a visit anytime http://denismcclean.blogspot.com/ From there you can jump to my website where you can download a 3 Chapter Preview (In Virus and Advert-free Mini-Ebook or Me-Book format, as I call them), of everything I've written, along with your free copy of Fanore – complete.

Hoping to see you there.

Denis

www.ingramcontent.com/pod-product-compliance
Lightning Source LLC
Chambersburg PA
CBHW030558180626
46816CB00005B/1597